Both danger and sex are inescapable in the Amber Zone.

Jaci Harmon was born a Sapphire, but after she's summoned to receive her final designation, the testing reveals she carries a gene slated for eradication. Within a day, she's sterilized and dumped in the Amber Zone, where the damaged are corralled away from the rest of New Atlanta. Scared and alone, Jaci would rather die than face her future as an Amber.

Born in the Amber Zone, Xander Dimos is a product of a lifetime spent under the oppression of the Repopulation Laws. Decades of suffering have taught the Ambers to make the zone a place where touch, sex, and unconditional acceptance ease the pain of their fate. Jaci has a lot to learn about her new home, and it's Xander's responsibility to guide her through the differences and the dangers safely.

With the simmering undercurrents of sexual chemistry growing between them, and in the midst of discovering the Gov's true motives, Jaci and Xander must overcome his secret and accept their love as undeniable… even if the time allotted to share it is short.

Books by Sylvia Ryan

New Atlanta Series
Being Amber
Being Sapphire
Being Emerald

Published by Kensington Publishing Corporation

Being Amber

A New Atlanta Novel

Sylvia Ryan

LYRICAL PRESS
Kensington Publishing Corp.
www.kensingtonbooks.com

First Electronic Edition: September 2013
eISBN-13: 978-1-61650-454-0
eISBN-10: 1-61650-454-4

First Print Edition: September 2013
ISBN-13: 978-1-61650-904-0
ISBN-10: 1-61650-904-X

Printed in the United States of America

Prologue

The first cases of the deadly influenza were identified January 22, 2050 in New York City. Martial law was declared and mandatory quarantines were enforced by the National Guard, but the spread of the virus proved to be aggressive and unstoppable. Death of an infected person usually occurred within seven days of the first signs of the disease.

Mortality rates grew exponentially and government services collapsed sixty days after the first identified cases. By that time, there were not enough people alive for society to carry on as normal. Millions of dead were left unburied and made cities uninhabitable for the few uninfected by the virus.

By the time the pandemic was over, an estimated ninety-two percent of the world's population had not survived. The majority of the deaths were the result of the virus, but some were a result of being cut off from food and water and from the chaos reigning in the aftermath of the pandemic. Those the flu left alone were left isolated throughout the world. Suddenly, mankind was an endangered species.

In the United States, remaining government and military leaders rallied quickly in an effort to save surviving citizens. Skeletal remnants of military forces concentrated on making three US cities--Chicago, Los Angeles and Atlanta--inhabitable. The densely packed skyscrapers of the downtown areas were left untouched, and loomed like ghosts haunting the new cities hastily constructed in their shadow. In outlying neighborhoods where the population had been less dense, corpses were buried in mass graves so their homes could be assigned to the thousands of people that descended in hoards to the closest of the three cities.

During this time, martial law ruled with brutal authority. Everybody participated in the rebuilding, except for the very young and the very old. Those who didn't fall in line were exiled outside the safety of the tall walls that surrounded the "new" cities. The area outside the walls, what would later be named the Onyx Zone, was unlivable and lawless.

As the population gathered, and the momentous, uphill struggle of rebuilding society began, it became clear that some genetic traits in humans, like blond hair and blue eyes, were on the verge of disappearing altogether. In an effort to propagate these endangered genes, and eliminate unwanted genes as well, the government decided that the repopulation of the US would occur slowly and under their supervision. Backed by a heavy military presence, the Repopulation Laws were enacted in 2052.

The Repopulation Laws mandated significant and difficult restrictions on the pandemic survivors all in the name of saving the unique and diverse qualities of the human race. They also established guidelines to eliminate unwanted genes, such as those that passed on chronic illnesses and mental health diagnosis. In time, they reasoned, the US would be completely populated with humans who had near-perfect genetic profiles.

By the end of 2053, all citizens living under government control had submitted to genetic, psychological and intelligence testing and were classified according to the results of those tests. Four classes were established and given corresponding color marks. Every person was required to bear the color mark of his or her class and follow the Repopulation Laws established for that classification. The ruling class, those determined to possess significant talents or have made significant contributions to society, were designated as Emeralds.

The overwhelming majority of people were classified as Sapphires or Ambers, with Ambers being the lowest and most restricted of the classes. Those marked as Ambers were determined to be of undesired genetic makeup, low intelligence or emotionally unstable. As a result, they were forced to make most of the sacrifices for the greater good of mankind.

Anger and insurrection from the Ambers swelled from the start as they were segregated from the rest of the population. Thousands of Amber women were sterilized, so many that a new term, fallow, was coined to identify those who were forced to suffer through sterilization at the Gov's hands. Feeling helpless and persecuted, the Amber population in New Atlanta started to organize and resist their subjugation. Their efforts began to successfully gain sympathy and sway public opinion against the Laws.

The Gov feared revolution and the leaders of the resistance movement were eventually asked to attend secret accord meetings to negotiate terms and accommodations for the people of the Amber Zone, in hopes to find peace and balance in the new social structure.

Eventually, they reached an accord that appeased the Amber Resistance. The Repopulation Laws remained, but several government concessions improved the quality of day-to-day life in the Amber Zone. In the end, the Gov granted the Amber population the liberty to police themselves with the stipulation that it would remain their right only as long as Amber citizens didn't impact society outside of their zone. If Ambers were successful at containing their population, they would be free from the National Guard and associated government persecution.

The message was clear. Once a person was designated Amber, the Gov expected him to be invisible to the rest of the population in the "new" cities.

The secret accord between Amber authorities and the Gov has stood since that time.

Chapter 1

The tightness in Jaci's chest nearly suffocated her. She closed her eyes and took a deep breath, trying to calm the nervous flutter in her stomach. She rubbed her damp palms on her jeans while her gaze darted around, taking in the barren walls of the cubicle. The pervasive pall of the Designation Center was bleak, right down to the ugly green tint of the fluorescent lighting.

She wondered how many people sat where she sat right now with their hearts beating in their throats and breaths coming quick and shallow. How many lives had been irreversibly changed right here? Goose bumps rose on her arms as the acute apprehension building within her exploded. The information contained in the large white envelope she held would impact every moment of the rest of her life. Once the designation was given, there was no turning back. The results would be her color until the day she died.

Hands shaking, Jaci opened the flap and pulled the top sheet of paper free from the envelope.

Dear Jaci Harmon,

As the result of score assessments in all three major areas of testing you have been given the designation of Amber...

Her breath caught in her throat as her vision narrowed to the underlined word.

...If after reviewing all accompanying paperwork, you have any questions regarding your designation, please com the contact listed on the back of this form.

You have been given the job designation of Painter. Your reporting date and supervisor name are enclosed.

You are assigned to Amber Housing Zone Building 17, Apartment 404.

Due to your genetic profile indicating the presence of an Automatic Disqualifier, you are to report to the Amber Sterilization Center for mandatory sterilization tomorrow, June 1, 2075.

Jaci let the page fall to the table in front of her. "Oh my God," she whispered numbly. Her face heated, and her ears filled with high-pitched ringing. She pulled the rest of the packet from the envelope and leafed through the pages. When she got to the IQ section, she studied the scores for all of the individual testing segments. They were all good. She had an IQ score high enough to be a Sapphire. A slight sense of pride washed over her. At least she was smart enough. But, that didn't really matter now, did it?

Jaci clumsily rifled through each remaining page, trying to find the reason why she'd been designated an Amber. Then, toward the back of the stack, she found her genetic profile and zeroed in on the highlighted section.

...An Automatic Disqualifier was found in genome CD247 indicating a genetic predisposition for scleroderma and probable perpetuation of the disease through offspring...

Scleroderma. She'd never heard of it but clearly, it was one of the chronic conditions the Gov was trying to exterminate. Information regarding the disease was highlighted but she didn't read it. She put the papers down and leaned back in her chair. All of the studying or talent in the world wouldn't have made a difference. There were some genes deemed undesirable in any person, and she had one of them.

Jaci sat stunned, her gaze unfocused, unblinking.

Like an animal helplessly looking up at its demise, she experienced a frozen panic. She was road kill, unable to make sense of the unexpected ruin that just hit her. She'd been leveled by the Repopulation Laws. There was no recovering from this.

Disoriented, she followed a woman to a different cubicle to get her tattoo.

"Would you like a design or a plain band?" A young man asked as he looked at her paperwork and picked the amber-colored ink bottle from it's place in the neatly ordered row of class colors.

"Band," Jaci said vacantly.

He paused and met her eyes, opening his mouth as if he was going to say something. Then, his gaze flicked over to the surveillance camera mounted on the ceiling and abruptly closed it, busying himself again with his work.

As he tattooed the one-inch yellow-orange band around her wrist, Jaci screamed inside. She lost her bearings as the room around her caved in on itself, receded to a pinpoint far, far away. Anger and panic rose within her as she sat rooted in a state of catatonic frenzy. Only the vibrating sting of the tattoo needle marking her wrist tethered her to the reality of her surroundings.

"Can I have your left palm please?"

Jaci looked at the man. Had he been talking to her? "What?"

"I have to give you your code," he said softly. "Everyone in the Amber Zone has one." He gave Jaci a glimpse of the code on his palm, and then her eyes traveled to his wrist. He was an Amber. She hadn't even noticed.

Jaci gave the man her hand. She didn't ask what the code was for. She didn't watch as the sting of the needle pricked the sensitive skin of her palm. She didn't care.

When the tattoos were completed, she was ushered to the waiting transport bus that would take her and her duffel bag to their new home.

The border that separated the Sapphire Zone from the Amber Zone was heavily guarded. Only Ambers with the correct clearance, ones that worked outside the Amber Zone, could pass into Sapphire.

Being raised as a Sapphire, one class up from Amber, Jaci never had any contact with Ambers before. She'd been educated early that there was no color mixing. Ambers were inferior human beings, weak, stupid, and riddled with disease.

Now, she was one of them.

The transport driver had a serious case of diarrhea of the mouth and either didn't notice or didn't care that Jaci was barely there. She watched the beauty of the Sapphire Zone disappear behind her while he droned on cheerfully with need-to-know Amber Zone facts.

As they approached the ugly high-rise buildings of Circle City, the driver's annoying buzz of words continued to permeate the protective barrier she tried to erect around herself.

"...twenty story high rise that looks exactly like buildings one through twenty-eight. The buildings themselves were built specifically for housing single Ambers. They form a huge circle enclosing an entire city within the ring. You won't need transportation. Everything you're going to need is within Circle City. When you get married, you'll be transferred to a town house or condo in the Amber Zone, but outside of Circle City."

The transport pulled up to building seventeen. Jaci exited, escaping the talkative driver, and walked in. She wove her way through the crowded lobby to the elevator and then rode it up to the fourth floor. The door opened to a congested hallway. She walked through small huddles of people, like a rat in a maze, confused and not quite sure where she was going. Then she stopped short, and for a second, stared at the door of her new home. She tried the knob. It was locked. She stood for a moment longer, having trouble keeping it together while trying to remain invisible amidst the crowd of people. She fought an explosion of tears and frustration as she stared at the metal 404 directly in front of her. Then she sighted the scanner on the left side of the door. She placed her hand on it. The scanner registered the new tattooed code on her palm, and a small *click* sounded as the lock mechanism released.

Jaci exhaled the breath she'd been holding, and stepped in. She surveyed her new home, a studio apartment with a small galley kitchen and a bathroom. The entire space was about the size of the family room at her parents' house. Being a single Amber meant she would be stuffed in and vacuum packed so she took up as little space as possible.

Jaci closed the door behind her and stood frozen just inside the doorway, taking the room in. White, it was all stark white, impersonal, sterile. One large bed centered on the wall of the living space monopolized the room. There were night tables on each side. Clothes, pictures and other personal items were strewn over the area closest to the large window at the far end of the room.

A huff of air escaped her as realization dawned in Jaci's mind. She would not be in this small space alone. Another person already lived there. But there was only one bed. It didn't make sense. She glanced to the side nearest to where she stood, to what she assumed was her side of the room. She was closest to the exit and the door entering the bathroom was on the other side of her night table.

A small flat screen hung on the wall opposite the bed, and two chairs were tucked into a small round dining table near the counter that delineated the kitchen from the living space. The kitchen was small and narrow, taking up the back wall of the apartment by the entrance. It contained all the basics, a tiny fridge, a sink, and a two-burner stove.

When she got enough strength and courage together, she needed to call her mother with a list of things to send from her bedroom. She wouldn't call now. She couldn't face it. If she heard her mother's voice, she would break down. She was barely keeping it together as it was.

All her parents would be told was that she'd been designated an Amber. They would have to endure her swift, brutal removal just like she would. That's how it had always been done when someone's designation changed, a clean break away from everything and everyone they'd known in their lives.

Two visits a year. That's all she would be allowed to have to her parents' zone. Over the years, Jaci knew of some Sapphire kids who'd subsequently been designated Ambers. It wasn't unusual for them to stop visiting after a while. Maybe their families made them feel inferior, or maybe they realized they didn't belong anymore. It didn't matter that there was nothing she could have done better to change her designation. Bottom line was that she didn't make the cut, and she would merely be a satellite member of her family from now on.

A compad sat on the counter to her left. Glancing down at the large envelope she held, she lifted the flap and pulled the papers free. She searched scleroderma, bracing herself for the results, fully knowing that since it was an Automatic Disqualifier the information she found would be bad. She scanned the list of sites brought up by the search and touched the screen to get to the site she chose. Focusing on the article, she let her eyes skip quickly over the information. Scleroderma. An autoimmune disorder meaning that the body attacks itself. Genetically linked. No cure. Thirty-four percent death rate within ten years of first symptoms. Significant and intensive long-term care for those afflicted. Tissues of the body hardened and froze, essentially trapping the person inside his or her own skin.

"Shit."

She exhaled softly. It made sense. Automatic Disqualifiers weren't diseases that killed efficiently. The Gov didn't mind the quick killers. Automatic Disqualifiers were the conditions that killed ever so slowly, leaving the afflicted person in need of extensive treatment and long-term care.

The bandage over the newly tattooed amber band around her wrist caught her attention. She ran her finger over it, feeling the sensitivity of her skin beneath. She'd been planning on getting a sapphire daisy chain as her designation tattoo. Plain bands were for her parents' generation. There were options now since the Gov loosened its restrictions. Simple designs were allowed instead of only a solid band. She'd been so blindsided at the time she didn't even look at the available amber designs.

Somehow, Jaci never actually believed this could happen to her, that she'd be designated Amber. Before she received her summons to appear for her designation, she daydreamed that her testing showed her to be so genetically clean that she was designated a Diamond. Those perfect people with the ideal mixture of good genes and the absence of bad, were instantly immersed in a life of privilege and pampering. It was like winning a lottery. She supposed a lot of people had that fantasy. However, she'd totally dismissed the thought that there was even a possibility of being designated an Amber.

Jaci walked over to the window at the far end of the apartment. It offered a bird's eye view of the curious circular city. The day was gray and stormy, suiting her dire mood and doomed life.

It was quiet and still in the shadowy room as she stared out the window, brooding. Now that the influx of new information slowed, her mind started processing other things. Things she hadn't dealt with yet because everything happened so fast.

Significant things.

Devastating things.

A tear overflowed the lower lid of her eye and streamed down her face. She tried to swallow down the tight knot in her throat as she focused on her reflection in the window. But the hard-core reality of her new life suddenly inundated her, impacting with full force and striking a blow so deeply that it cut her to her very soul. Her suffering flourished, becoming palpable to her, chilling the air and seeping into her skin. The mere beginnings of it laid waste to her insides.

Goose bumps rose on her flesh. She was an Amber now, and for the rest of her life until the day she died of that god-awful disease.

Her friends and family were gone, suddenly blinked right out of her life. She was alone, utterly alone here. Her stomach swam.

She was scared.

Thunder rolled deep and ominous in her ears, vibrating the windowsill. The colorless gray of the sky was the perfect backdrop to the tiny drops of rain that landed and gathered together on the glass, forming trails that flowed down like teardrops. The window cried with her.

"I'll never have a baby," she whispered into the silence of the room. Tomorrow she'd be sterilized.

Suppressing the pandemonium of feelings trying to crash out of her was futile. Disjointed fragments of thoughts and fears flew at her, and utter grief and pain raced unbridled through her mind. She felt violent, wanting to throw something, smash anything into tiny pieces.

A primal moan rose up from the depths of her soul and burst through her mouth, filling the room as she sank to her knees. Now, all she had was the wait for her defective gene to kick in, to make her pathetic and helpless, a prisoner within her own skin, before it finally finished her off. In the course of one afternoon, she'd lost everything. Even her life had been shortened significantly with the knowledge of the deadly gene she carried. Rage and despair came from so deep within her gut that she felt like she was going to throw up between the wrenching sobs. She cried, pounded and screamed an entire pathetic performance for an audience of none until there was nothing left in her. The feel of the cold floor on her face was the only thing she registered as she collapsed the rest of the way, settling into a shivering heap on the hard tiles. She curled in on herself.

Jaci remained there sorting through all of it in her head as the hours passed. Her cheek resting on the floor was cool and wet from the tears she'd released and let fall unchecked. It felt good against the humid, New Atlanta summer heat.

Finally, trembling, she lifted herself to her knees, then to her feet, and got into bed. She lay there with her eyes open, but not noticing dusk's shadows overtake the room. Hours of monotonous, opaque blackness enveloped her as she lay awake through the night. Sleep wouldn't come.

Jaci thought seriously about committing suicide. There wasn't anything left for her. She would spend the rest of her days waiting to be diagnosed with the first symptoms of the debilitating illness that would eventually kill her. She doubted a day would ever pass in her life that she didn't feel like she was waiting to die.

If she killed herself, there would be no impact on any other person in the world. Nobody would miss her now.

She thought about others who found their lives too hard, the pathetic throng of people who slouched in the plastic chairs of the waiting room for the Gov Assisted Suicide Program, GASP. Jaci felt sick thinking of the brick smoke stacks of the cremating ovens behind the building. The acrid smoke released from the burning bodies saturated the air with a revolting smell. GASP ensured a quick, painless exit for those who sought it. But Jaci would be damned if she was going to let the Gov take that last act from her.

Lying in the dense gloom of her new home, her mind frantically groped for a foothold, something to reassure, to comfort. But, the same hopeless thoughts rolled through her mind like booms of thunder refusing to be ignored.

Near dawn, Jaci fell into a half sleep, her mind still running through her new circumstances, still seeking a way to end her life. A pleasant way. A way that she would actually have the courage to follow through with.

When she opened her eyes again, a stream of sunlight slanted through the window. She glanced at the clock on her roommate's nightstand. About a half hour remained before she was required to report to the transport.

Jaci looked around. Despite the fact that someone's belongings were in the apartment, no one had come home. She went into the bathroom, brushed her hair and teeth and washed her face.

The dark hair and brown eyes looking back at her in the mirror illustrated the lack of genetic diversity she offered the world. Weariness and misery faded her features. She expected to look different, uglier. She felt uglier, smaller somehow, but she looked the same as always.

A half laugh, half snort of despair shot out of her. Eyes closed, Jaci bowed her head in defeat. Tears welled behind her eyelids, preparing to escape. When she opened her eyes, a steady stream wet her cheeks and her nose began to run again. She grabbed a tissue for now and one for later before walking out of the apartment.

Herds of people crammed the hallways, socializing and laughing. Most of the apartment doors were open, letting sunlight filter into the corridor. Quickly, she walked down the hallway, looking at her shoes. She encountered slight brushes from the bodies of people who encroached in her space as she passed them. At times, it felt as if someone was actually trying to stop her. She didn't look up. She didn't want to meet anybody new right now. She was nauseated, physically ill. She couldn't stop. She didn't stop.

The transport was waiting for her when she got to the front entrance of the building. She climbed in and was relieved when saw she was the only passenger. She plopped down, this time out of earshot of the driver and rode the entire way with her head in her hands, still looking at her feet.

Chapter 2

Xander Dimos looked up from his vantage point between Emily's legs to see her blindfolded and writhing with need.

"Rock, please," she hissed.

Xander had stopped the dance of his tongue over her clit to appreciate the sight before him. Rock had Emily's wrists clasped in one hand and leaned over her, sucking on the pink tip of one breast and kneading the other. She was breathtaking in the dim light of the room, pleading for more of them and groaning when her requests went unanswered. He dipped his head and took her clit between his teeth, raking it lightly. Her throaty groan was heated. She was close.

He moved to kneel between her legs and then hooked them in the crooks of his arms, spreading her wide. His cock nudged the glistening opening of her pussy. He waited for her pleas again before he entered her slowly. The sight of the mushroomed head of his cock and then the length of him, disappearing inside her in a smooth, warm glide, was intoxicating. Her quick intake of breath revealed that, even blindfolded, she knew it wasn't her boyfriend, Rock, entering her. She didn't know it was Xander acting as the third in her birthday gift. She didn't want to know. The who wasn't important, according to Rock. It was the act of having two men at one time that she craved.

Rock leaned over and brushed his lips over hers. It was a hot caress of breath that prompted another whisper of Rock's name to pass through her flushed, swollen lips.

Her breathing was heavy and erratic, and the shine of moisture on her skin reflected the flickering candlelight in the room.

Xander stopped his slow in-out glide and Emily immediately arched herself up, trying to recapture the cock hovering at her entrance.

"You want more?" Rock teased her.

"Yes." The word floated from her, a mere breath slipping through her lips. Her chin was upturned toward the sound of Rock's voice. Her face held the purest expression of love Xander ever saw.

Rock gave him a quick nod, and Xander pulled back but only long enough for Rock to roll to his back and pull Emily on top of him. Rock spread her legs wide so the woman straddled him, and he breached her pussy in one smooth stroke, revealing his easy knowledge of Emily's body. Both of his huge hands gripped her hips, holding her still. She undulated on top of him, trying to get more, squirming to pleasure herself by creating friction where their bodies met.

"Lie still," Rock ordered, as he spanked her ass.

A cry escaped Emily's lips, "Oh God, please fuck me."

"Shut it." Rock cracked her ass again and looked up at Xander who was positioning himself behind Emily.

Xander grabbed the lube and placed the end of the tube into her rear entrance squeezing a liberal amount inside of her.

"Fuck," she said again. Another crack on her pink ass stopped her from saying anymore.

The whimper that accompanied the slide of Xander's two lubed fingers inside her tiny anus made his cock twitch with anticipation. She tried to get more by leaning back into him, but she was at the mercy of Rock's big hands, holding her still. Xander worked her anus while her desperate moans filled the room. The sound was lovely and for an instant, he experienced a surge of longing for a woman of his own, someone who sweetly whispered his name with a thread of need woven into it.

He retreated for a moment to lube himself and then guided his cock to the entrance he'd so carefully prepared. Emily cried out as he popped the head in past the tight muscle of her ass. Xander met Rock's gaze in the flickering light of the room and he waited until Rock gave him a slight nod. When he finally got it, Xander penetrated her completely until his hips were against the beautiful, firm rounds of her ass.

"Oh God," she cried as Xander looked down at where their bodies met. He stilled when he was completely seated inside her, taking in the graceful slope of her back. He pulled back slightly, just an inch and rocked back into her, watching his cock disappear inside her again. He ground his molars together, striving to maintain his control while inside the exquisite tightness.

He withheld the moan he so desperately wanted to release. It was vital he be totally silent, so as not to give away his identity as their third.

Xander didn't want his interactions with Emily to change. He valued her friendship too much.

A leisurely, fluent give and take of Emily's body emerged between Xander and Rock. Being partners at work translated well into partnerships in other areas, including this one.

Drawn-out moans escaped Emily's lips as she tried to continue her writhing, searching for perfect positioning, for ultimate fulfillment.

Xander heard Rock turn on the vibrating cock ring before he felt the subtle buzzing travel through her, adding an extra layer of stimulation. The speed of the cooperative penetration between them quickened and Emily's cries intensified, becoming louder and more demanding.

Rock reached around and grabbed her ass in his massive hands and held her down hard against him, no doubt pressing her clit into the vibrations. Xander's penetrations ended with his hips slamming against the backs of Rock's hands. The pumps provided a steady rocking motion for her body to move over Rock's cock and graze over the vibrating nub.

She wailed unintelligibly, obviously deep inside her own headspace where there was pleasure and probably not much else. He gazed down at her feeling savage and followed his impulse to grab her damp curls, gathering them together and using the ponytail to tug her back into him as he thrust deep and hard into her ass.

Emily stiffened and froze for several pumps before an uninhibited wail of sheer pleasure sprang from her lips. Her inner muscles tightened, squeezed down on Xander's dick with tremendous strength. Her orgasm triggered his. He fought to keep his eyes open while he came. His gaze never swayed from the sensuous scene spread out before him. Emily's profile was stunning in the midst of her climax, and Rock looked at his beautiful girlfriend with an expression of reverence. Anyone with eyes could see he loved her. He loved her enough to give her anything for her birthday, and this was always what she asked for.

When Xander recovered from his climax, he freed his softening cock from Emily's ass, left the bed and silently got dressed.

He watched as Rock caressed Emily's smooth skin, inducing whimpering moans from her moist, swollen lips. The dim lighting caused her nude body to become a study in contrast, light and shadow, curves and planes.

Rock wasn't done with his girlfriend, but Xander's role in the night's sexual performance was in the first act only. Emily wanted to be overwhelmed by pleasure, to swim in it, to drown in it. Rock indulged her as much as he could and Xander was glad to help, but the rest of the night was for the two of them alone.

Xander turned and left with only the *snick* of the door closing behind him to announce his departure. He smiled as he wove through the people in the hallway. From Emily's multicolored curls and nipple piercings, to Rock's tattoos and bad-ass attitude, they were as delinquent as a cop and his girlfriend could get without being arrested themselves. Xander chuckled and shook his head. It had been a good night.

He liked the threesomes with Rock and Emily. It was the most satisfaction he'd gotten out of sex in a long time. Too bad it was only once a year. The wild, anonymous sex Xander sought out in Circle City during the last five years got him off, but as time passed, he gained less and less satisfaction from it. Lately, sex was like surgery--sterile, and done only when necessary. He sometimes yearned for love and intimacy like Rock and Emily enjoyed with each other.

He cut himself short. That was a dangerous train of thought.

Xander stepped off the elevator on the ground floor of Rock's building.

Normally, before his roommate Diana had gotten married and moved out of Circle City with her husband, he would have gone back to his apartment. She would have teased him about being such a slut and then he would fall asleep spooning her like every other night since the day she moved in.

Some men would have been happy to have a respite from the responsibility of their female, but he wasn't one of them. Without Diana to take care of, the apartment felt empty. It wasn't home anymore.

Lost in thought, he exited into the humid summer night and walked the path that meandered from building to building.

He was well aware he hadn't adjusted well to Diana's absence. It was ironic that he'd never realized how much he needed her until she wasn't there anymore. The responsibility of caring for her and protecting her created stability in a life that was self-destructive and wild when they'd first met. He realized now that her presence established a home for them both. No matter where they'd been or what they'd done since they crawled out of bed together that morning, there was someone to go home to--assigned family, but still family.

It wasn't sexual with Diana. Never sexual. But it was intimate. Her unconditional acceptance of his authority, and her warm body got him through many nights of rebellion and insecure feelings about his place in the world.

The soft *ping* of the elevator roused him from his rumination. The door opened and he found himself looking down the hall of his floor in building seventeen. Small crowds gathered here and there outside open doorways.

He walked through the first gathering and into the apartment beyond.

"Can I crash here?" he asked Caroline when he found her cross-legged on the bed, watching TV with a group of others.

"Xander, you know you don't have to ask," she said, moving over and making room for him.

"I'm working tomorrow. I have to set the alarm," he warned.

"No prob."

He climbed in the bed, finding enough room among the large tangle of people to get comfortable and fall asleep.

* * * *

"You wanted to see me, Cap?" Xander stepped into his supervisor's office.

"A fallow has been transported over from the Sapphire Designation Center. Jordan's covering her right now," Captain Rush said, without looking away from his compad. He touched his screen a couple more times then looked at Xander. "Looks like you're on. We need to have a strategy session. I notified the rest of the task force team. Take an hour for dinner. We'll meet at eight in the briefing room."

Xander stepped through the side door of police headquarters and lifted his face toward the thunderclouds and sprinkling rain. He breathed deeply. Anticipation and contentment swirled in his chest. He was ready to get back to normal, having a female assigned to him, someone to care for again. The practice of single Amber males caring for their assigned female suited him, fulfilled an inexplicable need in his personality. It made him a better man.

An hour later, Xander, Rock and Brady, the electronics specialist, as well as Wes, the homicide detective from the last fallow cases, were all gathered around the large briefing room table in Amber Zone Police Headquarters. The atmosphere was relaxed. Everyone knew one another. The officers assigned to the Circle City area were like family to each other. All of them, except the captain, were single and lived in Circle City as well.

Captain Rush's sharp eyes lasered in on the team members as he walked in the door. Rush reminded Xander of a predatory bird. His bald head and pointy beak nose added to the effect.

"Let me give you the overview of what we have so far," he said, getting right down to business. "The last three fallows assigned to Circle City from other zones have wound up dead within weeks of their placement here. The first, Stacey Adams…" He tapped his stylus on his handheld to bring up a projection on the board. "Was originally taken at face value as, what we thought at the time, was an obvious suicide by some kind of poisoning.

"A month and a half later, another fallow came in from the Sapphire Zone, Tanisha Washington." He projected another photo. "Three weeks after her placement in building nineteen, she was found dead in her apartment by her roommate. Her wrists were slashed. At first glance, this looked like a suicide as well. But after investigation, the evidence didn't support suicide. It looked more like a murder set up to pass as a suicide.

"The last victim, also a fallow from Sapphire…" Another picture projected. "…August Zayzinski was found drowned in the Circle City public swimming pool. Again, questionable injuries not consistent with drowning.

"The deaths were reported on the news feeds as suicides, and accident in the last case. We don't want this guy tipped off that we're on to him. We know his MO, which leads us to his obvious next victim. The captain switched the picture on the whiteboard. "Jaci Harmon. We've been keeping the female spot in Xander's apartment open waiting for the next fallow. She was transferred there this afternoon."

Xander studied the picture of his new roommate. She was pretty. A small feeling of trepidation washed over him. God he hoped she wasn't bratty like some of the other women transferred in from one of the more privileged zones.

"Jordan is covering the apartment now. As of her last check in, Miss Harmon hasn't left the apartment or let anybody in. According to Jordan, she hasn't so much as even turned on a light.

"Xander, along with Rock and Jordan will be responsible for surveillance. You guys have to put together a schedule. See that she's always covered. Brady will monitor bugs of the apartment as well as incoming and outgoing com activity. I'll contact the supervisor at her work assignment and place Jordan to work with her there."

They all spent the next twelve hours breaking down the previous cases with Wes, hammering out surveillance schedules and setting up the monitoring system that would track the chip in Jaci's com, giving her exact location as well as bugging her conversations and messages. It was late morning when the group finally left the station. Xander was exhausted by the time he headed out to meet up with Jordan, who'd been doing surveillance all night.

He sat with her, sweating his ass off, in the police cruiser parked outside of building seventeen. He just finished updating Jordan on the strategy meeting she'd missed and was delighted to be the one to tell her about her new job assignment as painter, when she pointed to the building.

"There she is. They're delivering her back home."

Xander watched Jaci as the sterilization transport staff pushed her wheelchair into the side entrance of the building. She sat unmoving, her arms wrapped around herself, and her gaze fixed down at her lap.

"Shit." His heart broke while he watched her being wheeled inside. She looked spent, like she had nothing left. "I should have been there last night and this morning. She needed me."

Jordan answered him with a sympathetic look and a pat on the shoulder.

A few minutes later, they watched the transport pull away. He sighed. "I'm beat. I'm going to get some sleep."

"Me too. I still have to talk with Caroline and let her know that I want to volunteer for the Sit-In Team. They'll probably show up within the next few hours."

"Sounds good. Come on. I'll walk you up to your new apartment. Oh, by the way, Brady's your roommate, in case you haven't figured that out already." He chuckled as he got out of the car and slammed the door behind him. "He's finishing up his surveillance setup."

"What was the chuckle for?" Jordan shot him a glare.

"No chuckle." He smiled down at her. "Brady's been waiting his whole career to have a case like this. I'm wondering if he'll even notice you're there with all his electronics, slash stakeout, slash contingency supplies there."

She smiled up at him. "Go ahead and yuck it up. You won't be when he saves your ass."

"Let's hope that never happens. I'd never live it down."

On the ninth floor, Xander checked in with Brady and picked up the bug he needed to plant in his own apartment, promising to plant it as soon as he walked in the door.

He was dead on his feet as he rode the musty-smelling elevator to the fourth floor.

It was silent when he walked into the apartment. He expected Jaci to be in bed, sleeping, and was surprised to find the bed empty. The window shade was pulled down, darkening the room. A slit of artificial light escaped from underneath the bathroom door. He planted the bug underneath the lamp on her bedside table and settled himself at the dinette set, waiting for her to exit. After a while, he listened for movement inside the bathroom. He heard none. Another couple of minutes passed. Still nothing.

Walking over to the bathroom door, he tapped lightly. "Jaci? Are you okay in there?" He waited, ear close to the door. No answer. He tried the knob. It was locked. He pounded with the side of his fist this time "Jaci. Open the door," he shouted, trying to force back the feeling of dread that crept up his spine.

Xander covered the three strides it took to get to the kitchen in seconds, and was back at the bathroom door, butter knife in hand, to unlock it.

He swung the door open and found her sitting on the floor between the tub and toilet. She was in a paper clinic gown, with her bare legs tucked up in front of her and her head drooping forward.

"Jaci?" He stepped in and lifted her chin so he could get a good look at her. She was an alarming shade of gray. An empty prescription bottle sat on the closed lid of the toilet.

"Goddammit," he yelled, as he fell to his knees, pulling her toward him, and then whirling her around until he held her upright, with her back to his chest, and his arm wrapped around her waist.

"Brady," he barked, loudly. "She's OD'ing on painkillers." He lifted the lid of the toilet, sending the pill bottle flying, and leaned her forward over the bowl. Her head bobbled on her neck as he stuck his fingers down her throat. The reflex was immediate as the contents of her stomach expelled into the bowl. A smattering of partially dissolved tablets plopped into the water, decorating the bottom of the bowl with light blue dots. He made her vomit again and again until nothing came up anymore. Then, he scooped her up and carried her to the bed.

Xander laid her down and felt her neck at the carotid. Slow, lazy thumps surged underneath the pad of his finger. Her chest rose and fell in long labored breaths.

He looked at her ashen face and the dusky circles under her eyes. His heart bloomed with the need to ease her anguish and protect her from the rest of the world. It was clear that the last twenty-four hours had destroyed her.

Xander's hand was on its way up to touch his ear bud to call Brady, when he walked through the apartment door, closing and locking it behind him. He dug through the bag he carried, finally pulling out a syringe. "Narcan," he said, holding it up before popping the cover off the needle and injecting her. "That's all I got in my bag of tricks." He met Xander's eyes. "I'm out of here, but I'll be listening in case you need anything," he said, turning around and walking back through the apartment door.

He stood in the darkened room with his blood boiling. His chest heaved as he raked a hand through his hair and paced back and forth next to the bed.

Then focusing on Jaci's form, Xander brushed a lock of hair from her face. Her skin began to lose some of the deathly gray pallor it exhibited only a minute before. Already, she looked better. She was going to survive this.

His panic dulled enough for other emotions to seep in. "Holy fucking hell. Dammit." He stormed, knocking a chair over and kicking it across the room. Then, he sat heavily in the one remaining by the table, leaning over, elbows on his knees and head in his hands. Air rushed savagely in and out of his lungs. He attempted to calm the fury he felt, taking long minutes to recover from the massive adrenaline surge.

Finally somewhat calmed, he took a deep breath and looked up at Jaci's unconscious body. This was his fault. He hadn't been here. She didn't know that she already had family here, had someone who cared about her, who would take care of her.

Well, there was absolutely no chance she'd get the opportunity to do something like this again. She was going to see just how seriously he took his responsibility.

Xander stripped down to his underwear and slid into the bed. He grasped Jaci's wrist firmly. She wouldn't be going anywhere without him knowing about it.

Soon, the hens on the Sit-In Team would take over. And the leader of the hen parade, Caroline, would be trying to shoo him out. He grunted. Good luck with that.

Chapter 3

She wasn't dead.

Disappointment settled, cold and painful, in the pit of Jaci's stomach.

When she learned there was no hospital in the Amber Zone and that she'd be transported back to the apartment after her sterilization, she'd been shocked. But she eventually realized that they gave her the easy out she'd been searching for. The clinic staff provided a bottle of painkillers to take home.

But it hadn't worked.

She cracked open her eyes. A quick sweep of the room told her it was dark outside. It was hard to see anything other than all the women who surrounded her. There were several in bed with her, touching her, comforting her. Jaci's head was on a pillow in a woman's lap.

"It's okay, Jaci. We're all here for you," someone whispered in her ear. It was the person caressing her hair.

"Are you my roommate?" Jaci's throat was dry, her voice gravelly.

"No, I'm Caroline."

"Why are all these people here?"

"Jenna from the sterilization clinic sent a u-com about you."

"They sent a universal com about me?"

"Only to building seventeen. It's standard procedure."

"So, everybody in the building…knows?" Jaci paused. "How humiliating," she whispered more to herself than anybody else in the room.

"Shhh, don't worry about that." Caroline raised her up so she could take a sip of water from a straw somebody else held to her mouth. "Oh, before I forget, your assigned com is on the night table when you're ready for it. A lot of our numbers have already been downloaded in.

"I would tell you everybody else's name, but you wouldn't remember them right now anyway." Caroline was still gently raking Jaci's hair with her fingertips. "Tomorrow, you'll feel much better and we'll all have plenty of time to talk. For now, relax. We're not going anywhere tonight."

For the rest of the evening Jaci succumbed to a hazy flurry of women everywhere.

She fell into a bizarre funhouse sleep with oddly realistic and suffocating dreams. Pain woke her occasionally, and each time she opened her eyes, she was still surrounded by women. Later, they slept with her. A tangle of females covered the big bed, their bodies pressing close to her and each other. It seemed like a dozen hands reached out, touching her. Their vigilance kept her prisoner in a cocoon of female flesh. The oddity of their behavior drove away her immediate despair and provided brief moments of respite from the amalgam of physical and emotional pain.

When Jaci woke up the next morning with a clearer head, Caroline and another woman, Emily, whose name she remembered only because of her purple-tipped hair, were still there. She recognized the two other women present, but she couldn't remember their names.

"How are you feeling?" Caroline asked when she realized Jaci was awake.

She pegged the woman with a foggy gaze, "Okay, considering."

"Didn't they send home any pain meds with you? I couldn't find any."

"I don't know," Jaci lied, closing her eyes.

"I brought some that were left over from other sit-ins when I couldn't find yours. Do you want one?"

"Yes," she croaked through parched lips. "Numb would be nice right now."

Caroline walked to the counter separating the living area from the kitchen and shook a couple of tablets from a bottle. She returned with a glass of water and two tablets in her hand. Jaci accepted them wincing slightly as she sat up enough to take the pills.

"Thanks for staying with me, but you guys don't have to stay anymore. I'm sure you have better things to do."

"Nope. You're it. We're the Sit-In Team and you're stuck with us until our job is done."

"Job?" Jaci shook her head. "I'm lost."

"The Team helps new fallows from other zones adjust," Caroline said. "I'm the Sit-In Team Leader."

"We've got a lot of things to talk about today," the woman in the corner said. "My name's Hannah, by the way, in case you don't remember from last night. You were pretty out of it." She patted Jaci's blanket covered leg.

"And I'm Jordan. We're gong to be working together once you're up and around."

All of the women sort of looked alike. All had brown hair and brown eyes like she did. She would have to pay attention to faces more closely since virtually everybody designated as an Amber had brown hair and brown eyes.

Caroline had shoulder length straight brown hair with bangs. Her face was scrubbed clean which gave her appearance of being a bit plain.

After Jaci swallowed her pills, Caroline took a deep breath and spoke first. "Well, welcome to the Amber Zone."

Jaci looked at her lap and then looked at the other women. "Thank you."

They all smiled back at her with kindness. Or was it pity she saw in their eyes?

"Living in Amber is going to be different from what you're used to. Are you up to talking now? Or do you want to hold off for a while?" Caroline asked.

"Now's okay."

"Good. Well, let's see. Starting's always the hard part." Caroline looked up at the ceiling for a moment as if she was figuring out exactly what words to use.

"I've been doing this long enough to know you feel like you've lost everything, that you've been dumped here. I also know what the other designations think of us, that we're stupid and diseased. Part of our job as the Sit-In Team is to help you understand that, for the most part, we're just like you." She took Jaci's hand. "You're already accepted as one of us and you never have to feel abandoned or alone.

Jaci looked down at their joined hands, feeling slightly weird about it. She hadn't held another woman's hand since she was a young girl reaching out for the comfort of her mother.

"The major difference about our way of life compared to the other classes has nothing to do with our eye color or IQ. Our zone is completely different though, better, in my opinion. But I need to fill you in on some of our social norms that are different from what you're used to."

Jaci's mind latched on to the word better and didn't track much after that. That woman actually thought life was better here? "Okay," she said, as if she was asking what the punch line was.

Caroline went on. "Let me go back and tell you the history. It'll help explain why things are the way they are. If that makes any sense." She laughed.

"About twenty-five years ago, as a part of an agreement made with the Amber leaders at the time, the Gov researched and developed a program to help the Amber couples who were free of Automatic Disqualifiers raise their one and only child in a way that would reduce the suffering brought on by the Repopulation Laws. Doctors and other professionals determined that social support was the best way to cope with the sterilizations and other crippling conditions, as well as the restrictions Ambers have to deal with regularly.

"Back then, our parents were miserable, and they wanted their children to be happier than they were. Mandatory parenting classes were developed that taught new parents how to raise our generation so that coping mechanisms are developed and in place from birth. They went to the classes gladly. Every parent was desperate to have their one and only child live a happier life than they had. They were hopeful that this program was the solution, so they rigorously followed the recommendations and totally immersed us in an environment of unconditional acceptance and almost constant touch.

"Now, people who have been born and raised as Ambers, our generation, have a stronger connection with each other. We have built in coping skills to help us deal with the Repopulation Laws as well as all of the inevitable catastrophic illnesses that many of us were diagnosed with at our genetic testing."

"Here in Amber, we don't have the invisible don't-touch zone around us like you had in Sapphire. Touching is no different for us than breathing," Jordan cut in. "We just do it. We don't think about it. It's such an intrinsic part of our lives that many Ambers have difficulty going periods of time without the support of someone else's touch."

Jaci studied Jordan as she spoke. She was short-haired, petite and fit. Definitely a no-nonsense type of woman. Somebody who would fit in with a crowd of men as well, or maybe even better than with a crowd of women.

"You may not realize it now, but we're helping you heal, emotionally and physically, with our presence, our touch and our support," Emily said.

There was a lull in the conversation. The women let what they'd said sink in. For long moments, a relaxed silence filled the room. Jaci looked at the four of them surrounding her, touching her.

Jaci closed her eyes to escape the scrutiny of the women. Just yesterday, she would have preferred death to life in Amber. Maybe it wouldn't be as bad here as she thought. A surge of hope took up residence within her. She did feel emotionally better today, surrounded by these women, than she did yesterday. Could it be true? Could she feel included, happy even, being Amber?

Jaci opened her eyes and looked at each one of them individually. She had the feeling they would sit there and wait for her, holding her, hugging her, raking their fingers through her hair as long as she needed it. Overcome by the depth of sincerity and acceptance she felt from these women, she nodded her head slowly in understanding.

"Let's take a break. I have to pee, and I need some tea and food," Hannah said, slicing through the silence. They all answered in murmurs of soft agreement, getting up from their places on the bed. Jordan and Emily went to the kitchen together.

When Hannah returned from the bathroom, she and Caroline helped Jaci from the bed to the toilet and closed the door behind them as they left.

After she went to the bathroom, Jaci took stock of herself. She noticed the removal of the mandatory birth control device that had been implanted in her arm since she was sixteen. She wouldn't need it now. She poked at the two small stitches in her skin from the removal procedure. They didn't hurt.

She lifted up the front of her hospital gown and took off the dressing covering her incisions. The two horizontal cuts in her skin were an angry red with vertical strips of tape keeping them closed.

That's it. It was done.

Jaci's emotions plummeted. Like falling through thin ice, cold anguish enveloped her. The quickness and magnitude of the plunge caught her off guard. She groaned aloud and fell to her knees, bracing herself on the edge of the tub. "Oh fuck, fuck, fuck," she sobbed almost imperceptibly.

It didn't matter. None of the things the women told her today mattered. It was a distraction, giving her false hope that her future here in Amber was going to be tolerable. Her life was not a fairy tale, and she wasn't going to find happily ever after here.

Jaci laid her cheek on the cool surface of the rim of the tub as she cycled through the physical and mental assault of her new life.

There was a tap on the bathroom door before it opened. Caroline entered and closed the door gently behind her. "I shouldn't have left you alone. I'm so sorry. I should have known better." She rubbed Jaci's back and combed her fingers through her hair, hushing her and whispering encouragements.

It took several minutes before Jaci pulled herself together and straightened her spine. "I'm okay."

"Let's get this redressed." Caroline helped Jaci up and grabbed the box of surg patches sitting on the counter next to the sink. She placed a fresh one on each of Jaci's wounds. "They've definitely perfected this procedure over the years. You'll be feeling pretty good by tomorrow," she said unfazed as if she always found women in crumpled heaps on their bathroom floor.

When they finally exited the bathroom, she found that the other women had laid tea, bagels, and muffins on a tray in the middle of the bed. They helped Jaci in, propping her on pillows until she was comfortable and sitting up enough to eat.

They ate in relative silence with only snippets about the food and tea breaking the quiet. It gave Jaci time to process the information from the morning and stabilize her mood.

"So, do the men take advantage of this touching thing? You know, sexually? I mean how do you know if a man is touching you because he likes you or just because it's what everybody does?"

"Now that's the question isn't it," Emily said, laughing. "I like the way you think. The mind seems to travel right to the guys, doesn't it? Doesn't matter if you're an Amber or a Diamond."

"You especially are going to have countless people, both men and women, touching you a lot," Caroline said.

"Why me especially?"

"Because you're a fallow. Women who've been sterilized before having their baby, the ones that had the choice to have a child totally taken away from them, are honored members of our community. Ambers have been raised to give special attention, support and acceptance to fallows. You've made the ultimate sacrifice. Your loss does not go unnoticed here. It's a part of our culture, and I think defines who we are as a community. We're always trying to make life easier to live."

"That's part of the reason why there was a u-com sent about you to the building yesterday," Hannah said softly, looking with kindness into Jaci's eyes. "Every woman here will be sterilized eventually, but after we've given birth to a child. There are fewer women identified with Automatic Disqualifier genes, resulting in less fallows than there used to be and even fewer from different zones like you, so you're a big deal."

"And the info gets around. The coms about your arrival yesterday were flying. Plus, people talk. Pretty much every woman in the building tried to stop by last night. I had to have Xander drive them away at the door," Caroline said.

"Xander?"

"Xander's your roommate." Emily piped in.

"I have a male roommate?"

"Yeah, we all do," Emily said. "Except for Caroline. She hasn't had a roommate for how long now Caroline?

"Over a year."

"How do they keep managing to skip over you?" Jordan asked.

Caroline shrugged.

"Anyways," Emily went on with a wave of her hand. "All single Ambers are paired up boy-girl."

"It's like having a built in big brother," Jordan said. "Well, at least that's what I think having a big brother would be like. It's reassuring to have some built-in family. None of us has siblings, and a lot of our parents are sick or have died already. Our roommates take care of us. It's expected."

"I'm pretty sure the boy-girl pairing started as a result from the Gov studies," Caroline said. "They showed that supportive touch from the opposite sex affects a person more positively and with increased strength."

"I agree," Emily said, smiling with an added eyebrow wag.

"Leave it to Emily to jump into a conversation as soon as it gets anywhere near the subject of sex," Caroline said drily.

"There are some roommates that end up hooking up and sometimes even get married. But more often than not, they're our protectors and best friends. Nothing else," Jordan said.

Jaci glanced between Emily and Jordan and immediately decided that she liked them both, especially Emily. If somebody could be that happy as an Amber, she wanted to get to know them better. Maybe some of that effervescence would rub off on her.

"Anyways, we'll be staying with you for a while, until you…well, won't freak when Xander wants to be touching you. You know, when you're both home, sleeping and stuff." Hannah said.

Jaci felt disconcerted by the thought of some guy she didn't know sleeping next to her, touching her.

"That look, right there," Caroline said, motioning to Jaci. "We'll stay with you until you don't have that look on your face when you're thinking about other people touching you all the time."

Jaci tried to wipe whatever look Caroline was talking about off her face.

"It has been hard for some women from different zones to adjust to the different culture and to being a fallow," Caroline said.

Jaci noticed the split second glances the women exchanged with each other, but before she opened her mouth to ask about it, Jordan quickly changed the subject.

"Believe it or not, the last twenty-four hours have been hard on Xander. Nobody knew you were here until the u-com was sent. You were already at the Sterilization Center by the time we found out about you."

"He felt like shit that he wasn't here for your first night. He was so upset today we couldn't get him to leave. We tried to get him to go, but he was being stubborn." Emily said. "I actually had to call his mother." Her smirk was devilish. "She imposed her motherly authority and forced him to go. She's one of the very few people that will take him head-on and not accept no for an answer. They're close, the two of them."

"I think he feels like he's let you down, without you even meeting each other yet," Jordan said. "If you're up to it, you guys can meet later. I'm sure he's going to try to get in here anyways."

"He's been sleeping around because he has trouble falling asleep by himself. His last roommate, Diana, recently got married and moved to the townhomes with her new hubby," Caroline said. "That's why he wasn't here your first night."

"Sleeping around?"

"Yeah, staying here and there instead of coming back to his own apartment."

"How did Diana's husband like the fact that she slept in the same bed as Xander?" Jaci asked.

Hannah shrugged. "It was fine. Half the time, he was here too." She paused. "Listen, you have to change the mindset that sleeping with somebody or touching somebody is sexual. Sometimes it is, but most of the time it's not."

"And there's going to be a lot of times that there are three, sometimes even four people in your bed, like right now. We're all here and will be here for another night if you need us. All of our roommates, including Xander, are on their own. They're sleeping with other people."

Jaci nodded then yawned.

"Okay, I think that's enough for one morning. Jaci needs some rest," Jordan said.

"You don't have to stay and watch me sleep."

"You guys go," Caroline said. "I didn't get much sleep last night anyways, a nap sounds good."

The women left and Jaci rolled to her side trying to get comfortable. She fell asleep easily to the soft caresses of Caroline's fingers sifting gently through her hair.

* * * *

The apartment was totally silent when Xander opened the door.

A few moments before, Jordan had checked in to report that she'd left to get some sleep. He was supposed to take over surveillance. He could have done that from outside the apartment, sitting with Brady and monitoring the bug from the ninth floor. But, bottom line, he needed to see Jaci, to make sure she was okay. He wanted to…Xander shook the thought away. Wanting to shake her and yell at her for what she'd done wouldn't be the ideal way to start off their new relationship. He slipped in and peered over toward the bed.

Caroline slept next to Jaci. Her hand was on Jaci's waist.

They were both turned away from the door, facing his side of the room. He crept in, walking past the bed so he could look at his new roommate. He wanted to officially meet her since she hadn't woken up at all before the Sit-In Team arrived and pestered him until he got out.

It was hard to step back and relinquish control of this situation. But, he understood why the women took over on these occasions. Caroline, the head of the Sit-In Team was a nurse and also a fallow herself. The other women who volunteered for the sit-in would become an instant circle of friends for Jaci. They would help her cope with the extreme culture shock coming from living her whole life in a different zone. And, even more importantly, help her through the heart-piercing struggle of coming to terms with her sterilization and the new life assigned to her.

His gaze fastened to the woman in the bed. A puddle of wavy, brown hair covered his pillow. Even while sleeping, a mask of misery veiled Jaci's face. It would have been preferable to meet her before her reassignment to Amber, before the operation. He would have been able to know who she truly was, not just the person she'd been forced to become.

Xander knew other women and men that came from different zones after being designated Amber. They'd all adjusted well, many preferring the Amber lifestyle to their previous designation. He was confident Jaci would too.

He stood over her, working himself up yet again about finding her near death the day before, when Jaci opened her eyes. She looked dazed while she tried to figure out where she was, and Xander discerned the exact moment when she put the pieces together in her head because a profound sadness emanated from her. Her eyes deadened.

Kneeling next to the bed, he whispered, "Hi."

He reached out slowly and ran his thumb across her cheek.

She looked into his eyes. "Hi."

"I'm Xander."

She smiled a sad smile. "Jaci."

"You're on my side of the bed," he said teasing her. He gingerly climbed onto the sliver of mattress available next to her. Their faces were inches away from each other, their bodies pressed close with only the covers as a barrier between them.

Chapter 4

It took Jaci an instant to suppress her surprise when Xander climbed into the bed next to her. His intense expression and his dark exploration of the features of her face raised goose bumps on her arms and sent tingles down the back of her neck.

"How are you feeling?" he whispered, reaching up to brush a lock of her hair aside. He placed his palm on the skin he'd exposed on her neck, his fingers curling around to her nape. His hand was hot against her cool skin. Her breathing quickened. It felt nice, his hand on her.

"I'm ready to come home. These women wouldn't let me yesterday," he grumbled. He gently petted the back of her neck with the velvet pads of his fingers.

"I'm not sure it's up to me," Jaci said, giving him a faint smile.

"Maybe I'll stay here and hide behind you."

"You could try, but I think I'd notice." The voice sounded from behind Jaci. Caroline was awake.

"Crap," he murmured.

"You just couldn't stay away, you goon," Caroline chastised.

Jaci rolled over onto her back. "It's okay, Caroline. He's not bothering me."

Caroline glowered at Xander while he gave her a self-satisfied expression.

She turned her attention to Jaci. "You need anything?"

"Bathroom."

Xander got up from the bed and walked around to where Caroline stood. They both helped her up and walked her over to the bathroom. Xander's arm circled her back. His hand slipped underneath the opening of her paper clinic gown. It was large and warm on her skin, gently cupping her hip, guiding her. Caroline went into the bathroom with her this time, as Xander stepped away.

* * * *

"Do you want me to kick him out?"

"No, it's his apartment too."

"He's going to want to sleep here tonight. Are you ready for that?"

Jaci was silent for a while. "He's not weird or dangerous or anything is he?"

"Ha! Xander? No way. He's just a whiny baby who can't stand not being in control."

Jaci smiled. She couldn't imagine that man having a whiny bone in his body. "I think it will be okay."

"It's nice to see you smile." Caroline caught her eye, obviously trying to read her, and then nodded. "Okay."

"I'll be out in a minute." Jaci raised her eyebrows expectantly, waiting for the woman to leave her alone.

Caroline nodded and smiled at her. "Okay." She grabbed the box of surge patches on the way out the bathroom door. "I'll have to take a look when you're done in there," she said, holding up the box.

When she exited the bathroom, Caroline was waiting. "Let's take a look. I'll spray the areas with the antibiotic spray and put new patches on."

Xander leaned against the wall by the window. His arms were crossed over his chest. It looked as if it didn't even occur to him that she may want some privacy. He wasn't going anywhere.

"Oh you don't have to do that. I can do it this time." She looked down. "It's kind of--yuck."

"I'm a nurse. I've seen a lot worse than this."

Jaci's head snapped down to where Caroline knelt in front of her. "A nurse? I thought Ambers couldn't have professional jobs."

"Sometimes I think the Gov spreads that disinformation on purpose because you aren't the first fallow to say that to me. So, it's understandable why you're confused. Plus, only the Ambers that don't have higher education work outside the Amber Zone, so there was no reason to think any differently. You can go to college online here as long as you do your twenty hours of work assignment every week. All of our professionals are Ambers. Everything here is done by us, for us. There are no other class designations that work in the Amber Zone.

"There, you're all set." She threw the wrapper from the new patches away, and led Jaci back to bed.

"My work assignment is painter. It's only twenty hours a week? And I can go to college for anything I want?" She looked back and forth between Caroline and Xander.

"Yeah, everybody works twenty hours a week. No exceptions," Caroline said.

"I don't get it, how do you earn enough money to live?"

"We don't earn money, we earn credits. It's illegal to have currency in Amber," Xander stated.

"Pretty much everything, you know, the basics, are provided by the Gov at the commissary. The credits are for extras like clothes and luxury items like scented soap, stuff like that," Caroline added. "That's one of the things the code on your palm is for."

Jaci must have looked lost because Xander added, "Your credits are deposited to your code. Whenever you need to pay for something you scan your hand and the credits will be deducted from your total."

Jaci looked at Xander with disbelief, then at Caroline waiting for her to contradict him, or start laughing or something. "You're kidding right?"

"No." Xander shook his head. "From teachers to trash collectors, nobody is paid with money, and everybody earns the same amount of credits every week. If somebody chooses to go to school to be a nurse, it's because that's how they want to spend their twenty hours of work per week, not because nurses earn more credits."

"Our quality of life here is probably as good, or better even, than those who are Sapphires. Of course, the sacrifices that are made are the price we pay. Some more than others," Caroline said absently scratching Jaci's thigh.

"What's your job?" Jaci asked Xander.

"I'm a police officer."

Jaci saw it in him immediately. He carried himself with authority. She scanned his face and body, taking everything in. He was handsome with his short cut, brown hair and intense, almost black eyes. His features were rugged, especially with the growth of whiskers darkening his jaw. His face could easily be intimidating. He also possessed an essence of danger.

Their gazes locked. He'd seen her taking him in, assessing him, and it looked like he'd been doing the same.

He wore an intoxicating look on his face that contained a promise of… Jaci sighed and the muscles of her neck and shoulders relaxed. His eyes promised refuge and security.

Caroline cleared her throat and then rolled her eyes. "Don't mind him, he knows he's good looking and it's gone to his head. He thinks he's

God's gift to the female of the species." She misinterpreted the moment they'd just shared. It's about time for another dose," Caroline said over her shoulder as she shook out another painkiller for Jaci.

Xander's jaw clenched as he eyed the pill bottle in Caroline's hand. But in the split second it took for Caroline to turn back toward the room, his expression changed to normal. In that moment, Jaci realized he was the one who'd found her after she took the pills. No words were necessary from him. His expression told her everything she needed to know. He was seriously pissed off about it and nothing like that would be happening again.

"So you only work twenty hours a week too?" Jaci asked, trying to change the subject.

"Yeah. I do two ten-hour days--Tuesdays and Wednesdays unless I'm working on an ongoing case. Then my hours adjust if they have to. It all eventually washes out to twenty hours per week in the end. It's a nice gig.

"We don't have much crime here, since there's no paper money and few valuables. Thieves try to sneak out of the Amber Zone to steal. Violent crimes are practically nonexistent. I think it's because people are rarely alone enough to get away with much of anything. Once in a while we'll get a call about a fistfight, usually it's over a woman." Xander reclined at the foot of the bed, propping his head up on his hand and absently touching the hills made by Jaci's toes under the blanket.

Their eyes met again. He was doing it on purpose, trying to catch her gaze. Instinctively, she looked away. Her face flushed. He was an intense man. When he looked at her like that, she felt like he knew every secret in her soul. She liked it. In that moment, she wanted him to look at her like that for the rest of her life.

Jaci glanced at Caroline, who rolled her eyes again. "Okay, get on out of here, Xander. Jaci has to clean up and change. She's had enough of you for now." Caroline shooed him away toward the door.

"Let me grab my clothes, jeez," he said, ducking away from her. "I'm going to take a shower at your place," he grumbled over his shoulder as he grabbed his clothes and strode out the door. Jaci's gaze followed him all the way. He was magnificent to look at and as she watched him go, something inside her shifted. Suddenly she wanted more of him. She needed him to come back.

"Now listen." Caroline's voice intruded on the longing that started to develop inside her. "We have a few more things to cover before tonight."

That caught her attention. "What do you mean 'before tonight'?"

A knock sounded at the door, and Caroline walked over to let Jordan in. The hallway was crowded with people.

"What's going on out there?" Jaci asked.

"There's a bigger gathering than usual because people have been wanting to come in," she said, closing the door and walking back over to the bed. "Our open way of living is literally that. Open. When we're home, we usually leave our front doors open. People come in and visit, watch a movie, eat, talk, sleep. You literally are never alone here. Most people stick to roaming their own building and you'll get to know the people on your own floor the best.

"Let's put it this way," Jordan said. "If your door is closed, you're either not home, showering or doing the nasty. And a lot of people don't even close their doors for that. You could spend a year here and never sleep in your own bed if you didn't want to."

"That explains the crowd I walked through when I left for the Center yesterday morning. People were touching me when I walked by. I didn't even realize they were doing it on purpose." Jaci shook her head in understanding. "So, people are waiting for me to open the door so they can just come in here?"

"Yep."

Jaci's heart beat faster with anxiety.

"You suddenly look nervous," Jordan said.

"I am. Meeting large amounts of people...I don't know...is intimidating. Especially when I look like this." She motioned to herself.

"You won't be alone. We'll be here. And we'll fix you up. You'll look luscious." Caroline winked at her.

Jaci rolled her eyes. "I don't think I've ever looked luscious." She laughed, and it felt weird to laugh so soon after the events of the past day.

"You might as well get used to people seeing you *au naturelle*. We're one big family here with a lot of brothers and sisters," Caroline said. "I think I have probably seen every person in this building in their pajamas. Hell, I've probably slept with at least half." She paused. "When I say sleep, I mean sleep...you know that right?"

Jaci smiled. "Yes. I get it. I want to take a shower. I feel stinky, and I'm dying to wash my hair."

"Oh," Jordan said standing up. "I'm getting a com. I have to take this. I'll be back ladies," she said as she slipped out the door.

"Can you manage the shower on your own?" Caroline asked while helping Jaci to her feet.

"I think so."

Caroline eyed her for a few moments. "Okay. You got anything to change into?"

"Not really," Jaci said, walking the last few steps to the bathroom.

"While you're in the shower, I'll find something for you to wear. When you get out we'll get you in some clean clothes, put some food into you and take it from there. Sound good?"

Jaci nodded and shuffled to the bathroom. After closing herself in, she turned on the shower and then released the strings at the neck of the paper gown she wore. She was so glad to get out of that crinkly reminder of the sterilization. She wadded it up into a ball and tossed it into the can. Pulling the curtain back, she stepped into the shower and stood with the spray hitting her back. The hot steam felt good. She felt   good? She wouldn't go that far. But, she was hopeful. She already felt like she had a place where she belonged.

Maybe she could withstand the loss of her old life.

The loss of her fertility.

The loss of her family.

"Shit." Bowing her head, she groaned. As soon as she started thinking, she started hurting all over again. The rush of feelings swarmed her, erasing any hope she'd accumulated that day. The longer she stood under the spray, the more she felt like someone ripped her insides out and left a hole there. Stark emptiness swam around inside her. Jaci got down on her knees in the tub and curled herself up in a ball, letting the hot spray sting her back. The waterfall of her dark hair created a dim, wet sanctuary for her face.

It was true. There was something in the touching and acceptance that eased her. It was the times she was alone when misery attacked, devouring all the emotional progress she'd made. This was all an illusion. She knew nobody cared about her, loved her here. It was impossible. She'd only been in Amber for a day. But she supposed pretending that someone cared for her made life bearable right now. Being connected with other people kept her from collapsing in on herself, from becoming a shell of skin with nothing of value inside. It helped her feel not so alone. It distracted her from suicide.

She inhaled the hot, wet air wafting around her face and then released a shuddering breath. The shower spray needled her back from the jets hitting the same place for so long. She shifted slightly to relieve the sting. If only it were that easy to dull the other pains.

In these silent moments, she felt too much, way too much. The emotions were caustic, like acid eating through her heart. She'd do anything to make the hollow loneliness that swam around inside of her subside. Caroline told her she didn't ever have to be alone in Amber unless she wanted to. In that moment, she didn't want to.

She called out. "Caroline?" There was only silence.

Then the bathroom door opened

"Caroline's not here. You okay?" It was Xander.

Jaci wasn't expecting him to be there. "Yeah," She struggled to sound normal. "I'm just being pathetic. I'm fine." She heard the click of the door close and sighed.

So much for not being alone.

She knew it was essential to get up and face the world. It was time to embark on her new life even if she forced herself to do it. The pity party she was currently throwing for herself wasn't helping anything.

Jaci flinched at the unexpected contact of a hand on her back.

"Come on, I'll help you out." Xander's raspy voice caressed her ears.

She lifted her head to look up at him, and a screen of wet, tangled hair stuck to her face. The spray of the water stopped. The bathroom fell silent.

"I can do it," Jaci whispered shakily.

"Yes. But you don't have to." With the soft warmth of a towel draped over her back and a firm grip on each side of her, he lifted her, unfolding her until she stood. Xander's gentle touch brought her to the verge of tears. He drew her into his arms and held her there.

Chapter 5

"Don't be embarrassed," Xander whispered into Jaci's ear as she made an attempt to hide her body from him. With shaking hands she groped for the edges of the towel, trying to pull it around herself to hide behind. He lifted her onto the counter next to the sink. "Your body is beautiful," he whispered, as he watched her violent blushing clash with her silent plea to be held. The fact that she was already suffering from the absence of physical contact was undeniable. She needed it as much as she needed the air that rushed in and out of her lungs. She sat for only a second, then hid from his scrutiny by leaning into him and resting her forehead on his chest. Her breathing was deep and ragged as she tried to pull herself together. "I've got you, sweet Jaci. We'll do this together." He wrapped his arms around her and stroked her back, expecting her to cry. She didn't.

For long minutes in the steamy silence of the bathroom, she didn't say a word. With her head resting on his chest, sheltering herself with his body, she took cover from the world They were a still life, the jaded and the lost making a connection, trying to make their lives a little less brutal, helping each other survive. Xander closed his eyes as he attempted to choke down his fury and did the only thing any Amber male ever did to help an Amber female, touch her…love her.

He felt as if he was experiencing firsthand the helpless rage that the first Amber men experienced during the mass sterilizations of their women. Those men possessed little control over anything in their lives. They were acutely aware of the fact they couldn't stop the Gov from victimizing them, and they couldn't take away their women's pain. So they did the only thing they could do, give them pleasure. And now he felt that compulsion too. He wanted to make Jaci feel better, to counteract her pain.

Xander was dragged back to the present by the subtle shaking of Jaci's shivers. He grabbed another towel and dried her hair, brushing it away from her face, and then he dried the skin she didn't have covered. He smoothed the towel slowly over her damp, chilled body. She was slumped over and, he suspected, purposely not meeting his gaze.

Jaci's innocence and modesty about her body was refreshing. It was an odd departure from the women who grew up in Amber and lost that sweet self-consciousness about their bodies at an early age. With the new parenting philosophy his generation was raised with, encouraging touch and physical openness, sex became a natural extension of that. Girls were used to being touched at an earlier age, and by the time boys in Xander's generation became men, they were exceptionally skilled at giving pleasure with their touch. Most boys were adept at bringing a girl to orgasm with their hands by age fifteen, and with their dicks by eighteen. As the men got older, many learned the fine art of blending pleasure and pain--of manipulating hormones and endorphins to create a state of total abandon and euphoria for their women in Amber. As a result of the Repopulation Laws, Amber men were possibly the most skilled lovers in the history of the human race. Jaci hadn't grown up with any of this, he reminded himself. She was unaccustomed to being touched all the time. Xander felt his hackles go up. She was probably a virgin. How was he supposed to protect that?

"You're the one who found me?"

"Yeah, sweetie, I did."

"Why didn't you just let me die?" she whispered.

"Because you're mine to take care of now." He leaned in close so that his lips were brushing her ear. "It's okay to stumble and fall. I'll be here to catch you. I'll take care of you Jaci, I promise." Xander squeezed the words out through a tight throat. "Come on, I'm taking you back to bed." He lifted her carefully, as if she'd disintegrate and fall to pieces in his arms, and hugged her close to comfort her, instinctively knowing it was what she needed.

He sat on the edge of the bed, settled her in his lap and tucked her into him, wrapping his arms around her to keep her warm and let her know she was safe. After a few beats of stillness, Jaci started shaking her head. Almost imperceptibly at first, but within seconds, a sob escaped her. "I can't…" She looked him in the eye as tears spilled onto her cheeks. "I can't do this. She looked at her lap again as her shoulders shook with heavy racking sobs. "It hurts to be alone in the world, to be forced to start your life over again. There's nothing to look forward to. They took everything from me, including my dreams.

"I don't want this. Let me die next time," she cried. "Please. Please," she sobbed. "I don't want to feel like this. I don't want to feel it anymore."

"That's enough," Xander growled. "I don't want to hear any more of this. I'm going to take care of you, Jaci. I'll help you chase the pain away. We'll do it together."

He was determined to be the crutch that propped her up and helped her through this, carrying her past it to the other side, settled and stable.

Jaci curled up into a ball in Xander's lap. He rocked her, peppering light kisses on her temple, cheek, and hair until her tears dried up. When he finally released her from the cradle of his arms, he settled her into bed. "Okay?" He looked directly into her eyes, tried to read her level of comfort, her unspoken thoughts and feelings. She returned his gaze with round eyes. He couldn't glimpse any other emotion. They were flat with no glimmer of life in them. They were as dead as she wanted to be.

He walked over to the small table for two and sat in one of the chairs with his back against the wall. Seconds later, Caroline flitted into the room like an excited hummingbird, clothes in hand and ready for her task. She walked over to the bed and handed Jaci a pale yellow, silky nightshirt. "I love the feel of this one against my skin. It makes me feel pampered," she said.

As Xander watched Jaci slip the shimmering fabric over her head and bare shoulders, he acknowledged the compulsion he had to fix it, to make everything better for her. His mind returned to the many ways he would help her forget all of this. She didn't want to feel. He knew how to get her to that place where the world receded, where her body chemicals took over. Enticing flashes of erotic scenes comprised the mental rundown of how he would get her there.

Son of a bitch. He was hard while his mind devised all the things he wanted to do to Jaci, with Jaci, for Jaci. He watched her get ready, still slumped over and looking at her lap. Caroline brushed her hair and then loosely braided it into a thick rope, falling onto her back.

He could help her tonight, if she'd let him. He opened his mouth to tell Caroline she should go, that he'd finish helping Jaci get ready, when Hannah and Emily blew in through the door bringing positive energy and fun banter with them. "We came with food. Fresh chicken, mashed potatoes with green beans," Emily said.

Caroline gasped. "Oh my God. Where did you get chicken?"

"Sid from the restaurant knew I volunteered for a sit-in and made it special for us," Emily said.

Xander watched as Jaci looked back and forth between the two women in confusion.

"Man, I haven't eaten chicken that hasn't seen the inside of a can for almost year," Caroline said. The thrill of the treat electrified the air as everybody looked at the small plate of chicken Emily brought from the restaurant she worked at.

"I'm missing something. What's the big deal about chicken?" Jaci finally asked.

"Fresh meat is hard to come by in the Amber Zone," Hannah said. "We're bottom of the food chain. There's always plenty of fruit, nuts and veggies, but meat is usually canned. Milk is usually powdered, and some things are almost impossible to get, like chocolate and coffee."

"Well, chocolate and coffee are hard to get in Sapphire too, but it sounds like Amber suffers more from the shortages than the other zones," Jaci said.

Jordan rejoined them, slipping into the apartment just in time to get a small portion of chicken. All the women ate together on the bed and filled Jaci in on some of the characters that lived on the fourth floor, trying to give her the lay of the land. Xander didn't eat the small plate of food Emily sat in front of him on the dinette table. He watched Jaci, tried to read her, tried to figure out how much he still had to worry about her. His heart lurched at the look of trepidation that flashed over Jaci's face as Hannah stood. "Are you ready to do this? You don't have to, you know."

"I guess." Jaci shrugged and then turned her head to look at Xander as if to make sure he was still there. "Might as well get everybody's curiosity out of the way."

Caroline got up from the bed and gathered the remnants of the dinner. Hannah straightened up the sheet and blanket, brushing off a few crumbs here and there.

Emily walked to the door, her curly springs of hair bounced with her steps. As soon as the door was opened, the immediate buzz of voices told Xander the hallway was packed with curious neighbors, just as it was the night before.

An endless stream of people visited Jaci while he brooded. Finding her rolled into a ball in the bathtub wrenched his feelings from their hiding spot, and the breakdown that followed tied his heart into knots. He was more worried about her after seeing her fall apart. He was sure the depth of hurt she felt was barely tolerable. It was hard not to be affected by it, not when standing there staring it down face to face. It took him several hours to pull himself together, and even though various people sat and talked with him, it wasn't until Rock came in that Xander started to tamp down the thoughts and emotions that sprung up from his time with Jaci earlier in the night.

Emily introduced Rock to Jaci, and then he crossed the room to sit next to Xander. The two of them spent the better part of the evening casually pretending that they weren't conducting the most intense stake out of their careers.

The apartment was loud and crowded by the time Gwen arrived. She grabbed Xander's hand the moment she got close enough to touch him. He registered an instant of surprise at the concerned look on her face. He thought he'd been hiding his turmoil well. "Somehow, I knew this would be hard for you," she murmured. "Are you okay?"

Xander glanced over to Rock who nodded, and then excused himself.

"It's fine," he said with the most convincing smile he could muster. But they grew up together. Gwen was his family, his adopted sister. She knew him. With a glance, she knew.

Gwen's mother died a few weeks after Xander's dad, leaving her young and parentless. Their mothers had been best friends, so it was a no-brainer for his mom, Allie, to take her in.

Having a sibling in the Amber Zone was an anomaly and a blessing. The two of them grew up together, sharing the common ground of knowing what it felt like to lose a parent. She always seemed to know what was going on inside him, probably because similar things were going on inside her. They were close, and he couldn't wait for Gwen to meet Jaci. He wanted to know Gwen's initial opinion of her. She was a good judge of character, and suddenly it was important for her to like Jaci, to give her stamp of approval on the woman. But tonight would not be the night to find out. The place was a madhouse.

Gwen sat and held his hand for over an hour. Then she left with plans to stop back to meet Jaci when there weren't so many people around.

The evening was excruciatingly long for Xander as the majority of people living in the vicinity paraded in to pay their respects to the new fallow of the building. He watched every person who walked into their apartment closely for some indication of stalking behavior, mental instability or even overfriendliness. He noticed nothing unusual from the visitors, but learned a lot about his new roommate.

Jaci handled the steady stream of people sitting and laying on the bed well. Every single person that came in the room that night touched her. It was obvious this was like nothing she'd ever seen or experienced before. She looked self-conscious at first when both men and women kissed her cheeks, caressed her arms, and ran their fingers through her hair. She seemed extraordinarily surprised that, to them, she was important. Special.

She was approachable, and even though she felt terrible, she made the effort to get to know people and return their touch. She got it. He was impressed.

Whenever anyone asked how she was feeling, "Good" was always her response. He knew she didn't feel good. But her strength of spirit, her pride, would not let her show her personal pain. It didn't look like she was feeling sorry for herself and she didn't want others to feel sorry for her either, and that made her all the more endearing.

Because he'd been watching the visitors so closely, Xander caught the play of emotions on their faces when they interacted with her. This was upsetting for many of the men, women too, he guessed, but probably more in a thank-God-it's-you-and-not-me kind of way.

He understood the Gov's desire to eliminate the genetic anomalies, reducing and eventually eliminating the diseased people who burdened the social systems that are only now functional again. Amber society helped themselves feel better by assigning the fallow a place of honor within the community. They patted themselves on the back, telling themselves it was enough and moved on. The truth, the fact that the fallow suffered in silence throughout their whole lives, was dismissed. Despite the questionable circumstances of the last three fallow deaths, statistics showed a significantly higher rate of suicide for them compared to the rest of the Amber population. Xander silently vowed Jaci would not be one of them. She would make it through all of this. He was going to be sure of it.

The evening wound down with no obvious suspects standing out. It was late, and Caroline was saying goodbye to the last of the stragglers. Rock, who'd been sitting with him again since Gwen left, nodded his goodbye to Jaci and left with Emily. Caroline closed the door after the last visitor left and met his gaze. Jaci had already rolled over onto her side and seemed close to sleep.

"You can go," Xander said. "I'll take care of her overnight."

Caroline stood looking between Jaci and him for a moment.

"She'll be fine. You've done enough for the day. Go."

With a sigh, Caroline picked up her purse. "Com me if you need me. I can be here in two minutes."

He nodded and ushered Caroline through the doorway, closing and locking the door behind her. He walked through the apartment, turning off lights and throwing away cups left behind by their visitors.

He got ready for bed in the bathroom, brushing his teeth and stripping off his jeans and t-shirt. He was excited to be back in his own apartment, his own bed again. This would be the first good night's sleep he'd have in weeks.

Coming out of the bathroom, Xander turned off the light and walked around the foot of the bed to get to his side. It was dark, but not so dark that he couldn't see. The moon cast a faint blue light in through the window, and he easily saw Jaci's face once his eyes adjusted to the dark.

He pulled back the blanket and slid in next to her. She faced him and was obviously fast asleep. He studied her face. She was lovely. The blueish light from the moon illuminated her. She was an angel with an aura of peaceful grace surrounding her. She looked less troubled than in her earlier sleep. He sighed with relaxation and relief.

"Jaci?"

"Hmm?"

"Roll over to your other side."

Jaci cracked an eye open. "Not enough room?"

"It's not that. I can't get up next to you if you're facing me. Unless you want to switch sides if that's better for you."

Without answering, Jaci rolled over so she faced away from him. She took a deep breath and settled back to sleep as Xander pressed his body against hers. The wall of his abs cradled the curve of her spine. The bare skin of her legs brushed up against his. He slaked his hand up her side, encountering the material of her panties and the yellow silk nightshirt. He clenched his teeth, wanting so badly to go underneath the shirt instead of over. Her hair brushed his face, smelling like vanilla and tickling his nose. He smiled, she smelled sweet, too. He gingerly let his hand fall around her, on the outside of her shirt, his elbow at her waist, his hand cupping her breast.

"Okay?" he whispered.

Goose bumps raised on her skin and the nipple under his palm hardened. Xander chuckled. "I'll take that as a yes."

* * * *

Rock faced away from the two women in his bed, listening to Journey ask all about Jaci and the goings on that evening. He loved to listen to them talk when they thought he was sleeping. The voyeuristic quality of eavesdropping, of hearing the side of a person they don't intend you to know, the secret side of them, was compelling.

Earlier, Journey had been petulant when he'd left for Xander's apartment. She was mad because he wouldn't let her go too.

But even now, he stood by his decision. Journey was a different kind of woman than most. She was small, shy and easily affected by others. In other words, the complete opposite of Emily.

He'd been clueless on how to handle this skittish woman when she'd moved in almost two years ago. It looked like she was about to cry from the sight of him alone. Rock assumed she'd probably gotten that way from years of moving from place to place after her parents died. It seemed like she wanted to make as little noise and take up the smallest amount of space she possibly could. He was so completely blessed to have Emily in his life back then. She embraced Journey with open arms and acted in Rock's place many times when he was clueless as to what to do because his mere presence intimidated the tiny mouse of a woman. Emily helped him soothe Journey regularly back then.

He felt fortunate his girlfriend and his roommate got along. He'd known many men who'd had to get rid of their girlfriends because they didn't get along with their females. Not Emily.

Journey had come a long way since her arrival at his apartment. What at first seemed to Rock like an impossible pairing, quickly became exactly right for him. She needed a strong protector and he was very good at the protection thing.

He was all she had, and he'd move mountains for her if she needed him to.

Rolling over, Rock met Emily's gaze over Journey's head. She was spooning Journey with both arms wrapped firmly around her. Journey looked over at him. Her eyes widened and her chatter suddenly dropped off when she realized he wasn't asleep.

"If I let Emily console you, do you think you'll be able to get rid of your hurt feelings and wake up tomorrow with a better attitude?" Rock asked.

He glanced back up at Emily. She smiled at him, and her eyes glittered with desire. He was well aware Emily loved soothing Journey. He didn't let her do it often. He didn't want Journey to become dependent on either one of them for touch or sexual gratification. She needed to learn and become comfortable with the process of making new benefriends. Which, he had to admit, she was.

Journey smiled at him. "I'm trying not to be bratty. And cross my heart, I won't wake up with an attitude tomorrow, whether you let Emily or not." She pouted. "I felt left out, that's all. I trust you to know what's best, you know that."

He took her chin, lifting it so she would meet his eyes. "That's my good girl." He released Journey and nodded at Emily.

Emily squealed. "I was hoping. It's been a while hasn't it, Journey?" Emily asked as she moved to her knees. "Come up here, on your knees, brat," Emily said with a giggle. The spark in Journey's eyes as she lifted herself to kneel opposite Emily captivated him.

One by one, Emily unbuttoned the small white buttons that kept Journey's nightgown closed. Her unhurried approach to seduction intrigued Rock. Mainly because he knew Emily was more of a fuck-me-hard-and-fast woman, but when it came to Journey, she was mellow.

When Emily finished undoing the buttons, she dipped her hands under the material and brushed the fabric from Journey's shoulders. Her hands lightly skated over the soft, pale skin as the nightgown pooled on the mattress around her knees.

Journey whimpered at the tease of Emily's caress. Her face was already flushed and Rock observed the slight tremble of her hands as she steadied herself after getting rid of the nightgown, and then placing them on the tops of her thighs.

"Lay back, Journey," Rock ordered as Emily got off the bed to remove her own clothes. Journey immediately complied, stretching her diminutive body next to him. The bright moonlight transformed her pale skin to ghostly white. Her nipples puckered as he raked his gaze over them. They were pretty, but Rock honestly lost all interest in any women other than Em.

Emily crawled back on the bed and knelt between Journey's legs. Reaching out, she swept two fingers through Journey's pussy. Rock held his breath as he watched Emily lift the fingers to her mouth, tasting Journey's cunt and meeting Rock's eyes.

She was teasing him, trying to get him to join her. He returned her manipulation with his best look of censure and a growl. "Who's the brat now?" he warned her. She smiled at him but quickly turned her attention back to Journey.

Emily crawled her way up Journey's body until her lips closed in slowly on Journey's. The profile of the two women as their lips met was a feast for the eyes. He watched their long, gentle kiss intently. The occasional peeks of tongue as they twined in the recesses of each other's mouths, stirred him. The women shared each other's air and moaned into each others' mouths.

When Emily separated her lips from the other woman's, she lowered her kisses to Journey's neck and then lower to her chest.

Emily's seduction was a performance. Rock could have come in his boxers when she bit down on one of Journey's nipples. In response, Journey arched her back up for more. The reaction was sheer perfection. A visual moment in time that would never leave him.

Emily continued her trails of kisses down Journey's body, occasionally replacing a kiss with a lick or a bite. Then she stuck the tip of her tongue into Journey's navel.

With a sweet moan, Journey brought her hands up and tangled them in Emily's black-and-purple curls. As Emily's ministrations traveled further south, Journey's body swayed under the slow advance and retreat of Emily's fingers, and the talents of Emily's mouth.

Watching every moment, Rock remembered Emily mentioning she'd been able to coax three fingers into Journey the last time they were together. He'd raised an eyebrow in response and laughed. "Let me know when you've worked your way up to fisting and then we'll talk." A jolt of lust had him clenching his teeth as he refocused to where Emily's hands worked Journey.

Fuck! His cock was going to explode just thinking about it.

Journey neared her peak, and Rock traced his gaze up to her face.

Sweet little mouse. He loved the expression on Journey's face when she came. It held a strange combination of acquiescence and triumph while the orgasm nourished her, coloring her cheeks and giving her what she needed to thrive.

While she hovered right on the edge of her orgasm, Journey let go of Emily's hair and grabbed his hand. The pale hand squeezed his tightly as she reached for her orgasm. Her body was fixed as she stretched to reach the zenith. She froze for a few seconds then suddenly, she tumbled, falling, crying out in her meager mouse voice. Pleasure and love whirled fiercely within him at the sight of the two women in his life.

Journey eventually crumpled and Emily collapsed onto the bed next to him.

Rock laughed a slow, menacing chuckle. Now Emily was going to suck him as repayment for her earlier teasing. He cupped the nape of her neck.

"Come here, Em…"

Chapter 6

Every morning since moving to Amber, Jaci woke up tunneled into Xander's body like it was a cocoon that surrounded and protected her from the outside world. This morning, the weight of his iron arm caged her as she lay there awake, unmoving because she wanted to soak up his…his what? What was it he gave her by holding her while they slept? She didn't know exactly how to describe it, but it was comfortable and safe and every morning, she never wanted it to end. But sadly, it always did.

When Xander left the bed after their first night sleeping together, she had the chance to see all of him in the light of day and she almost groaned aloud. With only a pair of shorts on, she saw that his body was perfection, powerful and sexy. He was tall and lean. His tanned skin stretched taut over his frame showing all the intricate cuts and edges of his anatomy. His shoulders and chest were broad and every muscle in his torso showed above the low-slung waistband of his shorts. When she looked at him with the morning light framing him, it was as if she admired the flawless art of God. He took her breath away. Her favorite part of her new life in the Amber Zone was waking up every morning engulfed by this masterpiece of a man.

Every morning, when he rose to go to the bathroom and get dressed, Jaci lingered in the bed, feeling a physical ache, a substantial loss, as if a part of her was gone too.

After a few days of this, it occurred to her that she wasn't going to be good at the touching not equaling sex concept because in her heart and mind, Xander's touch was pure sex. No matter how many times she'd tried to convince herself it wasn't. Her body reacted to him as if he were her lover. By the time he left the bed every morning, she was fully primed for him, her breathing deep and ragged and her skin screaming for more of his touch. In this time she relished most, she imagined them together in beautiful love scenes. They were everything to each other--lovers and friends, protector and protected, savior and saved. Daily, she tried to will it to happen, to telepath her fantasy scene into his brain. It didn't work.

Xander gave no indication he had even one sexual impulse toward her and no matter how much she wished his sexual desire for her to be there, it wasn't. Even when he held her in his arms and she pressed up close to his body, the sexual component on his part was noticeably absent.

Jaci's recovery progressed quickly. She spent the next few days adjusting. A lot of that time she spent with Jordan.

"It's time you got your lazy ass out of bed," Jordan announced one morning, walking over to Jaci's dresser and rummaging through it for clothes. "I'm getting you out of the apartment to tour the building." She turned to face Jaci. "Jeez, when are you going to get your clothes?"

Jaci shrugged. "I still haven't called my mom yet."

Jordan didn't reply. She didn't have to. Disapproval was blatant on her face.

"Come on." She threw some clothes at Jaci. "Get dressed."

They walked the building together. Jordan showed her the locations of the recycle shoots, laundry, solar cart station and social center, which basically was a big room on the ground floor used for everything from dances to memorials.

Jaci looked into the open doorways as she passed them in the hall and did a double take several times. She saw glimpses of people fucking, many times with others watching.

Jordan glanced over to Jaci and picked up on her expression.

"What?" Jordan asked.

"This is the norm?" Jaci pointed to another group sexathon, complete with gawkers, as they passed.

Jordan shrugged. "Yeah, pretty much. Not common in Sapphire?" she asked, grinning.

"No, you know it isn't." Jaci's mind chewed on this new information for a few moments. "You said this touching thing isn't sexual."

"We did, but that doesn't mean we don't have sex. One thing leads to another. Like back there," she said, motioning with her hand, "Probably started with some people hanging out watching a movie. Maybe a couple started kissing. The next thing you know, you're walking past their open door with your mouth gaping open." Jordan laughed. "You'll get used to it.

"We don't ignore our biological need to have sex. It's emotionally unhealthy. Everybody here has sex when they want to, whether they have a boyfriend or not. And, FYI, if the door's open, you're welcome to join in. I don't know if you're comfortable with that, but at least you know."

Jaci's stomach performed a perfect flip inside her torso. She wondered what it was like to be so comfortable inside one's own skin that joining in like that was as casual as going to a party. How would it feel to physically give and take without reservation, no self-consciousness, no fear of rejection, no judgment.

God, she bet it was good.

"Can I ask you a question?" Jordan murmured under her breath. "Just between us. You don't have to answer if you don't want to."

"Sure."

"I've heard that guys from the other zones are not that good in bed, I mean, you know, they're kind of clueless when it comes to getting a girl off."

"I'm not sure I'm the one to ask. I'm not that experienced, but the couple of men I have been with didn't have me pounding down their door for more. I can tell you that."

" I've heard that some women pretend to get off. Is that true?"

"Yeah."

Jordan was silent for a few beats. Her lips pressed together in a thin line. "Really?"

"You can't make me believe that the women in Amber never fake orgasms."

Jordan turned and looked at her as if she had two heads. "Have you pretended?"

Jaci sighed "Yeah." She lowered her voice. "Every time."

Her eyes widened and utter confusion clouded her face. "Why would you do that? It doesn't make any sense to me."

If Jaci hadn't seen Jordan's complete astonishment for herself, she would have thought the woman was joking around. "Because some guys are so clueless that you just want them to get off you."

"So, you've *never* had one with a man?"

"No." The word was an unsure whisper. In the long pause that stretched between them, Jaci wondered if her sex life had been this way because of something she'd been doing wrong. But the thought was cut short when Jordan spoke again.

"That doesn't happen here."

Jaci was skeptical. "Never?"

She shook her head. "No. They all know what they're doing. At least I've never been with or even heard about a man in Amber that didn't.

"It's probably the touching. Over time, the guys get to know a woman's body pretty well. Or, maybe they teach each other. I don't know," Jordan said with a hint of curiosity in her voice.

They rode the elevator in silence while Jaci turned over and examined this different perspective on sex in her mind. Maybe the Amber Zone had it right. It was a more honest and straightforward approach to relationships. There was no need for sweet talk or lies from men trying to get into a girl's pants when there were any manner of sexual offerings any time he wanted. And for the woman, there was no reason to fake an orgasm with a so-so lover, or settle and lower standards in a relationship because some sex, even if it was mediocre, was better than nothing at all.

Jaci reminded herself to revisit this when she had more time to digest this cultural peculiarity. Maybe she would try to get more info from Emily later when she came over with Rock.

"Come on. I've got to get you back or Xander will be mad that you're overdoing it."

"I'm fine." But Jordan tightened her grasp on her hand and headed toward the elevator.

"Okay, Jordan, relax."

"I'll relax once I get you back." The elevator door opened on the fourth floor. "Apparently, you haven't seen Xander when he's mad. I don't recommend it, by the way."

As it turned out, the rush back to her apartment was for nothing. It was empty when they got there.

"You need to talk to your mother. It's been too long already," Jordan said as she settled into one of the chairs at the cafe table in the corner.

Jaci sighed and fell silent, trying to think of another good excuse that would fend off this push to call. She couldn't think of one.

Originally, she'd been avoiding the call because she was embarrassed and ashamed of her designation to Amber. She didn't want to admit that to Jordan and she didn't feel that way anymore anyways, but she knew her mom would. She was hiding from her mom's reaction, from her pity. She couldn't hide forever. "Okay," Jaci said, shaking her head.

Jaci spent about ten minutes reassuring her mom that she was okay after telling her about the Automatic Disqualifier. Then, she gave instructions on what clothes and personal items needed to be sent. She ended the conversation promising that she would com again soon.

As Jaci touched her ear bud to disconnect, she knew she'd lied. She wouldn't be calling again soon. She'd made her mother too upset and to be honest, it made her upset, too. It felt good hearing the sound of her mom's voice, but it was also a harsh reminder of what she'd lost and of what other people think about her now. She was still the same person, but somehow the Amber label changed her in other people's eyes.

She and Jordan talked about life and the curves it threw until Xander got home and then Jordan took off, stating she had her own plans for the evening.

Xander had invited Rock and Emily over for a series marathon. Gradually, more and more old programming became available to watch through the video feeds. Some of the shows were so old it was like watching history. She looked forward to hanging out and watching the shows together, marathon style. She'd done it with friends in Sapphire and it was always a blast laughing about the language and clothes and drooling over the food people enjoyed back then. Plus, spending time with Emily always seemed to make her feel better, lighter inside, and that feeling was one she'd craved since she arrived in Amber.

When Emily and Rock arrived carrying food and drink, a storm of activity arrived with them. Emily sported a devilish smile, as always, and Rock oozed intimidation with his size, tattoos and rough, throaty voice. It took a lot to overshadow Rock's presence, but Emily did it easily.

They settled in quickly with all four of them sprawled on the bed, and started watching *Sex in the City*. The series was about the opulent, narcissistic lifestyle of women of the early twenty-first century.

When they paused the marathon so the men could get some food together for all of them to munch on, Jaci tried to gauge whether she and Emily were still within earshot. The men were in the kitchen making snacks, drinking beer and totally engrossed in their conversation.

Jaci had enough of a buzz to ask Emily the questions she'd been holding on to. They'd moved to the small round table on the other side of the bar, dangerously close to where the men were. But curiosity won out and Jaci went for it.

"I need to pick your brain," she said, leaning in toward Emily.

"Shoot," she said loudly. Jaci's subtlety was lost on her.

"When Jordan took me around the building today, there were some apartments that had groups of people having sex and some with other people watching them have sex like it's no big deal. This is totally new to me. You need to fill me in. Jordan said it was normal. No big deal?"

"It's not a big deal, not in Circle City anyway. I don't think it's that common with the married couples in Amber outside of Circle City. Most couples quit the group thing, if they were even into it in the first place, especially after they're married."

"Do you and Rock?"

"Once in a while we'll do something different than only the two of us. Actually, it's the only thing holding me back from saying yes to Rock's marriage proposals. I'm not sure I'm going to be satisfied with one person sexually right now, or for the rest of my life.

"Oh, my wounded heart," Rock cut in.

Emily looked up with a smirk and a fiery twinkle in her eye as she locked her gaze on her boyfriend.

"I'm going to get you to say yes this year, Em, so get your last flings in while you can." Rock's voice softened. "Plus, baby, you know I got more than enough in my repertoire to keep you going for the rest of our lives together."

Emily rolled her eyes and ignored him. "Where were we?"

"Group sex," Xander prompted in a gravelly voice.

Jaci's cheeks burned with a rising blush. "Okay, so I just walk in…and join them? Even if I don't know them?"

"Yeah." Emily shrugged.

Jaci was silent for a few moments, trying to fully process the information. "And it's totally no big deal?"

"No."

"What part are you hung up on?" Xander asked.

"Every part. The whole perspective on sex here is completely contradictory from the way I was raised in Sapphire. You guys are so, 'It's a biological need. It's totally natural.' While the attitude about sex in Sapphire is more like 'wait for the right person and don't be easy or they won't respect you.'"

"I've heard that from other people who've come from there. You'll like it better here. I guarantee it." Emily beamed.

"That's what Jordan said. She also said that the men here are better lovers." Jaci took another swig from her beer and knew that her face was full on flushed with embarrassment as she continued, "That they, you know--know what they're doing."

"We should. We've had lots of practice," Xander said smugly as his hot gaze traveled over Jaci's body and back up to her face. He searched her eyes as if he were trying to gauge her reaction.

It was the first time he'd done anything at all that could be interpreted as sexual and it flustered Jaci so much she looked away. "Well, I've had…I've had not as much as you." She lifted her chin. A conspicuous silence followed her comment and she felt compelled to fill it. "I'm not a virgin," she announced, trying way too hard to not sound like one. "But the experiences in Sapphire were," Jaci paused, "less than gratifying. It made me wonder what the big deal was about."

Xander and Rock flashed incredulous glances at each other.

"Don't worry about it. The guys do all the work anyway," Emily said, looking at Rock with arousal flaring in her eyes.

"I'm not worried," Jaci lied. "I'm actually kind of excited that maybe it will be better here."

"Jaci, it is definitely going to be better here." Emily winked at her. Then to Jaci's mortification, she continued, "Are you comfortable being naked? Because you're never going to be able to come if you're feeling self-conscious." She looked at Jaci expectantly as if she'd asked whether she liked the color blue or if she had read any good books lately.

"Uh, not particularly."

"I can help you with that particular problem," Xander said. He was obviously amused by the turn the conversation had taken.

Jaci looked over at Xander as he made his amused offer for help. Then Emily said something, but her voice receded. Jaci wasn't listening. Her gaze was locked with Xander's. He wasn't smiling anymore. He looked her over with X-ray eyes. She actually brought her hand up to check her shirt. Then her heart skipped a beat when his scorching gaze traveled there. It made her wet, and from the look on his face, he knew it.

Jaci spent the rest of the night confused. As they progressed through the marathon, she was hyper-aware of every miniscule movement, every changed facial expression from the man sitting next to her on the bed. All of a sudden, it seemed like she had to try extremely hard to keep her eyes off him. She was fucking losing it.

They all drank heavily and laughed hysterically at episode after episode of what Jaci could only describe as ridiculous clothes and mindless problems.

At some point, she'd fallen asleep and barely reached consciousness when Xander woke her up to get her under the covers.

She woke in the middle of the night curled up, as always, in Xander's arms with his hand gripping her wrist. When she opened her eyes, she was staring into Emily's sleeping face. Rock lay curled around her with his arm in a tight hold around her waist. The video feed was paused, frozen on a close up of the main character of the series they'd been watching.

She was surprised to see Emily and Rock were still there. She'd assumed that they would leave at the end of the night. This place was so fundamentally different from the Sapphire Zone that it was hard to anticipate other people's behaviors. She was constantly revising her expectations of what others would do or say.

Lying there in the still silence of the night was about as close as she got to having time to herself. For the most part, she didn't mind the absence of solitude. This way, she didn't have time to dwell on the negative. But she also didn't have time to make sense of the influx of new information about the Amber Zone. Jaci unpacked all of the tidbits that she'd tucked away so far. She needed to put them together and reason through everything in hopes of getting a better understanding of all the differences. She was beginning to understand her new Zone in its most basic form and the thought processes that drive the people here.

She figured Rock and Emily didn't leave because, as far as they were concerned, they belonged in this apartment just as much as anywhere else in Circle City. The whole city was theirs. It belonged to all of them. They all owned the same things, had the same furniture in their apartments, earned the same number of credits, and all of them worked for the good of the rest.

All supported all. She was hit with an ah-ha moment. This place was a commune, a society that lived, worked and loved each other without boundaries. Nobody was better than anybody else. There was no mine or yours, only ours. They recognized that every single Amber here needed everybody else in order to survive, in order to meet the physical and emotional needs of one another so that they all could cope. They worked together to confront and solve their problems because everything else worked against them.

"What's wrong?" Xander murmured from behind her.

God he was tuned into her. He knew she was awake even though there was nothing she did to alert him to that fact.

"Nothing," she whispered. "Go back to sleep."

He grunted and squeezed her wrist for a second before they both settled back into sleep for the rest of the night.

The following morning, Jaci was happy to see Rock and Emily leave early. She loved starting the day alone with Xander.

Now, she luxuriated in the comfort of his arms. The morning sun bathed their room with cheerful contentment as she listened to the even paced breathing of Xander's slumber. She thought about all the changes in her life since she'd arrived in Amber. She smiled to herself remembering the fun she'd had the night before and the friendships she'd made since arriving. So far, things were turning out better than she could have ever imagined.

She still missed her life in Sapphire. She was still sad, but the sadness was bearable now. She took a deep breath. Yes, it was bearable. She took advantage of the private moment to allow her mind to wander to the life she left, to touch upon the dreams she'd held close, of teaching and being a mom. She let her heart feel the loss. This was something she didn't often do. It wasn't productive. But, from time to time she let herself feel it. She couldn't pretend her grief didn't exist. It was still such a fresh pain.

A steady stream of tears rolled from the corner of her eyes, soaking into the pillowcase as she allowed herself to dwell on her losses. So many times she'd been forced to restrict the amount of time she let herself think about them, feel them. She always restricted herself, stopping before the pain turned into an anguish that overwhelmed her. She thanked God for the extraordinary gift she received when she landed here in Xander's arms. It helped more than she could even put into words.

When Jaci's nose began to run along with her silent tears, she slid out of Xander's clutch to get a tissue. When she returned to the bed, Xander was awake and studying her face as she got back under the covers.

"What's wrong?"

"I was thinking about my family. Sometimes I can't stop myself from feeling the loss. It sneaks up on me. It still hurts so bad. I wish the pain would go away, leave me in peace so I can move on with my life." Her voice wavered. "I don't want to feel it anymore."

He circled his arm around her waist and pulled her toward him.

"I'm not going back to sleep, Xander," she said as she resisted the pull.

"Relax." He pulled her tightly against his body and wrapped his arms around her. "We don't have to be sleeping for me to hold you."

They lay chest to chest. Xander rested his chin on the top of her head. For a long while, he held her in the silence, stroking her back softly. Jaci's heart sang while in the embrace. He cared about her, and God, it felt good.

She knew his actions meant so much more to her than they did to him. That knowledge tempered the moment, but she'd gladly take any attention he wanted to give her. She felt whole when she was in his arms and hope didn't seem like such a foreign concept. It was moments like this that kept her going.

They were too impossibly close for Jaci not to notice his erratic breathing and the erection growing between them. She pulled back and looked up at him. Their gazes met and held. A storm swirled in his gaze. He suffered a conflict of feelings. She saw the battle--right versus wrong, good versus bad. All of it showed in the black depths of his eyes.

"Xander, I--"

"Shhh," he said, holding her tighter, still stroking her back. "I can take it all away. The loss you're feeling. I can give you relief…just for a while, but I can do it. Do you trust me enough to let me touch you? No sex," he added quickly. "All that stored up pain can be released." His arms tightened slightly around her. "Will you let me do that, sweet Jaci?" he asked in a whisper.

Chapter 7

Jaci's heart fluttered. Trust him? God, she loved him. He could do anything. She'd never reject him. He was the foundation her life in Amber was built on.

"Yes. Do it." She was near tears when she tilted her head up and looked into his eyes. "Please."

He rolled her onto her back and brushed his lips against hers softly. She kept her eyes closed, afraid that if she looked him in the eye, he would be able to see her need, her pathetic desperation for him.

A small sigh was all she mustered in response to his gentle kiss. She was on her way to being lost to him. But hadn't she always been halfway there? Halfway toward surrender, tripping over her own cravings for his hands to be on her, for his body to satisfy her. Sate her.

Jaci moved to put her arms around his neck to pull him in even closer.

He took her mouth in another soft kiss. His tongue danced with hers. A deep growl resonated from low in his throat. It was a wild sound, a barbaric sound that made her want to submit her entire being to him. She wanted to be his to use forever.

He tangled a hand in her hair, grasping it firmly and tilting her head to one side. He bit her where her neck and shoulder met. It was a sharp bite and she gasped at the sensation of pain along with the heady feeling of his tongue on her skin as he laved over the spot. She moaned as he continued the sequence along the curves of her shoulders and neck.

She'd dreamed of Xander's hands on her, had fantasized about it. Her body responded to him, but her mind was still trying to work, sending up vague warnings to stop.

No sex? What was this then? There was a moment of mental struggle to turn off the nagging worry in her brain.

Then as if he read her mind, he whispered, "Relax. No thinking. Just now. Just the pleasure, moment to moment."

He was right. She needed to let go and simply be. Her life was in shambles. She wanted to feel alive, like she meant something to someone. She was sure Xander's touch was one of the few things that could get her there.

He slid his hands beneath the t-shirt she wore. The slight brush of his fingers on her skin teased her during the slow ascent of his hands. The last of his swift, gentle tugs pulled her shirt up over her head. She opened her eyes to witness his reaction to her nudity. His expression intensified as his gaze roamed over her. His nostrils flared as if he were a beast, a predator encountering his prey.

Jaci's nipples hardened. She tried to tame her labored breathing as her newly bared chest heaved up and down quickly. She looked up at him. He wore the mere glimmer of a satisfied smile on his face as he took in every nuance of her arousal. Then he put her hands over her head.

"Don't move."

She felt so exposed, vulnerable. It scared her. This man held the power to devastate her, to lay waste to her emotional grid. He possessed the ability to mow her down just as she was, only now, getting back on her feet again.

Her mind flashed to the scars from her sterilization that marred the expanse of her abdomen, and then to the total lack of interest he'd shown her up to this point. Doubt swirled inside. She desperately tried to get back to a place with no anxiety, with no fear of being hurt, when he leaned over her and kissed her again. His tongue expertly teased her mouth and rubbed lightly across her lips. She scraped her nails down his back, a plea for more of him.

"Uh-uh. Arms up."

She released a shuddering breath as he pushed them up again. The pad of his thumb caressed the hollow of her neck, her jaw, her cheek. His pace was slow and her need for more increased with every passing brush of lips and thumb. She closed her eyes and felt him. Electricity sizzled in the air between them when their lips were almost touching. She shivered as his lightest strokes raised goose bumps wherever his hands caressed.

He shifted slightly and with her eyes closed she found herself anticipating where the next touch was going to be. Her heart raced. She was panting and begging inside for her nipples to be his next focus. There was a light tug of her shorts and she inhaled a short gasp of surprise as they slithered slowly down her legs. He nudged her legs apart and knelt between them. He bent over and fanned a hot breath over her collarbone and fondled her breast. The surprise of the touch after the buildup of her anticipation sent a rush of moisture down to her core and a slow whimper from her lips.

He trailed his lips and tongue, kissing down between her breasts. She tried desperately to consciously slow her reaction, but she couldn't do it. Her pussy wept desperately for his attention. Her breasts begged for more after he scratched his growth of whiskers over the already impossibly erect peaks. The slow nuzzle of his face on her breasts was tender, sweet. She tangled her hand in his hair and arched up for more.

He raked a pebbled peak firmly with his teeth. Jaci sucked in a breath, surprised at the pleasure the rough treatment provided. Her reaction elicited a low chuckle from him, and to her delight, the same treatment to the other nipple.

He rolled her onto her stomach with firm, decisive hands, like he owned her. She reveled in it. She wanted him to own her.

For a moment, when she felt Xander retreat from the bed, she thought the seduction was over. The heat of his body disappeared. His touch left her. His teeth were no longer working small, beautiful bites on her body. She turned her head to look at him as he moved to his bedside table and opened a drawer. She had no idea what the item he selected was. She'd never seen anything like it before.

Xander glanced up at her. She expected him to smile, but his face was deadly serious as he held the...tool...in his hand fondling the individual strips that hung from it. "I want you to keep your arms above your head. And, I want you to trust me. Trust me enough to not stop me unless you absolutely need me to," he said softly. "Can you do that for me, sweetie?"

Jaci moistened her lips with her tongue. It was a seductive stall as her mind worked to figure out why she would ever want him to stop. She was suddenly nervous, but she trusted him completely. "Okay."

"Say stop if you want me to. Okay?"

"Okay," she whispered.

"Close your eyes and relax."

She followed his direction and settled into a comfortable position. The first brush of the leather strips against her skin felt like a warm caress. He spent forever lightly slapping her bare skin with the tool and Jaci fell into a relaxed lull. It felt good, seemed to release tension she hadn't realized she carried. As Xander started a third pass down her back, his strokes became harder and the bite of the leather stung. "Ow," she yelled and moved her arms to lift herself from the bed. "I'm not sure hitting me is going to help anything."

"Shh. Lie down." Xander flattened his hand on the middle of her back, pressing her into the mattress. "You promised to trust me, sweetie," he rumbled.

Jaci lowered herself back onto her stomach and raised her arms above her head again. "That was before I knew you would be hitting me," she muttered.

His body depressed the bed between her legs as featherlight fingertips met her core. "I know what I'm doing," he whispered, parting her labia and spreading her moisture with his fingers. He swept his touch softly up, in between the cheeks of her ass, and then back to her pussy. It was a slow, seeking investigation. "This will help you. Now tell me it's okay to begin again."

"Oh, God."

She groaned as he leaned over her, his chest covering her back, his lips mere inches from her ear. "Tell me." He waited for her consent, occupying himself with the taste of her skin. He took his time, moving over her shoulders and back, kissing and biting. All the while his fingers roamed, barely glancing over the parts of her that begged for his touch.

"Okay." The word escaped in the softest of whispers, dripping with fear, need and quiet resolve. She took a deep breath and consciously relaxed her muscles, allowing her mind to let go.

Disappointment rose within her as he retreated from the bed, leaving her absent of his touch once more. And then without warning, he began a series of steady, precise crisscross strikes. This time the contact of the leather strips and the tiny weights attached to the end of each one stung. Her skin sizzled under the blitz of leather blows.

As he worked his way down her back and bottom, she seemed to be sinking into the mattress, as if it were a sponge sucking her in like water.

After another perfect series of strikes to her ass, she was startled by the moan that released itself from her mouth. And then another escaped with the next strike. He added a smooth glide of his fingertips through her pussy without missing a beat, delivering the painfully beautiful marks he painted on her body.

Oh God it felt good. Her body and mind let go of the last remnants of lucidity as time slowed. She was submerged into a warm, hazy sense of being. She melted. The world around her faded away. All that was left was the blackness behind her eyelids, the blood pumping in her ears and the licks of pain and pleasure. Her long, evenly spaced moans made an intricate pattern of sounds when combined with the clap of Xander's leather against her skin. It lulled her even more. They were making music.

As the song played on, her desire grew. She'd never felt a build up of need like this before. She was a balloon ready to pop.

"Oh God. Oh God. Oh God," The mindless pleading rose out of her. This was torment and rapture combined. He drove her toward orgasm. The way he touched her, slowly building her need, stretching her limits. She was too far gone to focus on anything but the headspace she was in and the impending orgasm. Xander was brutal and unrelenting with his strikes to her back. He commanded her body. It was his.

The sound of her own wails barely reached her ears as her orgasm over took her. It assaulted her. Every cell in her body exploded. The exquisite release had an intensity that shook her to her soul.

And then she floated,

In a place of utter surrender.

He continued to stroke her, penetrating her with dexterity and expertise until waves of sensation loomed again. She cried out, but barely heard the sound. She shuddered and spasmed again, losing all control as he created a perfect ecstasy for her.

The air was a warm cocoon comforting her and carrying her effortlessly. The briefest of thoughts flitted through her head. She was high, drugged somehow. She was there--but not there. She was a scent wafting in the air. She was light.

She began to return back to him. She didn't want to. It felt so good, but she was merely a passenger on his ride. He held the power of these divine moments, not she. He kissed the inside of her thighs, caressed her calves, smoothed his hands over the thrumming skin he'd crisscrossed with leather. Up and down, he quieted her flesh. She felt the weight of his body depress the mattress as he leaned over her and caressed the hair away from her face. He kissed her cheek and then he trailed a finger from the back of her neck to the cleft of her ass, pausing for a moment at her rear entrance. She was aware of his movements, but she didn't flinch.

He rolled her and curled his arm behind her shoulders, lifting her. "Come to me," he whispered in her ear. "Let me know when everything becomes too much. I'll help you not feel it, help you get rid of everything bottled up inside you. I'll take care of it for you. I'll take care of you, always." He lifted a glass to her lips and she drank like an obedient child. He covered her with the blanket and then left the bed. The bathroom door snicked closed.

She was a loose puddle, clinging to the feeling of joy Xander provided for her. She lay there alone, happy.

As time ticked by, Jaci's body, and her senses came to her slowly.

No sex?

It felt like sex and something more. It felt like she gave him something from inside her. Relinquished her instinct of self-preservation and in doing so, she was completely defenseless against him now. She felt the familiar pang of sadness, the feeling of abandonment when she was in their bed alone. And it was felt more keenly this time.

* * * *

Xander shut himself in the bathroom. This endeavor challenged him to his highest limits, and they were a second away from total annihilation. His cock was rock hard for Jaci. It literally throbbed, throwing a tantrum and demanding satisfaction. He could no longer fool himself into thinking what he felt toward her was platonic. He was falling in love. He felt compelled to make her feel better, to provide the escape she so desperately needed. To make her world safe and…

He shook his head disappointed in himself as he shed his shorts and turned on the shower. He didn't know if he could do this again without fucking her.

He absolutely refused to allow himself to fall in love and he had to make sure that she didn't either. He didn't want to hurt her. Enough of that had been done already.

Jordan was covering Jaci's surveillance for the day. He had plenty of time on his hands. He needed a release of his own.

By the time he stepped out of the shower and wrapped the towel around his waist, he heard Jordan talking on the other side of the door. Shit. He hadn't brought in any clean clothes with him.

Going commando under his shorts was his only option.

After a quick run of fingers through his hair, Xander left the bathroom and was met immediately by a disapproving glare from Jordan. She'd recognized the aftermath of his actions, and it was obvious she didn't approve. He wasn't surprised. She'd never suffered such soul searing pain. Never needed the catharsis, the shelter of oblivion. She didn't truly understand the relief he'd provided Jaci. Trying to avoid Jordan's chastising scowl, Xander walked over to Jaci who was still in bed. She'd cocooned herself in the blanket from chin to toe. He searched her with his eyes. Her cheeks were flushed. Leaning over, he met her gaze.

"How do you feel?"

She met his gaze with foggy eyes and then parted her dusky-pink, rose-petal lips and sighed.

She was coming back to herself nicely. He was satisfied that she'd feel good, numb, for a while. It was exactly what she wanted and needed.

"She needed it," he said in Jordan's direction before he escaped from the women through the apartment door, closing it behind him.

Xander entered the elevator and pressed the button for the seventh floor. When he arrived there, he walked the hall, looking into the open doorways. It only took about twenty steps before he found what he was looking for. He stood in the entrance, absorbing the scene in front of him. He'd been with this group of people many times before because there were no feelings, no love or commitment between the people in this group, just sex, demanding, almost animal in its expression. Several people stood against the back wall of the apartment, watching the writhing, sweaty bodies rutting against each other on the bed. There were more men than women in the heap of flesh.

Xander wasn't interested in being with a man, but he couldn't have joined in with the men even if he was. Being gay in New Atlanta was against the law. The citizens were constantly fed the propaganda that this was an "illness" needing eradication from the population. The "offense" of being gay was overlooked by the Amber police force. But as a cop he was still expected to abide by the laws in public.

From the other side of the room, Sasha held her hand out to him. She was in leather that pushed up her breasts and gave easy access to the short landing strip of hair at her cunt. She'd been watching, or more likely, waiting for the right situation. They were benefriends and she knew his needs well. There was scant romance in Xander's sexual encounters and that was all right with Sasha. She liked rough.

With a few steps, she was on her knees in front of him, tugging down his shorts. A moment later his cock was consumed by the warm depths of her mouth. But there was no way he could withstand her talented mouth for long. He pulled Sasha up by her ponytail and bent her over the bed, holding her down with a heavy hand on her back.

Xander slipped his saliva-coated cock inside her and curled his body over hers, his abs conforming to the catlike curve of her back. He gripped each of her arms, holding them down on the bed. There was no warm up, no romance, just feral, reckless sex. He pounded into her, reaching around her body to stimulate her clit.

She begged for more of him when he came inside of her. He continued to pump his hips until she came, screaming her pleasure, as her body clutched and spasmed around his cock. The encounter took less than ten minutes.

"Thank you, my dear," he whispered into her ear before he kissed the back of her neck and rolled away from her. Xander sat, looking away from the bodies woven together on the bed beside him.

Dread collected in his gut as he pulled his shorts on and left the room. This hadn't worked. He walked away from it only slightly more relieved, but also more aware that, in his head, it was Jaci he'd fucked. Jaci's cries that echoed in his ears. It was all Jaci.

Chapter 8

Her day had been perfect. What Xander did released all the pent-up emotions and stress she'd been battling. It drained right out of her. She couldn't wait to see him and thank him for the relief. She couldn't wait to talk to him about it, feel him out. She wanted to know if he had similar feelings for her or whether she was making something out of nothing. Had he done the same types of things with Diana? Somehow, she doubted it.

Most importantly, she wanted more of it. But when he arrived at the apartment later that night, and she had the opportunity to talk with him, she didn't sense a change in the way he looked at her or acted around her. She had a hard time bringing it up after that. When Jaci realized that nothing had changed between them, that Xander immediately returned her back into the friendship category, she was crushed.

Confused and hurt, she wasn't sure if she could play this game. She didn't think she was strong enough. But she had too much pride to show even the slightest hint of what a sucker punch this return to friendship status was. And, because she seemed to have no self-respect at all, it was still easy to crawl into bed with him at the end of the night.

When Jaci opened her eyes to the sun in the morning, she was nervous. She had planned a day of exploring with Xander. He was supposed to take her through Circle City for the first time. But their "not sex" sex the morning before loomed over her. The day felt like a disaster waiting to happen because it was impossible for her not think about, and he seemed to have no clue as to what he'd actually accomplished. He'd flipped a switch within her.

She needed more of him, more of what he'd done.

Xander stopped in the doorway to the kitchen and leaned on the jamb, looking her up and down. "Come here," he rumbled as he held his arms open, ready to close them around her when she went to him. Instead, she stood frozen in place for a moment. The pleading words that weighed heavy on her tongue were a breath away.

Again please. I need it again. I need you again.

She saw the command and control, the restraint he forced onto his face, into his eyes, as she reluctantly took the few steps into his arms. He wrapped them tightly around her and swept her off her feet, carrying her to the bed and cradling her on his lap. "What is it?"

She looked down, away from his searching gaze.

He sighed. "You were hurting, and my instinct was to make you feel better. I did that in the only way I know how. I want to be close to you, to be your friend and help you through this. I want you to know you're safe with me."

He sifted his fingers through her hair and she raised her gaze to his, fully knowing that all her feelings were there for him to read.

"You're a beautiful woman and I'm not going to say I didn't enjoy myself yesterday morning, because I did." He paused as if trying to choose his words carefully, but the sinking feeling inside was already settling in. It didn't matter how he worded it. There was a but coming.

"You and I will be living together a long time and having a relationship with you, a true bond, is more important to me, means more to me than sex. I can get sex anywhere and so can you. I want something different for us." He took her chin and tilted her face toward his. "I have never had a girlfriend, never loved a woman in a romantic way, and I don't intend to start. I like my life the way it is, uncomplicated.

"I'll take care of you for as long as you need me to. And that includes doing what we did yesterday if I feel it's what you need. And I will love you, already do really. But what you're thinking…what you're hoping for is not going to happen.

"You have to trust me. Have to trust that I know what's best for both of us."

Jaci lowered her gaze and turned her face away from him, swallowing hard because she was choking on her heartache. Devastated. She was absolutely devastated. She tried as hard as she could not to cry. She didn't need to add humiliation to the long list of emotions she was dealing with. "Okay."

Xander held her for several long minutes stroking her hair and holding her, before he gave her a couple of soft pats to the rear and stood, setting her on her feet. "Come on."

He took her hand in the elevator on the way down to ground level and led her through the rear lobby. Her heart still soared when he touched her.

No matter how rejected she felt and how it's-not-happening he was, hope sprouted at his touch. She yearned to be the kind of woman he wanted, the kind of woman he could fall in love with.

Jaci's breath caught in her throat when she exited the back entrance of building seventeen into Circle City. The perfectly landscaped courtyard was filled to the brim with mature trees, colorful flowers and a fountain. The ballads of songbirds mingled with the sound of trickling water and lifted her spirits. They stepped onto a winding path that held shady nooks with benches to stop and rest along the way.

"It's nice, isn't it?" Xander smiled at her reaction. "This green space is a complete ring. It juts up against every rear entrance of the Circle City buildings, leading from building to building, rimming the whole of the city. There are two main streets that cross, splitting the city into quadrants. Building seventeen is in the south quad. If you ever have to travel to a far end of the circle, you can grab a solar cart to drive. But, the only place carts are allowed is on the two main streets. The north-south street, which is over there," Xander pointed, "is Peachtree Street. The east-west street that dissects Peachtree Street in the center of the city is Marietta Street. They walked together on the courtyard path until it met Peachtree, and then started making their way north toward the center of the city.

There were no cars, busses or trucks. No pollution. Solar carts zoomed quietly by on the paved paths that were surrounded by beautifully manicured vine covered trellises and flowers of every kind. Bridges arched over koi ponds and beautiful shade trees provided shelter from the New Atlanta sun on well-manicured grass. The feel was reminiscent of the kind of small town main street seen in some of the old TV shows from the last century. There were shop windows to look through and outdoor cafes to stop and rest. Circle City was a perfectly hidden secret within the twenty-eight ugly buildings that created its perimeter.

"I don't understand how it can be so gorgeous here. I expected it to be like the rest of Amber."

"We don't need a thing from the Gov to grow gardens. It's something we have control over. Ambers in Circle City take pride in what they have here. It's a simple joy to be surrounded by beauty, but every little thing helps and everybody works to keep it special.

Xander still held Jaci's hand as they crisscrossed the circular perfection. She watched the efficient bustle of men and women in grey uniforms emptying trash, sweeping walks and caring for the landscape. Hand in hand, they strolled the morning away, passing shops, restaurants, the recreation complex, and dance clubs. When they decided to stop and figure out the rest of their day, they chose a table shaded by an oversize umbrella on the patio of cute bistro. They sat together in the shade, smiling and relaxed with a moment of awkwardness before Xander spoke.

"So, do you want to go to Tri-C to sign up for classes?"

"Tri-C?"

"Circle City College. All the courses are online, but you would have to register for classes at the administration office. It's not too far from here."

Jaci found herself at a loss as to what she would to register for. Before she was designated Amber, she wanted to be a teacher. But now, she wasn't so sure she wanted to work around kids for the rest of her life, now that she would never have any of her own.

"No, not yet," she said softly.

A waiter came up to their table. "What can I get for you today?" he asked as he looked down at the two of them. "Oh, Jaci?"

She smiled at him. "Yes?"

"You probably don't remember me, I dropped Hannah off at your apartment a few days ago for the sit-in. I'm her friend, Asher." He leaned over and kissed Jaci on the cheek and shook hands with Xander. It looked like they knew each other, but only in passing.

"It's so nice to see you up and around."

"Thank you," she said, squinting up at him.

He was gorgeous with wavy sable hair that tousled in the breeze. His large brown eyed gaze traveled over her face and then her body, exploring her. Jaci was not confused trying to decipher this look. He was definitely checking her out.

She felt her cheeks redden. "It feels nice to be up and around."

He smiled at her. "So, what can I get you guys?"

"Do you have beer today?" Xander asked.

"Not till the end of the week. We have a hard mix on special--owner's secret recipe. It's on the fruity side."

Xander glanced over at Jaci. "You game?"

She nodded.

"We'll take two."

"Do you guys want anything to eat?"

Jaci shook her head. "No, not really."

"Okay, be right back." Asher turned and walked back inside the bistro to get their drinks.

"You've never told me about your family," Jaci said to Xander.

"Well, not much to say. My mom lives in the Amber Zone burbs, close to the Sapphire border actually."

Syvia Ryan

"Are you close with her?"

"Very. She is only now starting to learn how not to hover. Being a mom has always been her favorite role in life. It was hard for her when I turned twenty-one and was assigned my own place. I think she was at a loss for a while, but she's doing better. I've weaned her down to a few coms a week," he said with a chuckle. "She's already invited you over a couple of times by the way, so let me know when you're ready to be overwhelmed with well meaning doting."

"Next time she invites me, set up a day. I would love to meet her."

Xander nodded his head "I will, but don't say I didn't warn you."

Asher came back with their drinks. "Is there anything else I can get you?"

"No, I think we're good," Xander said.

Asher looked at Jaci and touched her arm. "Hey, listen, would you like to go to the next mix with me?"

"Uh, maybe. What's a mix?"

Asher flashed a brilliantly beautiful smile at her. "The first Friday of every month, every Circle City building has a party. Going to your own building's mix will be great way for you to get to know everybody. I'd love to take you," he said as he caressed a wayward strand of hair from Jaci's face.

Jaci glanced at Xander. He smiled slightly, and raised his eyebrows when their eyes met, like he was encouraging her and happy that she was being asked for a date.

If he was fine with Asher asking her out, she would be too.

"I'd love to," she said.

"Great, I'll get your com from Hannah. I'll be in touch with you soon. We'll hammer out the details."

* * * *

She'd been subdued and overly polite, stiff, all morning. The sadness from the gentle rejection he gave her earlier still shone in her eyes. He'd done that to her. He'd confused and hurt her, and he didn't know what to do to fix it.

Now, he was forced to grin and bear it no matter how much he hated the idea of Jaci going anywhere with a man like Asher. Asher sported a reputation with the girls much like his own. A lot of benefriends with no emotional attachments. Jaci needed more than that from a man. She wasn't acculturated to Amber enough to know him and exactly what a man like Asher wanted from her.

Xander knew he must let Jaci get out and meet people. But he hoped she would meet other women, not someone intent on showing her his superior skills of seduction and sexual play, then leaving her until the next time they ran into each other. He also knew if he safeguarded her from everybody, they'd never catch the person who was going after the fallows.

Still, Xander wanted to rip the man's pretty face right off his skull. It took some balls for Asher to ask her for a date while she sat with him. After all, he didn't know if there was anything between the two of them.

After Asher left them alone again, Xander tried to shake it off and settle his temper by concentrating on Jaci. He watched her slightly glossy pink lips move as she spoke, and her perfect white teeth peeking from between them when she smiled at him. Her body was relaxed, leaning back in the chair with her bare legs crossed. She was interesting and animated, talking with her hands.

They moved past the "tell me about yourself and your life" conversations and on to other topics. The fact that she was informed and easily discussed other subjects drew him in. He listened to her talk about the Gov's recent attempt to retrieve fine art from the Onyx Zone.

She was smart, articulate. No dizzy, ditzy woman here. She was more than, "How do I look?" and "Don't you love these shoes?" It was refreshing and attractive. Her self-confidence emerged and Xander realized this was probably what she was like in Sapphire, before life changed so drastically for her. He took a deep breath. Nice. Really nice.

After having a few drinks, Xander and Jaci walked the city. They took a long break in the late afternoon, finding a spot on shaded grass where a lot of people lay on blankets.

"As the summer gets hotter, this whole area will be filled with people sleeping at night. It's too stifling hot in the buildings. Some are worse than others."

They watched people pass doing their errands or meeting up after work. She lay with her head in his lap under the sun-dappled branches of a tree looking up into the cloudless sky beyond.

While she was lost in her daydreams, Xander looked at her stretched out before him. His desire for every perfect part of her raged within him. Her breasts rhythmically advanced and retreated with her slow breaths. The tempting band of skin where her shirt ended and her skirt hadn't yet started invited him to touch. Her slender legs. He wanted to be between those legs.

Xander's fantasy was interrupted by a sudden shift of the atmosphere around them. The difference was easily discernable. It seemed like even the air changed from relaxing to tense, and the birds quieted their song. Jaci sensed the change and sat up, turning to see what altered the peace she'd been enjoying. Together they watched a group of soldiers, some with guns drawn, marching a woman down Peachtree. The woman's hands were cuffed behind her and a loop of rope encircled neck as one of the soldiers led her with the pole attached to the loop.

Her gaze followed them. "What's going on?" She turned and gaped at Xander.

"National Guard," he whispered and then signaled Jaci, shaking his head almost imperceptibly. She picked up on the slight gesture and stayed silent.

One of the huge, vicious dogs walking alongside the group of Guardsmen, eyed them as he passed. The predator in the animal was barely concealed and Xander instinctively tensed to protect Jaci if she needed it.

"I can't believe people used to keep dogs in their homes," she hissed.

He turned to look at her, and her face confirmed what he'd already felt. She was in a swell of fear, her eyes were dilated and her breaths were coming short and fast.

"That's one thing I wouldn't do even if we were allowed."

After the group of soldiers passed, she looked to him for an explanation.

"The Gov keeps Amber on an extremely short leash." He snorted. "Sometimes literally, as you've just seen. The National Guard is never a welcome sight here."

"What do you mean?"

"National Guard has come to mean something different to the people of the Amber Zone. It's ironic really. The troops that once inspired feelings of safety, now strike terror into the hearts of people in Amber."

"Why?"

"Because the people they escort out of here don't come back." Xander scrubbed his fingers through his short hair and sighed. "Ambers are like the Gov's pets. We live where they want, eat what they give us, and are expected to be well trained or serve the consequences. Sometimes the consequences are removal and redesignation to Onyx." Xander nodded his head toward the soldiers that were almost out of sight. "They provide everything for us. But they also use that to control us. We have no money.

No personal modes of transportation. No voting rights. No right to own firearms. They supply an abundance of alcohol and drugs to keep us as docile as possible. The Gov wants us to be pacified, silent and to remain forgotten until, eventually there are no Ambers left.

"The Amber Zone polices itself. And, for the most part, the Gov leaves us alone until someone's behavior impacts their control in the other zones. They are still ultimately in charge. When they do step in, it is full force to send a clear message."

"What kinds of things does the Guard get sent here for?"

"Who knows what they consider punishable. It's not like the rules are written down anywhere. At least not where we can read them. But we all know on some level that their main concern is to keep us contained to our zone as much as possible, mute to everybody outside of Amber."

Xander looked around. "Never talk about this stuff with anyone else." He looked Jaci straight in the eye. "I want you to understand. You don't know who you can trust here. There are people planted in the Amber Zone who report back to the Gov about Ambers that are problematic. People they deem subversive or problematic either get publically removed, like her." He jerked his head toward the soldiers. "Or just disappear."

Xander reached up to rub the pad of his thumb over the furrows that formed between Jaci's eyes. They betrayed the thoughts that ran through her mind.

"Don't worry, sweetie. Just keep in mind that they monitor us. They track us through our codes." He absently held up his hand to show the code tattooed on his palm. "They know where we go, who we congregate with, where and what we eat, and what we buy with our credits. There are eyes and ears everywhere." Xander cupped Jaci's face gently. "It's essential that you fly under the radar as much as possible. They will be watching you more closely since you have ties to Sapphire." He dropped his hand and pulled her close to him until they were shoulder to shoulder. "Talking to people of other designations could be hazardous to your health. Keep that in mind when you go to visit your family. You might disappear if you say too much, or the wrong thing. Not only that, but they could disappear too. I think a lot of people who've been redesignated to Amber don't contact their family in their prior zones because it's just safer that way."

"Why do you think they're here now?"

He shrugged. "Who knows? But the coms will be flying with speculation soon."

"The more I learn about this place, the more fucked up it seems. Why did Caroline feed me all that shit about how great it is here instead of letting me know the good and the bad?"

"You know the answer to that question already. Who do you trust? You could be a plant for all she knows." Xander was still mumbling.

Jaci nodded her head, her mind was, no doubt, working on all of the information she'd received today. She leaned against Xander as he caressed soft strokes up and down her back. From time to time, he looked at her profile. Her expression had turned serious. She was a million miles away while they sat silent.

"Ready to go back?" she finally asked.

"Whenever you are." He stood and offered a hand to pull her to her feet. "I wanted to show you one more place on the way back if you're not too tired."

"I'm fine." She looked up at him and then down at their hands as he took hers in his. He was contented by her automatic acceptance of their connection. It was becoming second nature for her.

"I can't believe I didn't think of bringing you here this morning," he said as they approached the front of a building tagged with a sign Holistic Wellness Center.

"The pills you took too many of when you came back from the sterilization Center." He flashed her a stern look. "Are the only pharmaceutical medications you'll see in Amber, but you can take care of practically everything else here."

"There are hundreds of herbal remedies you can get here for everything from a rash to insomnia. There's a huge garden behind the building where they grow what they need. They also have other services like hypnotherapy, acupuncture and chiropractics. There are a lot of self-help classes here too. It's actually where I learned how to help you to that zone like I did yesterday." He looked down at her when he spoke the last sentence so that he could assess where she stood emotionally, but she didn't meet his gaze. "They have other classes too, like yoga and meditation."

They investigated the inside of the building together, peeking in on some classes in progress. Jaci grabbed a card from the reception desk on the way out. They strolled the path back to building seventeen at a lazy pace. Jaci was still quiet, pensive on their walk back. It was obvious that her brain chewed on all the information she stored throughout the day. When they arrived at their building, Xander left her to go to their apartment by herself. "You go. I'll be up in a minute," he said as she stepped into the elevator.

"Do you want me to wait?"

"No, I have one quick errand. You go on."

As soon as the elevator door closed, Xander sent a group com to the team about Asher, and then he sent a com to Rock letting him know Jaci was covered until she started work with Jordan the following morning.

* * * *

Jaci met Jordan in the courtyard outside the back door of building seventeen. It was a beautiful morning, sunny and cool. Within an hour or two, the sun would eat up the dewy coolness and replace it with the unforgiving heat that was summer in New Atlanta.

Jordan was dressed in a white, paint splattered jump suit and carried two travel mugs. She handed one to Jaci as they started walking through the courtyard.

"How was your day with Xander yesterday?"

"Okay."

They walked in silence for a few minutes, sipping their tea and saying "good morning" to the people they passed.

"I got asked out to the mix."

"By Xander?"

"No, one of Hannah's friends, Asher. Do you know him?"

"Mmm, Asher. Nice," Jordan said with a grin. "He's sexy as hell. Not a relationship prospect though. You'll have fun."

"Yeah."

"Why do I feel like you're only half here?"

"I don't know." Jaci sighed. "I…" She shook her head. I'm feeling kind of lost."

"Lost how?"

"Lost like I'm out of my element. Like I'm not going to be able to fit in or adjust to the way things are here." Lost like she didn't want to spend the day apart from Xander. Jaci swallowed the enormous lump in her throat. "I'm getting kind of attached to Xander."

"That's good." She turned toward Jaci. "Isn't it?"

"Yeah. I guess."

When they reached the Circle City Public Services office, there was a bustle of people. Landscapers were grabbing their tools and loading them in specifically equipped carts. Men dressed in matching coveralls were walking to the waste removal carts that featured a flat area in the back for filled garbage bags.

Jordan led Jaci into a small office. She met her supervisor, Chet, who handed her a set of coveralls like Jordan's. While Jaci put them on, he handed Jordan their assignment for the day.

"Building twenty-eight," Jordan said as they got into their loaded cart and made their way to the west quadrant. "I've heard twenty-eight is practically empty now. There's less Ambers than there used to be."

When they arrived, they parked next to a special maintenance entrance on the side of the building. Jordan scanned her hand to unlock the door and they unloaded their paint supplies.

Jaci could tell as soon as they walked into the building that twenty-eight was, in fact, practically deserted. There were doors open here and there but the overwhelming silence and absence of people gave the place an eerie vibe.

When they reached the apartment, the door was unlocked. The space was clean and empty, except for the standard-issue furniture that seemed to be in every apartment in the Circle City buildings.

They painted in silence for an hour or so while Jaci's mind wandered back to the time she spent with Xander the day before. When she thought of him, her stomach twirled with frantic excitement until her brain remembered the feeling was unwarranted.

She needed to stop it, to just fucking stop thinking about him.

Jaci was starting to hate the person she was becoming. She was falling in love with the hulking deadly serious man she shared her bed with, and every morning she got out of that bed and donned her ever-growing burden of please-love-me-back. It was pitiful.

Even after he'd tried to set her straight, she still hoped. It scared her. It scared her more than all the unknowns she'd encountered so far in Amber.

To fall in love with somebody who didn't feel the same way could be the tipping point for her. She recognized how emotionally unstable she'd been, that she balanced precariously on the line between a bearable state of being and an unbearable one.

What a damn mess she was making of her life.

Jaci forced herself to switch gears. She thought about Asher. Would his touch have the same effect on her? Maybe she clung to Xander because he was the only one around to cling to. She shook her head. Jesus, she was back to Xander again. This was beginning to turn into an obsession and it mixed her up inside. She felt like a puzzle with the outside frame completed. All the pieces in the middle, the ones that created the intricate pattern of who she was, were mixed up or missing. Xander fit in that puzzle somewhere. She was sure of it. But maybe she was attempting to fit him into a place he didn't belong. She wondered if she was so pathetic that she would fall for any man who showed her any attention at all right now. If she slept in Asher's bed, surrounded by his hard, warm body, would she fall in love with him instead?

Interesting question.

She was going to go on that date with an open mind, leaving any thoughts of Xander behind and whatever happened, happened.

She owed it to herself to make an honest attempt at finding out if she liked Asher. And, if she discovered anything about herself in the process, it would be a bonus.

Chapter 9

Xander sat at the small two-person table watching Jaci get ready for the mix. Earlier, Hannah arrived brimming with excitement because Jaci had connected with her friend, Asher. He listened to Hannah chatter about a lipstick recipe she'd gotten from one of her friends while Jaci brushed her hair until it looked like shimmering threads of brown silk.

He studied her as she put her brush down and picked up a small jar of lipstick. She leaned in toward the mirror as she put some on with her finger. The back of her dress became dangerously short, flirting with her rear end the further she leaned in.

He was off duty tonight. Rock was going to be doing surveillance until Jaci got home from the mix, then Xander would cover her until morning. The problem was, Xander wanted more than anything to be on duty for the surveillance tonight.

He trusted Rock to protect Jaci. But not being there, not knowing where she was or if she was safe, provoked anxiety. It felt like his heart was preparing to walk around outside his body.

Brady started investigating Asher as soon as he got the com reporting the man's contact. He'd already found a connection between Asher and Stacey Adams, the first victim. They worked close to each other, he at the Bistro, and she next door at the media lending library. Plus, Asher walked Hannah to all four sit-ins, Jaci's included. Jordan confirmed this fact in casual conversation with Caroline earlier that day.

This guy was a good suspect and Xander's blood pressure spiked just thinking about Jaci being with him.

The women cleared out of the bathroom. "See you later and have fun," Hannah said, hugging Jaci and grinning from ear to ear. It was obvious Hannah was delighted at the turn of events. He glanced back to Jaci. She didn't look delighted. She looked nervous.

"Do you think this is too much?" Jaci asked, looking down at herself.

Xander looked her up and down, studying every detail, every feature, curve and expanse of skin. Her face was made up to perfection, making her eyes look bigger and the pout of her lips more inviting. She wore a little black dress that covered one shoulder and left the other bare. A surge of jealousy jolted him as he looked to where the hem of her dress ended at midthigh. Her long legs were punctuated by high heels with her painted pink toenails peeping through the ends.

Possessiveness swelled within him, pounding on his chest to get out. His dick stiffened, and his jaw clenched tight. "You look great," he forced out.

Jaci picked up her com from her night table and inserted it in her ear. "Play." She paused, and then said, "Reply." She paused. "See you there."

Xander looked at her waiting, to see if she would share. She didn't.

"So, when do you think you'll get to the mix?" she asked him.

"Not sure," he said in the most disinterested tone he could muster.

"Well--" She looked at him as if she was waiting for him to stop her. He almost did. "I'm meeting Asher before it starts, so I better be going." Jaci looked through her bag, not meeting his eyes. Was she stalling?

"Where are you meeting?"

"In the courtyard. I don't know where we're going from there."

"I'll look for you when I get to the mix," Xander said, walking over to her. "Have a great time." He opened his arms to her and she stepped into them without hesitation this time. He smiled at that. Things were better between them. He squeezed her tightly, not wanting to let her go. He was forced to when she pulled away from him.

"I will."

Jaci left through the already open door, with Xander's gaze following her the whole way. The apartment was suddenly still and the jealousy and possessiveness he'd been feeling moments before disintegrated into something even more perilous. His mutinous body no longer followed his brain's dictates. It lusted for her. His cock was rigid, ready to claim what was his.

He steeled himself before he shot a com to Rock notifying him of her change in immediate destination. Rock replied acknowledging receipt of the message. Rock would be in touch with Brady who tracked her from the position chip in her com.

Xander tried to relax. Rock and Brady had it covered. He trusted them.

He stood and adjusted the still stiff cock in his pants, and then pulled some clean clothes from his dresser and headed to the shower. He was preoccupied, barely aware of what his body did, because his mind was on overload. It was as if once he acknowledged the feelings he had lurking beneath the surface, an onslaught of them rushed at him.

When he learned he was getting a new roommate, it never occurred to him that he'd struggle to maintain an appropriate emotional distance from her. It didn't even cross his mind. His previous roommate, Diana, was like a sister to him. There was love, yes, but not sexual in nature. He'd been blindsided by these feelings for this new woman in his life and now he was in trouble.

His attraction to Jaci had flourished and was now barely in control. She was beautiful, but it was the part of her no one saw that lured Xander's heart. She retained a gentle strength of spirit and an innocence he'd never seen in a grown woman before. He wanted to show her everything, then step back and watch the expression on her face as she discovered it.

Xander stepped into the shower.

Was he falling in love with her?

Yes, fucking yes. Dammit!

How could he let her go with that fucking Asher guy? He was a sleeze, pouring through woman faster than water through a sieve, no emotional investments, no serious relationships.

Just like him.

No, he was different. He lived his life this way for a damn good reason. Not because he was shallow and uncaring.

He shook his head. He had let her go and did it with a smile on his face. He punched the hard shower tiles with side of his fist. What was he thinking? An emptiness settled into a suddenly hollow chasm within him. It felt like her absence physically altered his body and his mind.

Xander lathered his hands with soap and started washing. As he bent over to wash his feet, he remembered the sight of finding Jaci there, right where he now stood, curled up in a ball, naked. The scene would never leave his mind as long as he lived. He didn't love her then, but he suspected that was the moment when his feelings for her took root. He hadn't taken much notice of her nakedness at the time, but his mind had no problem thinking about it now. He saw the knobs of each vertebra in her spine when she'd been curled into herself. He'd glimpsed the small rounds of her ass as she cowered underneath the shower spray. He had seen her perfect breasts with those perky, hard nipples, and the merest glimpse of her pussy when he'd helped her up.

Xander lathered his balls and palmed his stone hard erection. How he wanted her there with him right now. He wanted to lather her body. To brush his fingers between her legs and find her wet for him. He braced his left hand on the tiled wall of the shower in front of him and stroked his cock with his right.

In his mind's eye, she was there with him, her soapy body rubbing against his, her hands roaming, slippery over his skin. She knelt in front of him and opened her mouth. Pink lips caressed the crest of his cock. Her tongue and teeth grated gingerly against the sensitive skin. She took him into her mouth. All of him. Her hands cupped his balls firmly as she worked him, sucking him hard.

Xander's muscles locked as an almost painful sounding cry flew out of him. His orgasm was intense. Exquisite. His fantasy of being surrounded by her mouth, of being skin to skin with Jaci was overwhelming.

She was a need now. He had to have her.

His insides lurched. His heart was doomed to be quietly breaking, longing for someone he could never openly love. This was a whole new kind of hell. It was custom made for him, testing his resolve to do the right thing. As usual, the correct road was the one that was an immense challenge and miserably hard to travel.

Xander never thought he would feel this way. In fact, he'd counted on not ever feeling this way. But Jaci slipped unnoticed under his skin. Her presence ambushed his resolve and annihilated the safe, uneventful world he'd built for himself.

He stepped out of the shower and dressed.

Now what?

He was at a loss. Every approach, every idea was tossed away as not possible because it ultimately ended with him being a helpless burden to the one he loved.

Loved. Shit.

Xander put his com in his ear. He had a com waiting. "Play."

"Hey it's Rock. He took her for a walk through the gardens. He isn't wasting any time he's got his hands and lips all over her. I knew you'd want an update. Later."

"Erase." Xander paused "Call Rock."

"Yeah?"

"Where are you?"

"Sitting outside CoCo's"

"I'm on my way."

Xander met Rock at a solar cart parking area that allowed a great view into the corner bar's front patio.

"Can't stay away?" Rock asked with a raised eyebrow.

Xander didn't answer.

"Heard about your session with her. According to Brady, Jordan almost had an aneurism."

"Tell Jordan to butt out. Jaci is my female. It's my job to take care of her. She's my responsibility, case or no case. I gave her what she needed."

"Maybe waiting until the case is solved…"

Xander didn't answer. Didn't need to. They'd been partners a long time, long enough to know that Xander was giving him a silent "fuck off."

He glared in the direction of Coco's and found the two of them. They sat close together at a small two-person table. He grabbed the binoculars out of Rock's hands and lifted them to his eyes. The late day sun reflected the highlights in Jaci's hair giving her a radiant aura. Like an angel. Asher was smooth and handsome. His hands were always on her and his gaze focused on her like she was the only person who existed. He must have a great repertoire of date material because he maintained her full attention. Xander understood how a woman could fall for Asher's well-honed seduction skills. It looked like he definitely knew what he was doing.

She looked happy. She was having a good time.

Xander wasn't. His teeth ground together. His shoulders tightened.

"You think he's the guy?" Xander asked Rock.

"It wouldn't surprise me. But…I don't think so. He's been too public with his contact with her. They walked the park, went to the bar."

"He told Hannah about his date too. Plus, what's the motive? None of the girls were sexually assaulted."

Long, long pause while he continued to glare through the binoculars.

"Com me when they're headed back so I can supplement your surveillance as soon as she arrives at the mix," Xander finally said as he handed the binoculars back to Rock. He didn't wait for an answer from his partner. He stalked back toward his apartment, trying to blow off some steam. He needed to at least appear social when he got to the mix.

But, by the time Xander arrived back to building seventeen, he was miserable. He didn't want to go to the mix. He didn't want to see Jaci having a good time with Asher. He lumbered through the courtyard, up to the apartment and then shut himself in.

"That's it, no more of this tonight," he mumbled to himself. He jerked open the refrigerator, pulling a beer from the stash he'd been saving and sat at the undersized table for two. He declared himself officially off-duty. He wasn't going to let this case consume him. He tapped the com in his ear.

"Call Gwen." He paused until he heard her voice.

"Xander. What's up?"

"You busy?"

"No."

"Come over?"

"Sure, what time?"

"I'll be here all night."

"Is everything all right?"

He hesitated. "Yeah."

"Kay, be there in about an hour."

She disconnected.

Xander took a deep breath and forced his mind to think about other things.

He was on his third beer and sitting in the dim twilight of the apartment when he heard Gwen's knock at the door.

"It's open," he yelled.

"Jesus, Xander, what the hell is going on?" Gwen asked as she came in and closed the door behind her. "You're sitting in the dark for God's sake."

"You want a beer? I've been saving it for a special occasion," he grumbled.

"Looks like I'm going to need one," she said, eyeing him. "Only a woman could make a man look as dire as you do right now. Who is she?"

Xander didn't answer in hopes the question would be forgotten. But Gwen wasn't going to be distracted. "Jaci."

His silence told her more than if he were speaking. "Ohhh, and...she doesn't feel the same way about you?"

"She did. But now I have no idea."

"Why not? You've never had any problems talking the language of love with other women." She snickered. Then her look became serious again when she saw humor wasn't going to cut it with him tonight. "Is it because she's a fallow? Oh, Xander, please don't tell me you're holding back about your feelings because she's a fallow."

"It's not."

"Then what?"

"She's involved in a case I'm working on."

"And?"

"I haven't told her. I haven't told her that she's my roommate because I'm part of the task force assigned to her. She doesn't know her com and apartment are bugged. She doesn't know her work assignment was arranged to be with another undercover. Since she's arrived, pretty much everyone she's met and everything she's done has been set up or monitored by the CCPD.

He braced his head in his hands. "I let her go on a date tonight," he said, the low rumble of his voice amplifying with each new word. "I didn't say anything. I can't tell her my feelings, and I didn't warn her she might be in danger. It's tearing me up, Gwen."

"Well, tell her! Tell her everything. Now, before it goes any farther."

Xander slumped at the table across from his sister, pressing the heels of his hands pressed on his eyes. "I can't."

"You can't tell her she's a work assignment? You can't tell her you have feelings for her? Which is it? Or is it both?"

"Both right now. I can't be romantically involved with an assignment. As it is, I've already crossed that line a little bit."

"What do you mean a little bit?" She raised her eyebrows.

Xander shook his head and looked straight into Gwen's eye. "I have already done some things that could be interpreted as sexual.

"Plus…Gwen, I never planned on falling in love. Ever. You know that."

Gwen looked at Xander with an expression of dawning understanding. He saw the stream of thoughts rushing through her brain. Now she knew precisely what held him back.

"You can't let that stop you from love."

"I can, and will."

"Well then, you're fucked. I have no advice for you, little brother."

* * * *

Asher was too charming, too confident. His compliments combined with his amusing stories were told as if by rote. Everything seemed like a well-crafted formula to achieve his end game. He was like saccharine, sweet, fake and left a bad taste in her mouth. After having a couple drinks with him and then heading back toward her building for the mix, Jaci's negative feelings concerning Asher only intensified.

She longed for different company and searched for Xander when they arrived at the mix. The room was huge and dim. A small stage held the seated form of a man playing acoustic guitar and singing. Small handfuls of people stood around the bar, talking and laughing. The scattered love seats held groups of two or three lounging, kissing and fondling each other. After her gaze made several passes around the room, she realized

Xander wasn't there. Her disappointment was tangible. It weighed solid and heavy inside her. He'd said he would protect her, take care of her, and she hoped for his help with Asher.

Since the date began, Jaci's internal red flags triggered regularly. Asher was constantly in her personal space. She didn't like it at all. And even though she kept an open mind, acknowledging that his behavior was typically Amber, she couldn't shake the feeling that being with him didn't feel right.

She felt cornered by his continually errant hands, but she remained polite and smiled in response to his attempts at flattery and seduction. But bottom line, Asher was like a silk flower, pretty to look at but not authentic in any other way.

She didn't want to keep up the charade with him any longer.

"Let's sit over there." Jaci pointed to a love seat in the corner of the room away from the crowds of people. As they walked toward the darkened corner, she knew by Asher's grin that he got the wrong idea about her desire to sit with him away from everybody else.

"Listen, Asher," she said as they sat, "I'm flattered that you asked me out but I'm not feeling anything between us. I'm sorry." Jaci tried to be gentle and kind.

His expression fell for a split second, then he smiled at her. "You can't fault me for trying. You're a beautiful woman, Jaci." He cupped his hand on her cheek. "It's definitely my loss." He exhaled a long breath of air. "Would you like me to walk you upstairs?"

"No, I'm going to hang out for a while."

"Are you sure? I don't feel comfortable leaving you here by yourself."

"Actually, having some time to myself would be nice, but maybe outside would be better."

"How about I walk you out."

Asher stood and took Jaci's hand, pulling her up from the love seat. He kept her hand in his as they wove their way through the crowd and walked out of the building into the dark. Strolling in silence for a few minutes, they followed the courtyard path. In the slight breeze of the beautiful balmy evening, Jaci thought it ironic that it was actually the most comfortable she'd felt with Asher all night.

"I guess I should be going. Do you want me to walk you back?"

"No, I'm okay."

He stopped, leaned over, and kissed her on the cheek. "Com me anytime," he said with a sly smile.

"Thanks, Asher." Jaci hugged him and started walking away into the darkness of the green space. The night was warm and humid. She listened to the trickle of water from a fountain in between the slow *click, click, click* of her steps on the path. Faint moonlight penetrated through the trees, illuminating random patches ahead of her. Crickets chirped their slow, lazy, night music into her ears.

She was alone. It felt weird and good at the same time. Now that she was recovered from her surgery and adjusting to the Amber Zone, being alone wasn't as depressing as it had been those first few days.

Jaci strolled and started to get lost in her thoughts when she heard yelling and scuffling behind her. She turned to look at what was going on but couldn't see around the curve of the path. She turned and walked back toward the direction of the noises and found Rock's imposing form on top of Asher. Her jaw dropped as she took in the scene that was unfolding. She moved near the two, and Rock caught sight of her.

"What are you doing?" she yelled.

Rock's knee was in the center of Asher's back while he retrieved cuffs from their holder at his waist. He cuffed Asher, then hit his com and called for backup.

"Are you okay?" he asked breathlessly as he got up from the grassy area where he took Asher down.

"I'm fine. What's…"

Jordan ran out the courtyard doors of building seventeen, gun in hand. She looked at Jaci. "Are you okay?"

Jaci looked at Jordan, at Jordan's gun, then to Rock.

"I'm fine. Are--" She looked around again because she was having trouble understanding what was going on. "Are you guys watching me?"

"I'll meet you at HQ," Rock said to Jordan, without looking at Jaci. He lifted Asher off the ground and walked him through the darkness of the courtyard.

"Come on, I'll explain everything on the way there," Jordan said as she holstered her gun at the small of her back and covered it with her shirt.

Jordan tried to turn Jaci in the direction Rock had gone with Asher.

"You're police?" Jaci asked as she resisted going in the direction Jordan tried to lead her.

Jordan stopped to face Jaci. "Yes."

"Do you work with Xander? He's in on this too?"

Jordan hesitated for a moment. "Yes. We've been watching you, trying to protect you. We think someone is trying to hurt new fallows. Come on, we can talk about this at the station."

Jaci's anger was like a storm gathering little by little. Once it came together and was at full force, it would be treacherous for anybody in its path. "Where's Xander?"

Jordan pressed her lips together and then looked down at her shoes.

"It's his night off."

She looked at Jordan with disbelief. Her mind worked hard to reform her reality to fit the facts she had only now learned. Feelings of betrayal simmered the blood in her veins. Then, as the extent of everyone's deceit became clear, her blood boiled.

"Am I under arrest?" Jaci asked. Her stubbornness took root.

"No."

"Then, I'm not going anywhere with you." She seethed as her heart beat furiously in her chest. She was beyond words as she turned and walked away from Jordan.

"Jaci, come on," Jordan said as she started following her toward the building's entrance.

Jaci whipped around. "Stop following me," she gritted through her teeth as Jordan caught up to her. "I'm going to my apartment. Leave me alone." Jaci's tone escalated to a shout. She was on the verge of making a scene when Jordan finally retreated from her.

Jaci turned and stepped into the building, and thankfully, Jordan let her have the head start up to the apartment. But, she was positive Jordan would follow to make sure she got there okay.

When the elevator door opened on the fourth floor, the hallway was uncharacteristically empty. Jaci saw a woman standing outside their apartment door. It was the woman who held Xander's hand that first night they had their door open. She was sensuous, mysterious looking with her bronze skin and cascade of straight hair that gracefully tickled the small of her back. She was locked in an embrace with Xander. A flash of jealousy joined the fury that already engulfed her as she watched from the elevator.

The woman gently cupped both hands on Xander's cheek and looked into his eyes. "Love you," she said to him.

"Love you too," Xander answered. "Thanks for coming. Next time your place. I promise."

The elevator door began closing as the woman turned in Jaci's direction. "Hold the door," she called.

Xander turned to look in the direction of the elevator and locked eyes with Jaci right before the door closed in front of her.

She stood stunned and alone in the elevator as it made its way down to the lobby. She stared at her blurry reflection in the stainless steel door, and the strong urge to scream rose within her and bottlenecked in her throat. Her shoulders heaved with every drowning breath.

Xander had a girlfriend. He was in love with somebody else.

By the time the elevator opened on the main level again. Jaci's ear bud signaled an incoming com from Xander. She pulled the bud out of her ear and threw it to the floor as she exited the elevator. She turned toward the front entrance of the building, toward the exit that led out of Circle City.

Away from Xander.

Chapter 10

When the elevator door opened again, Xander and Gwen were standing face-to-face with Jordan.

Jordan seemed surprised to see them standing there. Then with an increasing look of dread, she asked, "Where's Jaci?"

"She never got off the elevator," Xander said. "She saw me hugging Gwen in the hallway and she never got off."

"Shit," Jordan said. "We've got problems. She's pissed as hell."

"What's going on?" Xander demanded.

"Rock took Asher down. Wait," she said quickly, presumably to stop the deluge of words that were about to spew from his mouth and crash down all over her. "I don't know why. He commed me for back up. Looks like Rock jumped the gun though and Jaci knows that we're watching her. I tried to take her down to the station to get it all worked out, because I wasn't sure what happened either. But once she found out what was going on, she wouldn't come with me.

"She was livid. I gave her some space to cool off. Dammit. She said she was going to the apartment. She must have come right back down again because I only gave her a minute head start."

"I tried to com," Xander said. "She didn't answer. Jordan, get a hold of Brady. He'll locate her with the position finder. I'm going down, maybe she went into the courtyard or back to the mix." Xander looked at Gwen. "Sorry."

She smiled at him. "Maybe this will turn out for the best. Don't blow it when you get your chance to talk to her."

The three of them rode the elevator down together. Gwen said her goodbyes when the door opened, leaving Jordan and Xander to coordinate their next steps. They agreed to meet back in ten minutes after Jordan called Brady, and Xander checked the mix and the courtyard.

He headed toward the mix, trying to com Jaci again. And again, he got no answer. He walked into the huge room that held the monthly party. It was packed. The dim lighting, noise and crowds of people made it almost impossible to find her. He scanned as he walked the perimeter of the room, twice. He didn't see her. She wasn't there. This operation had turned into a dismal mess in less than a minute, just the short time it took for an elevator to ride up to the fourth floor and down again.

He hadn't wanted Jaci to find out about everything this way. He'd planned on telling her in a way that would help her understand why they kept the whole operation under wraps. At least that way he would have had a chance of her understanding the reasoning.

Learning about the operation like this, in combination with overhearing Gwen and him at the door, definitely gave her the wrong idea. It looked like everything was a lie. God, he'd hurt her again. He'd hurt her so badly she felt she had no other choice than to bolt.

He exited the rear doors of the building and jogged up the courtyard path in both directions.

Nothing.

Brady probably knew where she was by now.

He met Jordan back at the spot where they had separated.

"Did you get a hold of Brady?"

"Yeah." Jordan opened her hand and held it up for Xander to see. It was a com.

"Jaci's?"

"Yeah."

"Fuck!" He took a deep breath and let it out slowly in an attempt to calm himself. He looked down at the floor and scrubbed the top of his head while he pieced a game plan together. "All right, let's get the team to the station. I'll call Captain Rush."

Xander went back up to the apartment to put Jaci's com on her night table in hopes that she would take it with her if she came back.

He sat on the edge of the bed for a few moments looking at it, trying to think about where she would go.

Caroline.

Xander dressed in his uniform for the first time in almost two weeks, holstered his police-issued revolver and stopped at Caroline's apartment. The door was closed. He knocked. No answer. He put his ear on the door. No noise came from inside. Caroline was probably at a mix in a different building since he hadn't spotted her at the one downstairs. He shot her a com asking her to hit him back if she knew where Jaci was.

As he headed toward the station, he was deep inside his own head, lost in his thoughts, replaying what he and Gwen said and did as they were saying goodbye. It was obvious Jaci thought Gwen was his girlfriend based on what she saw from the elevator. She'd heard them say, "I love you" to each other.

She probably thought he was hiding a girlfriend from her too. The thought of what he did with her the other morning crept into his conscious mind. Thoughts about that morning hadn't been too far from his awareness since it happened. The realization that she would think of him as someone who took advantage of her and cheated on his girlfriend made him flinch. She was going to think she didn't mean anything to him, to any of them.

The thought shot ice-cold fingers of dread down Xander's spine. Jaci thought she was truly alone. Fear began to penetrate, overtaking everything else. If she was despondent enough, would she attempt to kill herself again?

He groaned at the thought.

* * * *

Jaci slipped off her high-heeled sandals and started walking. Even in the dark, the Amber Zone outside of Circle City was urban ugly. Plain, square buildings that housed manufacturing and processing plants dotted each side of the street. It was picture perfect urban sprawl, depressing and dirty. It was what she thought all of the Amber Zone looked like before she arrived there.

Tonight was a massacre. Jaci's heart physically ached. Her feelings for Xander were not only *not* returned, they would never be returned. He'd already chosen someone else to love, probably way before she'd ever even walked into the Amber Zone. She choked down a sob, refusing to cry. The true reality of the situation was that Xander wasn't even her friend. She was a work assignment to him. He was under cover, acting out a roll to fulfill his job duties.

She thought he cared about her.

She'd been kidding herself, maybe because the lie was so much kinder than the truth. The truth, that she meant nothing to anybody and was completely alone in a strange place, unanchored her soul and set it adrift. She was lost, like a cork bobbing in an endless ocean, trying to find its way to shore. She'd take any shore right now. She needed solid ground, because she felt close to drowning.

Reality was heartbreakingly brutal, and she no longer had the luxury to pretend that it wasn't. To survive, she would have to develop some calluses fast. She needed to suck it up and let the wounds make her stronger, let the bitterness curdle the illusion of her phony life in Amber and reveal it for what it was, spoiled beyond saving.

After about an hour of walking away, both mentally and physically, from the painful, disturbing mess her life had become, Jaci noticed that a neighborhood with townhouses, schools, and strip malls replaced the businesses and manufacturing plants closer to Circle City.

She stopped walking and let out a deep sigh as her butt met the curb in front of an elementary school. The street was deserted. She was exhausted.

It was late. Too late for transports. She fixed her gaze on the traffic light in front of the school. It continued its cycle of green, yellow, and red despite the absence of drivers to follow its commands. The air was still and quiet. It was eerie to be alone in the dark so far away from…she snickered. Home? Where was that exactly?

Now that some of the initial hurt and shock had been walked off, the emotions remaining ate away at her. Anger at herself took root in her tired mind. She was a trusting fool who'd been easily scammed and knocked on her ass as a result. She was disappointed in herself the most. She would have liked to think she was smarter than this farce. That she wasn't some gullible dumbass that would believe any sweetly told lie.

God, she didn't want to go back to the apartment tonight. She wanted to hide away from the world.

She wished she could go home and cry on her mother's shoulder. She needed to feel loved. Being in familiar territory, even if only for a day, could shore up this newly found determination to survive and help her face whatever awaited her when she returned to the Amber Zone.

There was no reason why she couldn't go into Sapphire tomorrow.

Jaci looked around the area. She needed a place to lay low until the sun came up and the transports started running again. There was a playground on the side of the school, and in the center, a structure she could spend a couple of hours in before she continued her walk to the Amber-Sapphire border.

She stood, brushed herself off and walked toward the playground. She barely fit onto the platform in the center of the jungle gym. The small space was hidden from view outside the play structure. She lay down on the cool, damp wood and stared up into the star-filled night.

Tears welled in her eyes and then overflowed. She'd never been in love before and hadn't realized how crushing the experience could be.

How could the same emotion produce such fantastic highs and heart-wrenching lows? She would never have guessed that a simple rejection from a man she cared about could make her so miserable.

She sobbed quietly. She was not good enough to be a Sapphire and not good enough to have the man she loved love her back.

Jaci cried herself to sleep.

* * * *

She woke to the sound of a transport's brakes squealing. Peeking out to look in that direction, she saw a group of adults, with travel cups in their hands, descending the vehicle's stairs and walking away in different directions from the stop.

She crawled from the hidey-hole, stood and brushed off her clothes. She was surprisingly unwrinkled, but way overdressed, still wearing the black over the shoulder number she put on for her date with Asher. Jaci slipped on her shoes, raked her fingers through the tangles in her hair, and walked toward the transport stop. Fog weighed heavy in the morning air and cool, wet grass tickled the exposed parts of her feet as she padded to the front of the school. It was too early for the scorching summer sun to have dried the dew and burned away the fog.

She hadn't been standing at the stop long before another transport came, unloading a new group of people.

Jaci stepped into the vehicle. "I'm trying to get to the Sapphire border. Does this transport go near there?"

"Close enough that you could walk the rest of the way to the border crossing," the driver said. "Have a seat." She motioned to the empty one behind her. "I'll tell you when to get off."

It wasn't long before she found herself at the gate, waiting to get through the border. The National Guardsman at the pedestrian turnstile scanned her code and then waited, staring at the screen of the device until it indicated she could pass.

"You have twenty-four hours. It's seven minutes after nine," he said in a bored tone. He was already shifting his attention to the man standing behind her.

Jaci was too exhausted and depressed to be nervous when she went through security. Since she woke that morning, she wavered between not caring about anything anymore, and vowing to toughen up. It was easier to not care. The strong desire to lose herself in her depression clamped

Syvia Ryan

down and hung on to her. She might as well have the National Guard attack dog's viselike teeth piercing her skin and taking her down. The damage to her would have been about the same. But still, the small voice inside her whispered that she could make it through anything.

She needed to move though life without the expectation of it being good. It was never going to be good and the hurt wouldn't be so devastating if she expected it. Lowered expectations equaled less disappointments, less pain.

When Jaci finally spotted her childhood home in the Sapphire Zone, she nearly ran to it. Her throat constricted. Overcome, she swallowed down the emotion and held it together as she opened the back door and called for her mother. There was no answer.

She looked around. The house was as comfortable as an old friend and the only home she'd ever known.

Her muscles seemed to sag on her bones, releasing the rigid tension they held. She walked out of the kitchen and down the hall. It was probably for the best that her mother went out for a while. She needed a couple of hours sleep. Jaci schlepped her tired body to her bedroom looking forward to the comfort and familiarity of the bed that she slept in growing up.

She turned the corner into her room and stopped abruptly. The ground beneath her feet melted away. She was in emotional free fall until she landed, crushed by what she saw. Her bedroom was not her bedroom anymore. All of her belongings were gone. The room was now an office complete with a desk arranged to appreciate the view out the window and a comfortable sitting area to read.

She blinked and looked again, then closed her astonished mouth. Jaci slid down the wall and sat on the floor. The new-carpet smell lingered in her nose. She stared at her old bedroom. There wasn't a shred, not one tiny indication that she spent her childhood there.

Nothing could have done a better job of telling her that she didn't belong there anymore.

Was she that easy to disregard, to toss aside? Take advantage of? Lie to? What's next? She pounded her fist on the floor. What was the next fucked up thing she was going to find out and have to deal with?

Furious, she realized she was at a crossroads. She could either curl in on herself and give up, or become a survivor.

The old Jaci would have cried at the sight before her, but she didn't seem to be that person anymore.

No. This wouldn't break her. Jaci became stone, hard and cold.

The total eradication of her presence from her parents' home was the last blow she would ever take lying down.

As she left to return to the Amber Zone, she acknowledged the small treasure of strength born from the trials of the last couple of weeks.

Chapter 11

Xander sat with the rest of the team in the conference room at the Amber Zone Police Station. Every person in the room turned to look at Captain Rush expectantly when he walked through the door. "I made an official inquiry at the border guard station. Jaci went through gate two into Sapphire about an hour ago." The room stilled immediately. "I told them it was an informal check because her roommate didn't know where she was and she was not wanted by the Amber PD. Hopefully, she'll stay underneath their radar.

"Rock, Xander, cover Gate Two until she returns. Pick her up after she crosses back over the border," Captain Rush ordered. "Bring her back here. Give her the ground rules she needs to follow until this case is closed."

Xander breathed a sigh of relief. She was with her parents in the Sapphire Zone. That knowledge freed up some neurons so he could now accommodate his other worries.

In the police cruiser on their way to the border gate, all the ways he'd fucked up this situation ran through his mind and absolutely no ideas on how to make it right followed.

Xander and Rock sat in one of only two Amber Zone police cruisers out of sight of Gate Two. While they waited long hours, they verbally reviewed possible suspects, motives and opportunity with each other. Asher had been released and subsequently ruled out as the person they were looking for.

They sat there for the rest of the day and through the night. At sunrise, the twenty-four-hour time limit for visits fast approached and Xander became increasingly irritated. He tensed and the speculative back and forth conversations with Rock ended. If she stayed past the deadline, the Gov would be looking for her, too. And that wouldn't end well for Jaci.

Minutes before the deadline, Xander received a com from Captain Rush. He tapped his ear bud. "Captain?"

"Jaci reentered Amber through gate one."

"How long ago?"

"Long enough to know she's long gone from there by now."

"Thanks, Cap. We'll keep you posted. Son of a bitch," he spat to Rock. "We missed her. She reentered through gate one."

"She's probably back at the apartment. Relax. Let's go back there. If she's not there, we'll wait. I need to get a shower and some sleep anyway."

Xander nodded without looking at Rock. "She did this on purpose," he said, staring blankly through the windshield of the cruiser. "She knew we would be waiting for her. It was a big 'fuck you.'" Xander fumed, clenching and unclenching his teeth. A steely mask hardened on his face.

She was in so much trouble.

When they reached the apartment, they found a whole lot of early morning sun and a dark emptiness profound enough to mute the sunlight coming in. Jaci wasn't there and it didn't look like she'd been there.

Through the afternoon and evening, there was still no sign of her.

As her absence continued through the next day, Xander moved past annoyed and fuming and proceeded on to raging. He used all his effort to hang on to the rage because the only other applicable emotion was fear. And if he gave in to fear, if he let his mind touch on the reason he felt it, he wouldn't survive. He paced back and forth in the apartment and gave off his best don't-fuck-with-me vibe to the people who came and went. Intermittently, he cursed out loud. Mostly, he stewed in his own thoughts and argued with himself about his determination to stick to the life path he'd chosen. But the overwhelming need to possess Jaci still continued to clash violently with those plans.

At the end of the second day of waiting, Xander was in a dark place. He silently existed, a seething black hole seated in the corner of the apartment. He was tormented and serving his sentence, his punishment for the secrets and lies of omission. He barely contained himself.

He shook his head and an involuntary growl rumbled from his throat. When he got his hands on her, he was going to inform her what the consequences of any future behavior like this would be. He wanted to spank that ass to bright pink until she promised him she wouldn't do anything like this again.

He was responsible for her. She would not run from him or cut him out. It was just not the way things were going to be between them. They were family. He was going to protect her, even after the fallow case was closed. She needed to understand he was a part of her life now. Like a brother.

A brother my ass. The persistent voice of his guilty conscience would not shut the fuck up. Who the hell was he kidding? He wanted to make her his, kiss her savagely, possess her until she had no defense against him, until she submitted to him with her body and her heart. And there was so much more.

Xander stopped thinking about the more of it. His cock responded with just the slightest thought of the more.

His feelings raged out of control. Therefore, he sat, afraid if he did anything at all, he would lose the tenuous grip he maintained on himself. He was a breath away from being dangerous.

* * * *

Jaci pushed through the turnstile, reentering the Amber Zone through gate one. It was on the opposite end from where she left. They wouldn't be expecting her to re-enter there.

She wasn't going back to building seventeen. She got off the transport and after she entered Circle City, walked into building twenty-eight. Jaci found an unlocked, vacant apartment on the ninth floor, locked the door behind her and slept until it was dark.

When she woke, she stayed on the bare mattress, in the deserted apartment and listened to her stomach growl. She knew it was possible to be tracked by scanning her code, so buying food was out. She did not want to be found.

Jaci left the apartment and wandered the empty building until she found an open door on the first floor. She walked in and was greeted with smiles from a small group of people listening to music and talking.

"Hi," she said as she stuck her head into the apartment. The whole group looked up at her. "Uh, I was wondering if you had any food that I could grab. I haven't eaten anything all day, and I'm too beat to go to the commissary tonight."

"Come on in. Don't be shy." A man got off the bed and started walking toward her. "I'm Matt. This is my roommate, Noel." He gestured toward a woman sitting at the dinette. "And the rest of our band of misfits, Shane, Dave and Alison. All three of them waved from the bed.

Matt placed his hand at the small of Jaci's back and ushered her into the room. He pulled out the other chair at the dinette. "Here, sit. I'll make you a sandwich."

"Oh, that would be great. I'm Jaci, by the way."

"Are you squatting here?" Noel asked.

"Yeah, for a couple of days."

"What building are you assigned to?"

"Seventeen."

Noel shook her head. "Hmm, I don't think I know anybody from that building"

"Does your roommate know where you are?" asked Matt.

Jaci glanced over her shoulder into the kitchen. "No."

Matt quit making her sandwich and frowned, looking her up and down. "Did he…do something wrong? I can com the police for you."

"No, nothing like that. I needed some time alone to adjust. I haven't been in Circle City long and things are so different here."

Noel perked up. "Did you come from a different zone?"

Jaci nodded. "Sapphire."

Noel's eyes widened. "Wow." She looked as if she was going to interrogate Jaci when Matt rounded the corner and crossed to her, setting a sandwich down on the table.

"Fallow?" he asked.

"Yeah." Jaci didn't meet his gaze. "Thanks for the sandwich," she said softly.

"You're welcome." Matt leaned against the bar that separated the kitchen from the rest of the space. His arms were crossed over his chest as he watched her eat.

"Why are you so dressed up?" Noel asked.

"I just didn't want to go home and this is what I was wearing when I made that decision.

"So you're all dressed up with no place to go?" Matt's voice was deep and sexy and his words resonated like a purr.

Jaci looked down at herself. "Well, I'm here, so technically I had a place to go."

"And I'm so glad you're here," Matt said as his smoldering gaze explored her.

"I've got some clothes you can borrow." Noel stood, surveying Jaci quickly. Then, she walked over to a dresser and pulled out jeans and a t-shirt. "I want these back," she said smiling and shaking a finger at Jaci.

"That means you're going to have to come back and give me the gossip of why you're squatting." She looked over her shoulder. "Flip-flops?"

Jaci nodded and almost smiled, almost. Noel reminded her of Emily. They both flashed that perpetual devilish spark in their eyes. "I'll get them back to you as soon as I can, promise." Noel carried the bag of clothes back toward the dinette and Matt stepped forward, taking the bag from her. He proceeded to the kitchen and filled it the rest of the way with crackers, fresh oranges and a few other things.

"Do you think this will be enough?" he asked, meeting Jaci's gaze.

"I think so. Thank you so much. This should keep me going until I figure out…" She shrugged and sighed. "I should get going."

"Why don't you stay for a while?" Noel asked.

She glanced over her shoulder at the group on the bed. "I don't really feel like…" She wrung her hands together.

Matt didn't wait for Jaci to finish. "Not this time, Noel." Matt extended a hand to Jaci. When she took it, he pulled her out of the chair.

She turned to say goodbye to the group. In the short minutes since she arrived at the apartment, the action on the bed had started heating up. Clothes were falling away and bodies were meshing, weaving together in a mass of skin on skin. She quickly turned back.

"Thanks," she said to Matt. "And thanks," she said again to Noel as she reached for the bag. Matt held it outside her reach. "I'm going to walk you to where you're staying."

"You don't need to do that."

"I know, but I will anyway." He took her hand in his. "Come on. Lead the way." They walked together, hand in hand, to the elevator and Jaci pushed the up button.

"In my experience, I've found that running away doesn't solve problems, it only delays them."

She didn't reply.

"I'm sure your roommate is worried about you. At least let me com him and tell him you're okay."

They stepped into the elevator together and Jaci pressed the button for the ninth floor. "No."

He sighed. "It will get better, Jaci. I promise it will." He squeezed her hand.

She looked up at the man standing shoulder to shoulder with her, holding her hand.

"It can't get much worse." The elevator door opened to a deserted corridor. When she stopped in front of the apartment she'd been staying in, she turned to face him.

"I understand you're looking for some time alone." He let go of her hand. "I'd like to check in on you tomorrow. If that's all right with you." He ran his hands down her arms and goose bumps raised from the light caress. "Sometimes being alone isn't all it's cracked up to be."

Jaci looked up at the sexy man with the full lips and brooding eyes. "If I get lonely, you'll be the first to know."

He looked pleased. "I'll peek my head in on you tomorrow. And next time you stop by, make sure you can stay a while." He smiled at her, handed her the bag of food and clothes and hugged her hard before he turned toward the elevator.

When Jaci opened the door, she realized she already thought of this apartment as hers.

* * * *

It was late the next night when Matt popped his head in the door and called out Jaci's name. She sat in what was fast becoming "her spot" in the apartment, right underneath the window. When he walked into the total darkness, he whispered, "Jaci?"

"Over here."

Matt's shadowy figure moved closer and sat down next to her, wrapping an arm around her shoulders and pulling her into him.

And they sat there. He didn't speak and neither did she.

After sitting with him in the dark for so long that she was on the verge of sleep, she experienced an epiphany. That this man, this relative stranger, was willing to sit for hours on the hard floor, with his arm wrapped tight around her, explained everything about Amber with no words at all. Instinctually, she knew. Only a person who'd been where she was, struggling in quiet despair over something she couldn't change, would know this was exactly what she needed. She had no doubt that someone did this for him when he needed it. With great pain came great compassion, and almost everybody in Amber showed compassion.

Two more days passed with the silence and speed of a shooting star, one moment there and the next--gone forever. It amazed her how easy it was to spend a day inside her own head, fantasizing about what her life would have been like if Xander loved her instead of that other woman.

Then, when she came back to herself in the bleak room, she mourned the loss of him all over again.

Jaci sat on the floor under the window and watched the summer sunshine fade to twilight and the bright whites of the walls turn murky grey.

This would be her third night of escape from Xander and Jordan. She had to report for work tomorrow morning, and they knew it. They would be waiting so they could continue following her. At least they didn't have to pretend to be her friend anymore.

There was still the unknown of why they were following her in the first place. But after mulling it over and over in her mind, Jaci decided she didn't really give a shit. If someone was stalking fallows, she didn't care. She didn't care about much of anything anymore.

The last few days had been productive. The disastrous mess she walked away from three days ago had slowly been thought through, laid out and decided upon. After the first twenty-four hours of wishing for things that could never be, she forced herself to put on a pair of reality glasses. She saw things the way they genuinely were now, not how others wanted her to see them.

She wasn't going back to live in building seventeen. She would stop there after work to pick up some clothes and toiletries, but she was not staying.

She had been made a fool of, but she knew in her heart it wasn't intentional on their part. She would be kidding herself if she said that was the reason she wasn't going back. The truth was, it would hurt too much because Jaci had counted Jordan as a friend. And Xander, a friend and so much more. In the short time she'd been there, he was the one who truly healed her heart after the sterilization. When he touched her, she felt like she was whole, like there were no pieces of her missing anymore. She had fallen in love with him a little more every day with the hope that, someday, he would feel the same way about her. He never would.

She accepted that now. But she wouldn't survive having it rubbed in her face everyday. It was imperative she separate herself from him or she'd never be able to get over her compelling need to be with him, to seek comfort in his arms. He had been a Band-Aid on her heart and it was time to rip it off and heal the rest of the way on her own.

The woman she saw Xander with was beautiful, exotic almost. Jaci couldn't compete with that. She wanted to. She wanted so badly to be his, but…

She shook her head and fisted her hands. She most definitely would not be able to stand by and watch him love someone else. That would be the final shove that pushed her over the edge.

Yes, her fake friends made her feel like her life could be good here. It was a cruel hoax. Now that she had her head on straight, she realized she'd have to start from square one again. She had to put in the effort to rebuild her life. She'd already started making friends.

Several times over the past few days Jaci wondered if Emily or Caroline were in on the big act. She didn't think so. She could probably count both as friends, which was ironic, because it was no secret that the two women didn't like one another much.

Jaci hadn't clicked with Caroline the way she clicked with Jordan and Emily. She appreciated everything Caroline did for her, but generally, she was not the type of woman Jaci would choose as a close friend. Truth was, Caroline had all the personality of a saltine cracker. She was all about the I'm going to take care of you, and not much else.

She'd call Emily and probably Caroline, too. She didn't feel up to it yet though. She still wanted to sit in her empty room and withdraw from life for a while longer.

The emptiness was comforting. There was no chance of getting hurt.

Chapter 12

Jaci saw Xander and Rock in uniform and looking impatient when she finally arrived at work the next morning.

"You're coming down to the station with me. Now," Xander said to her. His jaw was clenched and it seemed like he was barely keeping his anger in check.

"Am I under arrest for something?" she asked sarcastically.

"Yes." Xander grabbed her wrists, wrenched them behind her back and cuffed her.

Jaci whipped her head around and met his pissed-off glare. He grabbed her arm, guiding her toward the cart parked outside.

"Let go of me," Jaci said between her teeth.

"No." He stuffed her in the back of the cart while Rock got in the passenger seat. When they got to the end of Marietta Street, Xander ditched the cart, walked Jaci through a door in the gate that connected the buildings and into the waiting police cruiser outside of Circle City.

"Xander," she said more softly. "Let me go, I haven't done anything wrong."

She got no reply.

"Xander. Dammit, answer me."

Still nothing.

When they arrived at Amber Zone Police Headquarters, Xander removed her from the back of the car and guided her inside. He led her to an empty room with painted white cement block, harsh, too bright lighting, and a table with two chairs.

"I'll be right outside," Rock said to Xander as he left the room, closing the door behind him.

"Let me go." She shot him an acid glare she hoped would burn and eat at him like he was doused with drain cleaner. She was mad and she had to stay mad at him, or she'd never be strong enough to do this. It would also help immensely if he was angry at her too. Today, she wouldn't be able to survive the nurturing, protective man she loved.

Loved.

She was a mere second away from tears when she turned away from him so he couldn't see her face and headed for the door.

With a long stride Xander pinned her between his body and the door. "No, you're going to sit over there and listen to me." His voice was low, dangerous and right next to her ear.

With her hands still cuffed behind her back, the stray thought that they must be dangerously close to his cock while he was pinned up against her made an unscheduled and unwanted appearance in her mind.

Then, as if he were psychic, he took a step back, grabbed her cuffs and led her into a chair. "You are going to listen to me."

"Why? You want to make excuses for the necessary lies? The sex that wasn't sex? The woman in the hall?" she spat.

Xander paced past her chair, eyes flaring, jaw muscle working, then stood silent for a long minute.

"Where have you been?" he asked her calmly.

"None of your fucking business," she hissed back.

"It is my business. I'm supposed to be protecting you." He watched her as she took the time to inhale slowly, calming herself, and pulling it together before she spoke.

"Protecting me?" She snorted. "You stupid ass." She was calmer now, except for a slight quaver in her voice that betrayed the devastating explosion of feelings lurking beneath the surface. "You hurt me more than any psycho that's out there. You pretended to be my friend, made me think I would be okay here. When I was at the most vulnerable and painful point in my entire life, *you* hurt me, Xander. You should have told me. You should have told me you have a girlfriend. You should have told me you and Jordan were nothing but my temporary bodyguards, not my friends." She cleared her throat and looked down at the table in front of her. "You knew I was falling in love with you and you took advantage of that." She waited for his response.

"Me being your roommate is not temporary. It works like the designations, once you're assigned, it's final. At least until you get married...or die." Jaci couldn't hide her expression of surprise as he dropped that little nugget of information. "It's done like that for a reason. It's designed to be like built-in family. And, like real life, sometimes you like your family, sometimes you don't. But you can't change who they are. Just like you can't change the fact you are assigned to me. It's my job to care for you and you're going to let me."

"Sounds like a lot of backward bullshit to me."

"Maybe. But this is where you live now and you'll have to learn our ways and conform to them. This isn't some arbitrary rule set up by the Gov. It's done this way for a reason."

"Which is?"

He sighed and sat down across from her at the table. "When human beings have no control and next to nothing of value in their lives, coping is," he scowled, "a bitch. But it's eased by close ties with other people, with family. The problem is, many of us in Circle City don't have any. This is the next best thing.

Women need to be nurtured. They need to be important to somebody. They need to be cherished and loved. And men need to have some control over their environment and their personal lives, they need the authority that comes with being a man. And since the Gov has taken all of that away from us, this arrangement gives some of it back. You, Jaci, are my number one priority, and other than my job, my only true responsibility. It was the same with Diana. Do you understand?"

"Don't bother yourself with me anymore. I can take care of myself." She looked away from him so that he wouldn't see any of the sadness she felt. "I'm not trying to be difficult. I just don't think I'll adjust well to Amber if I'm still living with you."

He stared icily at her. "You disappear without letting me know where you are again and there will be consequences."

"You can't arrest me for staying somewhere else."

"No, but I will put you over my knee and spank you if I need to."

The thought of it heated Jaci's cheeks. She ground her teeth together, trying to stay mad, trying to hate him.

He walked around and gently unlocked her cuffs. "I was doing my job, sweetie. Same with Jordan. I wanted to tell you…" Xander fell silent. He had no acceptable excuse for how things played out.

"Can I go now?"

"Wouldn't you like to know why we're following you?

Jaci shook her head. She wanted to defy him. She wanted to hurt him. "No. To be honest with you, I don't really care."

He huffed in exasperation. "You *are* in danger. Someone is killing fallows."

She looked at him with true anger rising, resolute in her conviction. "I should be dead already. Maybe next time it will stick."

She gained a small measure of satisfaction at the expression of agitation and stunned silence that followed.

He held out his hand and gave Jaci her ear bud. "Keep this with you at all times. Your coms are being monitored and you're under surveillance. Don't talk with anyone about this operation. Behave as if you don't know we're there. You also need to go back to living in building seventeen. If the offender can't find you to make his move, we won't be able to catch him."

"I wasn't planning on living in building seventeen anymore."

Xander raised his eyebrows. "That's not an option."

"Fine." Jaci stood up and started heading toward the door. He reached over her head and slammed it closed as she opened it.

"We're not done."

Jaci felt Xander's breath on the back of her neck. Her back skimmed his chest with every ragged inhale of air. She closed her eyes and just felt, wanting to remember the nuances of the moment. Wanting to remember everything right down to the smell of him. He stepped closer. She drowned in the exquisitely comforting sensation of his broad chest pressed up against her.

"Our official business is done, but we're not done, you and I," he growled.

She turned to meet his gaze.

Without warning, a keen sadness replaced her anger. It was so hard to be furious with this man. Cupping his face with a soft touch, she leaned into him and kissed him tenderly. The light sweep of their lips felt bittersweet to Jaci and demolished any anger she had left.

She turned back to face the door before she spoke again. "There is no you and I." She whispered the words without turning to look at him, and then opened the door and left the room.

Xander followed her without another word.

Hovering near tears, Jaci distracted herself from the dismal atmosphere in the police cruiser on the ride back to Circle City. She listened to multiple coms from Caroline demanding to know what was going on. Jaci called her back.

"Jaci, what the hell? Where have you been?"

"No hi, what's up? How are you?" Jaci teased.

"Hi, what's up? How are you? Where have you been?"

"I needed some time to sort things out."

"Let's get together. Tonight?"

"Um, tomorrow night would be better."

"Kay, I'll be over between six and seven. We'll do something fun and you can fill me in on what needed to be sorted out."

"Sounds good. Later."

Jaci touched her ear bud and disconnected the com as the solar cart pulled up to her work. She exited the back seat of the cart and didn't glance back at the two men still sitting in the front. She felt their eyes on her, but she resisted looking back at them.

Jordan was sitting in Chet's office when Jaci got there. She tried to maintain a neutral expression when she walked in. As with Xander, she tried to stay mad. She didn't want Jordan to know how hurt she felt.

"Well, Jordan said you'd be back. I'm glad you are. I have another apartment that needs to be painted in building twenty-eight." He handed Jaci the work order. "You probably still have enough time to get the majority of it finished today."

"Thanks, Chet," Jaci took the work order, deliberately avoiding eye contact with Jordan and turned to exit the office. Jordan followed close behind. They loaded up their solar cart in conspicuous silence and rode together to building twenty-eight.

As the two of them unloaded, Jaci heard someone call her name. She looked up to see Noel walking toward her, waving.

"I thought that was you. You haven't stopped by," she said accusingly with an exaggerated frown face. "And Matt asks me every time he comes back to the apartment. I think he's worried about you. We're having another get together tonight. Please come. We could use another girl. Plus, you have to give me my clothes back," she said, pointing to the clothes Jaci still wore.

Jaci's first instinct was to decline the invitation, but she stopped herself. She'd already decided during her three days of self-imposed solitude that she needed to make new friends. She never would if she didn't put herself out there. And if sex became part of the equation, that was okay too. Ambers had a healthier point of view about sex than she did. Plus, it might ease the pain that smothered her when she thought about Xander. It was all win-win. "Sure, what time?"

"Anytime after eight would be good. I'm going to the commissary for alcohol now. I was thinking about making some fancy fruity drinks for us. You up for that?"

"Count me in."

"Great." She hugged Jaci. It was a sneak attack she hadn't been ready for. Some things weren't second nature to her yet. "Later," Noel called as she turned to go.

Jordan and Jaci arrived at the assigned apartment and prepared it for painting. Jaci still deliberately avoided Jordan, and she felt ridiculously high school, giving her the I'm-going-to-pretend-you're-not-there routine. But she honestly didn't have anything she wanted say to Jordan because frankly, "Were you ever my friend?" or "Did I ever mean more to you than being just a work assignment?" was way too pathetic.

So, while she painted, Jaci concentrated on the get together she'd drop in on that night. Ever since the day Jordan took her around building seventeen for the first time, Jaci's mind occasionally wandered back to the openness of their sexual culture.

Intrigued from the start, she was positive she'd enjoy it. She needed it. Thinking about the sex brought up feelings within her, the need to be touched, to be loved, cared about. It would be easy to pretend the man who satisfied her body loved her, cared for her. That's all she needed right now, the temporary illusion that she meant something to someone. Plus, pleasure, even for a few moments would be a blissful escape from her mind's ruminations.

Jaci smiled to herself. To be able to have sex whenever she felt the physical need was actually a major positive about the Amber Zone. It would be liberating to be able to openly satisfy herself without all of the complications and niceties that came with dating or the judgment that came with what they considered meaningless sex in the Sapphire Zone. Here, it wasn't meaningless. It was a healthy way of life.

Jaci was excited. A small butterfly of a feeling whirled in the center of her chest. It was anticipation.

"I'm sorry," Jordan said, interrupting Jaci's thoughts and pulling her back into the moment.

She didn't answer right away. She didn't know what to say. The sticky strokes of the rollers laying down paint filled the cold silence between them. "Okay, thanks."

Jordan hesitated before speaking again. "I want us to be like we were before. It doesn't have to be different. We were friends."

"No, I was a friend. You were a fake, a character you put on and took off when you needed to. You were a deception. That is not what friendships are based on," Jaci said dryly.

"Ow. Okay, I deserved that. But Jaci, you had so much going on when you first got here. We couldn't add to that. I know, we should have told you at some point, but I think, after a while we knew it was too late and nobody wanted you to be mad at them. I love you, Jaci. You are my friend. I don't want to lose that."

Jaci stayed silent. Her throat clamped shut. In even strokes, she rolled the fresh white paint over top of the old white paint. Silent tears rolled down her face. "You guys hurt me so much."

Jordan put down her roller and walked over to Jaci, wrapping her arms around her. "I know. I'm so sorry."

They hugged each other in the silence of the abandoned apartment for a long time.

"Okay then, let's get the rest of this done so we can get out of here," Jaci finally said, straightening her spine.

They spent the rest of the workday talking about the other fallow cases, and Jordan told Jaci exactly what happened the other night with Rock and Asher.

Their friendship was repaired by the time they were done painting and had cleaned up.

* * * *

Jordan handed over the proverbial baton with a quick com to Xander. It was his shift to watch Jaci, and tonight he'd be on high alert. She was on her way up to the apartment and apparently, on her way back out again.

When she got there, she gave him a quick glance and a mumbled, "Hi," went to her dresser for clothes and then locked herself in the bathroom.

After what he thought was an unnaturally long time, she entered the room looking stunning. Sexy. His eyes took in every detail. She wore her hair long, waving around her shoulders. Her beautiful brown eyes were accentuated and looked even deeper and more alluring than usual. Her strappy, almost see-through shirt left nothing to the imagination. He saw the subtle thong lines underneath the short, black, clinging skirt.

"Are you following me tonight?"

Xander swallowed hard. "Yeah."

"Okay, I'm going to a get together in building twenty-eight. How close are you going to be following me?"

"Close enough to know you're safe. What floor will you be on?"

"I'll be fine."

"What floor?"

"First."

"Take your com with you."

"Already done."

Jaci turned to leave, ignoring whether he followed her or not. He drove behind her in his own cart as she shot up Peachtree to the opposite side of Circle City.

Xander parked his cart off to the side and called Brady as he watched Jaci walk into building twenty-eight. "What did you come up with?"

"Luckily the name Jordan heard was unusual. Noel Cavanagh lives in apartment one fifteen. That will be to the right side of the building if you're facing the front, fourth one from the end. It shouldn't be too hard to find her specific apartment window from outside. Building twenty-eight has very few tenants."

Xander brought up his binoculars and scanned. "Found it already. Any links between this girl and any of the previous vics?"

"None that I could find."

"Okay, keep me posted." Xander cut his com link, sat back, and watched.

He moved closer to the building as the sun set, welcoming the slight relief from the oppressive summer heat. For almost an hour, he sat in the balmy darkness of the outside courtyard. Inside Jaci was with a group of people, four men, two women. They were on the bed talking, laughing and drinking. The room was dark except for the light emanating from the video screen on the wall.

He watched, viciously feeling the rift between them when she smiled at a man that wasn't him.

She was on her third glass of whatever it was they were pouring when one of the men inched closer to her. He stroked the hair falling in waves down her back. She lifted her chin and closed her eyes obviously enjoying the touch.

Another man came around to the front of her, placing soft, slow kisses on her lips, her neck. Xander clenched his fists, at the dawning realization of exactly what kind of get-together this was becoming.

The other woman and two men also started kissing, fondling. Clothes began to fall off all of them.

"Oh fuck no," he cursed between his teeth. He wasn't expecting this. He wasn't prepared to eyeball the scene unfolding in front of him. He was halfway to standing, ready to break up that party, when he forced himself to stop.

He had no right to stop her. He closed his eyes and bowed his head.

He'd done the same thing, finding comfort, trying to fulfill his needs with someone other than her.

He knew she needed this. How long had she gone without touch? Since she disappeared three days ago? This would help her, comfort her, make her happy.

He sat and watched the man in front of her reclined figure as he pulled the scant lacy piece of fabric away from her pussy. It was the last barrier between her bare skin and his mouth.

She tensed for a moment, but then she closed her eyes and relaxed into their touch.

Xander's throat burned from the lump formed there. His heartache settled heavy in his chest. He desperately wanted to be that man. He wanted her to look at him with pleasure instead of the piercing glare she'd shot at him several times that day. Those eye daggers shredded him like shards of glass from a hot exploding bulb.

He lowered his head. Misery fell like a shroud over him, so heavy it slumped his shoulders. She was moving on. That's what he wanted, right? He wanted her to find happiness with someone who wasn't going to be a burden to her in a few years, someone who would be able to take care of her when she got sick.

He glanced up. They all were completely naked now. The two men that attended to Jaci looked like they've played together before. One concentrated on top, nipples, lips and neck. The other concentrated on bottom, using his mouth and fingers.

The scary thought, that Jaci may have gone looking for the pleasure and pain he'd given her, had him jerking his head up to look again more closely. No, this was just straight sex, none of the more intense games that he liked to play. There were no cuffs, spankings, or toys.

As he watched the scene in front of him, feeling the most heart wrenching pain he'd ever experienced, he had an odd realization. She was the one. He was sure of it. Jaci was the one he would have married if things were different. She would have been a good wife for him.

His pain rose to a whole new level as the muscles of his chest constricted. He wanted her. He wanted her body, her mind, her heart, all of it. God this was going to kill him.

Jaci's back arched, and Xander watched her face as she came. Her eyes were closed, and her mouth opened slightly. Her skin glowed hot and moist. Her painted nails dug into the shoulders of the man running his tongue over her breasts, her neck, her lips.

The man between her legs still worked her, worked every last drop of her orgasm from her before he rolled her over, hitched her ass up in the air and penetrated her.

The other knelt in front of her. She eagerly raised the top part of her body so she was on her hands and knees, and then she took him deep into her mouth.

Xander let out a groan. He wanted her to be happy.

He wanted her to feel better, but he was in agony.

He shook his head in defeat. Love was supposed to make a person feel good, not tortured.

Chapter 13

"Come on, I'll drive you home," Xander said tenderly as he drew near to her. He held a hand out in her direction. For a moment it looked like she was going to tell him to go fuck himself. But as he predicted, two hours of sex tamed her. She wasn't mad anymore.

"Was that your first time?" He asked her as he drove south toward building seventeen. "With multiple men, I mean."

Her head swung around, eyes round. A slight blush crept over the delicate contours of her cheeks. "How did you know?"

"I had a pretty good view through the window...for the first hour anyways, then I moved to the entrance of the building."

She was silent.

"I'm sorry," he said.

Jaci released a deep breath. "I don't want to talk about it. I don't even want to think about it. I finally feel a little normal after four days of feeling like crap. Leave it. Just leave it, for now."

He felt grim as his gaze roamed over her, assessing her body language. It screamed tired and defeated. "Okay. For now."

Their ride in the elevator continued the silence and when they entered the apartment, Jaci went straight to the bathroom and took a shower.

Xander stripped to his boxers and crawled between the sheets. He couldn't wait to be next to her again, to feel normal again.

She exited in a towel and a cloud of steam as she flicked the bathroom light off and walked over to her dresser. She grabbed a big t-shirt, threw it on over her head and let the towel fall to the floor.

A sigh floated to his ears as she spread out on her side of the bed. Xander smiled to himself. It sounded like she was glad to be home. He reached over and caught her by the waist and pulled her into him. He curled around her, but he didn't sleep. It seemed he couldn't sleep without her, and now he couldn't sleep with her.

His mind buzzed. Stray thoughts of Jaci with those men hung on like a case of the flu. The surge of greedy possessiveness turned his stomach and neutralized the peaceful serenity he should have felt as Jaci melted into him.

* * * *

Jaci opened her eyes in the middle of the night. Shifting slightly, she glanced over at Xander and was startled to find him looking right back at her.

"Hi," he whispered.

"Why aren't you sleeping?"

With a beats-the-hell-out-of-me expression on his face, he shrugged his shoulders.

Jaci took a moment to look at him, to really see him. He looked worn, diminished in some way, but he tried hard not to show it.

"Okay, so let's get it over with," she said, sitting up.

"What?"

"Cut the crap, Xander. You know what."

"The woman?"

Jaci rolled her eyes. "Yes, the woman. And, what's between us."

"The woman you saw me with was my sister, Gwen. I've told you about her."

Jaci was stunned into a long silence. Her three days of planning on how to handle what was between them went up in smoke. "Not a girlfriend?"

"No."

She studied his face. He gave her nothing more. "I thought she was a girlfriend."

"I know."

"And what's between us?" That uplifting twinge of hope appeared again in the depths of her chest.

"I explained that to you at the police station."

She looked at him trying to decipher any hidden meanings through his expression or body language. He looked as depressed as she felt. There was still something wrong. His joy seemed to have been sucked out of him. Just a shell that resembled the old Xander remained. She pegged him with a speculative stare. "I think it's time for both of us to be honest with the other person."

He nodded. "I agree." He closed his eyes for a moment and swallowed hard. "I know you have feelings for me, and believe me when I say, I'm having a hard time keeping my feelings for you in check. But we need to get past this, sweetie. I don't plan on ever falling in love or getting married. It was a decision I made a long time ago, before I ever met you. It's the right thing to do, for me--for both of us. We have to put whatever this is…" He motioned between the two of them. "We have to put it behind us."

With that one sentence, the stupid fucking optimism she tried so hard to not to have, crumbled. She sat surrounded by the remnants once again. The want and desire that once made up that lighthearted feeling of hope shattered into tiny pieces. She looked away from him so he wouldn't see the crushing disappointment she felt. So quickly the tables turned. Now, it was her that was a shell of her old self.

Xander placed his hands on her shoulders and looked directly into her eyes. "And please don't think the way I feel has anything to do with a shortcoming you have. It's all me. I'm the one with the flaw, not you. I am the one," he said, touching his own chest.

"I don't understand. Why are you doing this?" Jaci asked softly.

"I know this will sound like a cop out, but it's personal." He paused. "Maybe someday I'll share it with you, but not now."

Jaci's eyes filled with unshed tears. "I don't want anybody else. I want you."

Xander shook his head. "We'll walk our paths together until you don't need me anymore. Someday you'll find a man who will love you with every cell in his body and take care of you when you need it the most. That's what you deserve, sweetie."

"It's because I'm a fallow." Her head hung low, and tears flowed freely down her cheeks, falling onto the t-shirt she wore.

Xander's face turned dark. "No. And I don't want you to ever think that again." The anger in his voice was apparent.

Jaci's protective barriers crumbled as she sobbed openly, grieving the loss of something she never had.

She was a mangled mess of negative feelings. The last week had been more emotionally painful than the first few days after her operation and placement in the Amber Zone. But, without the subtle kindling of sexual tension, without the daily unfettered fantasy of his body on top of her, inside of her, without the hope Xander would love her someday, the hurdle of adjusting to Amber seemed too large.

She was going backward.

Losing ground.

Losing her mind.

Losing her will to make an effort toward having a normal life in Amber. Xander pulled her to him, cradling her head on his chest.

"I'm not sure I can do this. Every part of my heart hurts every minute of every day."

"You're not alone in this, Jaci. I'm here. I'll always be here." His chest rumbled underneath her ear. "I'll take good care of you. I promise. And I want you to promise me no more running and honesty between us from now on, Okay?"

She nodded, her head tucked firmly against his chest. "Xander?" she whispered.

"What, sweetie?"

"I need what you did to make all the hurt go away last time. I need that place that wiped away all the pain. Please." Her voice cracked. "Please do it again. I need the respite. I need a place to hide from all this, even if it's only for a while." She waited with her eyes closed and her head tucked against his chest. Hope and anticipation exploded with a flourish in her chest again.

"No, sweetie. I think that's what got us into this mess in the first place. It's too sexual. I don't think either one of us can handle that right now."

She freed the breath of air she'd been holding and slumped with defeat. "I'm not sure I'm going to survive this place," she whispered so softly he'd probably not even heard her. Jaci attempted to steel herself and pulled away. She smiled at Xander in what must have been the lamest attempt at looking okay that anyone ever tried. "I guess that's that then." She got up from the bed and walked to the bathroom closing the door gently behind her. She put the stopper in the tub, turned on the water and sat at the edge, knowing that she used this bath as a way to escape, because she'd been in the shower a few hours ago. Her feet slowly submerged as she sat on the side of the cool white tub.

Idiot.

She just had to love someone determined not to love her back.

Jaci thought about the sexual encounter she had the night before. For a while, it was delicious. It felt good. Somebody wanted her even if it was only for an hour or two. But she'd found the experience a little like eating a rich dessert without having a meal first. She didn't feel satisfied and it didn't sit well inside her.

She slipped into the hot water and laid back so her ears were submerged. She felt her hair waving around in the bathtub currents and listened to the steady rhythm of her breathing. The *thump-thump, thump-thump* of her heart was easily heard with her ears water-filled.

An isolated heartbeat in a solitary world.

* * * *

It was the right thing to do. He felt like shit about the here and now of it and hoped that after a week or two of being friends, with the other feelings suppressed, maybe it would work. If not for both of them, at least for her. She was suffering now, though, and he pondered her request for the relief she so desperately needed. It wasn't fair to her that she suffered when she could so easily get a measure of relief. He'd never trust anyone else enough to have Jaci seek relief from someone other than him. No, he was the only one he trusted enough to supply her with the endorphin surge pain provided. But he could find another to provide the pleasure part while he supplied the pain. Xander's mind worked quickly from there.

He dressed in a pair of jeans and a t-shirt and then looked at the time. It wasn't even five am yet. His surveillance shift would be over at eight.

Sasha was the only person he trusted to be discreet--and good. He grabbed his ear bud. "Call Sasha." He paused, waiting to connect. "Hello, my dear," he rumbled. "I need a personal favor. Can you come down?" He chuckled "I'll be waiting."

Ten minutes later, he talked with Sasha in the hall about what he needed from her. They returned to the apartment together and waited for Jaci to exit the bathroom. Sasha was gorgeous as always, kneeling at his feet in black, as always, ready to play, as always.

He was dressed in jeans only. The bed was prepared, and the anticipation of what lie before him danced in his veins. His cells hummed as his senses became sharp. He focused on the bathroom door. Jaci needed this, and he was pleased he'd found a way to relieve her of her pain. It had been a long time since the thrill of what was to come raced along his nerve endings. Tonight would satisfy a need building within him as well.

When the bathroom door opened, Jaci was a silhouette in the doorway.

"Lie down on the bed, Jaci."

Chapter 14

Jaci stopped short when she spotted Xander holding the flogger with a woman kneeling at his feet. His eyes flared at her when she exited the bathroom, and joy rushed at her when she heard his words and realized that, for whatever reason, he'd changed his mind about helping her. Or, maybe the woman would do it. She glanced down at the woman again.

"That's Sasha." He reached down and ruffled his fingers through her hair. "Sasha has generously agreed to serve me this morning." He lowered his voice. "She will be serving you also. Now, get on the bed, Jaci." He looked intently at her as she sheepishly let go of the towel wrapped around her body and complied with his order.

"Sasha, my dear, prepare her for me." Immediately, Sasha scurried toward Jaci and began positioning her. She slipped soft, braided rope around her wrists and then suddenly pulled it taut until they were bound together. Sasha brought Jaci's arms over her head, rolled her onto her belly and then firmly attached the other end of the braided length to a small hook in the wall that was hidden by pillows.

Xander's chuckle sounded again, floating to her ears from the shadows in the room. "You're quite good at this, but it will take more than rope work to impress me, Sasha." Jaci glanced over at the woman kneeling on the bed next to her. She might as well have been completely nude because what she wore didn't cover any important things that usually needed covered. Sasha's nipples were puckered and beaded like dusky rosebuds. Her chest rose and fell sharply as she turned her head to look back to Jaci. Sasha smiled at her and then licked her lips slowly with a slightly glazed look in her eye.

As Sasha grabbed a pillow and turned toward Jaci's legs, Jaci got a glimpse of her hairless cunt. It stole her attention while she was being moved into position. She ended up with her hips over pillows so her ass remained up in the air. Jaci sucked in a breath as she felt her right leg pulled tight toward the corner of the bed.

"No, Sasha, leave her legs free. Jaci won't move from that spot, will you, Jaci?"

All she could do was swallow and shake her head.

"Come to my feet." He stood at the side of the bed, extending a hand toward Sasha. She took the proffered hand and sank to her knees. Sasha's face was in her direct line of sight, nuzzling Xander's thigh "Jaci, what do you say to me if you want me to stop?"

She smiled at him. "Stop."

He nodded. "That's right, sweetie. Now, listen to me carefully, You will not move, and you will not come until I say so.

She nodded, the sheet shifting slightly under her cheek.

The first lash of the flogger on her ass struck hard, followed quickly by more.

"You may pleasure yourself now, Sasha. There may be no time for that later." The strikes continued to fall as Jaci watched Sasha trail a hand down between her legs. Jaci groaned. She couldn't see anything else from her angle. She was missing what the woman's hands were doing. But she studied the slow build of pleasure expressed on her face.

The sting of the flogger increased as the scent of Sasha's arousal filled Jaci's nostrils. The woman took her time. The lashes Xander delivered and her moans seemed to weave together, as if they were in sync with each other. Time progressed slowly while Jaci watched this gorgeous woman's face as she got closer to her climax. Finally, she watched Sasha cry out while she came, with her head flung back and lips parted, releasing shouts that eventually slowed and transformed to whimpers of pleasure.

The strikes from the flogger multiplied rapidly as Xander worked it down her back and legs to the soles of her feet, and back up again. Jaci closed her eyes. Her brain welcomed the release of the heavy emotional burden she'd been carrying. She gradually became lighter and lighter, almost floating, but the air weighed heavy on her skin and kept her on the mattress.

Slight fingers ran through her channel from anus, all the way to her clit. The strikes to her body slowed, but still maintained a steady rhythm and pattern along her skin. The sound of her own moan surprised her. She hadn't realized she'd been making any sounds at all.

Xander spoke and his voice floated through the thickness of the air to her ears. The pleasure it held was evident. "Go ahead," she heard him say. Immediately a vibrator sprung to life and Jaci felt it slowly penetrate her.

It was good. Another door in her mind slammed shut as Jaci floated further from reality.

Gentle kisses on her clit narrowed her focus within herself even more, and the pleasure she received from Sasha's mouth expertly, methodically, slowly built her arousal.

Layer upon layer it grew as more of the outside world fell away.

Sasha and Xander were relentless with their full body assault. The woman's hot tongue rolled over her clit at a slow, steady pace. Jaci knew she couldn't hold on much longer.

The sting of the flogger's weights continued in even, controlled strokes while Sasha tongued her clit and fucked her hard with the vibrating dick that stretched her.

Small tremors in her thighs began as the initial recognition of an impending orgasm skitted through her mind. But as if Xander sensed it, the strikes momentarily stopped and he whispered next to her ear, "Don't do it, Jaci. Not until I say."

The world narrowed until only she and the need existed. The tremors increased and her spine curved, rounded up. Jaci froze and locked down tight as she exerted rock-hard control over every muscle in her body to stall her orgasm.

"Please." She heard herself screaming. It echoed off the walls as her lungs emptied of air and struggled for more.

Xander increased the velocity of his strokes and then spoke the words she'd been waiting for. "Come now, Jaci."

And she did. She let go, screaming her pleasure and her pain at the same time. The orgasm lasted forever and then she was inside her own head, lost inside her own skin.

No part of her reached out or acknowledged the world around her, neither in thought nor in action. Her senses and her awareness were turned off. She experienced a total displacement of reality.

* * * *

Xander released Jaci, rolled her to her side and slid in behind her, covering both of them up. She was so deep inside herself that he was able to gain some relief from Sasha before she left to go back to her apartment. She'd swallowed his cock and his cum eagerly, but a small part of his brain niggled at him. It was the part of him that knew Jaci ached to be the one to do that just as much as he ached to have her as his, and his alone.

He shook himself out of that train of thought. It was dangerous and something he needed to keep in check. Sunrise approached and with it Jordan would take over surveillance and protection duty. The two would paint all day, and then Rock would cover for the few hours after that until it was time for bed.

Xander had the day and the evening free. And, as if his mother sensed the lull in his schedule, she had commed the night before to ask if he wanted to have dinner with her. He'd agreed and looked forward to getting some one on one time with her and her spaghetti.

He left the apartment when Jordan arrived a few minutes before eight. Jaci hadn't fully recovered from their session, but she was awake, her gaze following him from the bed as he got ready to leave. Her face held a slight smile of contentment and every crease created by worry and stress had been ironed out of her beautiful face. He kissed her forehead and whispered, "I'll see you later," before he left.

There was some spring to his gait when he left the building and followed the path in the courtyard. He loved the mornings in Circle City. The gardens and fresh air, before the stifling summer heat took over, were calming.

He needed some time in nature to center himself and strengthen his resolve after their early morning activities.

He loved her. He loved her enough to let her go. This was his mantra now.

Later that day, Xander sat with his mother at the cozy table in the dining room of the house he grew up in. The room smelled like a garden and was made significantly smaller by the crowd of plants and cut flowers. His mother loved the outdoors and managed to capture an old English cottage essence to the room with all the foliage and lace she crocheted herself. The worn round table that sat there all these years fit into the room more perfectly with every nick and scrape it acquired. The two place settings in front of them were as chipped and worn as everything else. But his mother would have argued that her belongings had character.

She placed two serving dishes between them and took her seat. It wasn't hard to tell from the expression on her face that she had something on her mind.

"What's wrong, Mom?"

She looked up at him but didn't answer the question.

He served himself spaghetti and salad and then waited, realizing something was wrong with her. He studied her during the silence between them. She was in her fifties, and wore the small telltale signs of her age well. But then, what boy didn't think his mother was pretty? But she was also nervous, fidgeting a lot and not looking directly at him.

"What's wrong?" he prompted again in a softer tone, touching her forearm.

She looked at him. Her brown eyes were serious. "Well, now that I have you here, I don't know where to start. I'm feeling kind of...hesitant. I guess I might as well jump in." She paused. "Gwen told me you have feelings for Jaci, and she told me why you're not acting on them."

Xander was silent. He felt his expression turn stony, unreadable as his mother gauged his response. "Mom, I--"

His mom raised her hand. "No, let me get this out." She took a deep breath and went on with a quavering voice. "I'm so sorry, Xander. I thought I did a good job of shielding you from our pain when your father was sick." Tears welled in her eyes.

"It's okay, Mom. We don't have to talk about this."

"Yes, we do. This is important to me." She set down her fork and pushed her plate away. "I'm sorry that your point of view of Dad's illness and our marriage was so negative." Her eyes, swimming in tears, locked on his. "Mostly because it wasn't. At least not all of it."

"Xander, I loved your father more than anything. The years we spent together were the absolute best in my life, even when he was sick. We spent so much time together toward the end," she said wistfully. "We grew about as close to each other as two people can get."

She wasn't looking at him now. Her eyes focused on a long gone past. "Some of the best times of our marriage were when he was sick. We laid together in bed and enjoyed a lifetime's worth of intimacy. And we appreciated every second of it. We reminisced about all the wonderful times we shared. We talked about our dreams for you. Your father..." she choked back a sob and swallowed hard, "would have been so proud of the man you've become. I'm proud of the man you've become."

She looked directly at him and locked her stern gaze with his. "But it's an insult to him, to us, to our parenting, and our marriage that you somehow took from your childhood that your dad was a burden to me, or that our marriage wasn't good because he got sick. That you couldn't fall in love, couldn't get married because you'll get sick."

A sour squeeze attacked his stomach, when he saw his mother's anguish. The realization that he was hurting her stabbed at his conscience as he tried to reason out a solution that would make her feel better.

She grabbed his wrist, capturing his full attention again. She met his gaze with determination. "You can still have a wonderful marriage, the love affair of a lifetime, even if it ends sooner than you'd like." She covered her face with her hands until Xander closed in on her and knelt next to her chair wrapping his arms around her and comforting her while she sobbed quietly in to his shirt. Finally, wiping her eyes, she looked up at him. Their faces were inches apart. "I have failed you so badly if you've changed your life, avoided love because of your father and I. Don't you see that love was the only thing we had in our life that actually made it worth living? That, and you." She sighed and sat back in her chair. Her tears remained a constant stream rolling down her face. She looked down at the uneaten food as if she wasn't sure how it had gotten there. Xander covered her hand with his. She looked at him and continued.

"I miss him so much. But I wouldn't have changed it for anything. The only thing that keeps me going some days is the thought of you building your life, finding a love like what we had. It was rare and wonderful. I want you to know what it feels like.

"Please, please don't make me carry the responsibility, the guilt that you're alone because of your father and me. I don't think I could shoulder it for the rest of my days."

Xander looked down at his own uneaten plate of food and pushed it away.

"Mom, it's the right thing to do."

"No it isn't," she shouted. "I am so sorry that you inherited the same genetic markers as your dad. But I am more sorry that you came away from your childhood thinking you would be a burden to the woman who loves you. Your father was never a burden to me." His mother thumped the solid wood table with the side of her fist. "Never. Can't you see that love is the only thing in Amber that we have that's ours, purely ours, untainted by the Gov. Don't let them have that much control over how you live your life.

"Maybe the love of your lifetime is Jaci, or maybe it's someone else. But you have to find her, Xander. Find her and don't ever let her go. Promise me. Promise me, please."

Xander looked away from her and digested what she'd said. Her perspective was radically different from his, and he'd never considered the affect his decision would have on his mother. God, this was hurting her, too.

She squeezed his arm. "Promise me, please."

He stood and took his mother into his arms. "I promise, Mom. I promise." He pulled her to him, and held her while she wept in his arms.

Chapter 15

After a full day's work, Jaci spent an eternity in the bathtub, soaking away her delicious aches. When she finally surfaced from her liquid heaven, she was wrinkled and relaxed.

Half-dressed, she ducked out of the bathroom to answer the knock the door. She expected to find Caroline and was surprised to see Emily instead.

"Hey," Jaci said as she backed up to let Emily in.

"Hey, girl. You've been making yourself scarce these days." She gave Jaci a hug. "Okay, give me the scoop. I know you haven't been home, but Rock is cheap when it comes to giving info, so spill." Emily flashed a beautifully wicked expression of anticipation. The look revealed that Rock already shut Emily down and she was being defiant by not dropping the subject all together. Little did Emily know that Rock probably heard everything she'd said because of the bug in the room.

"Come on into the bathroom. I have to finish getting ready. I have plans with Caroline tonight."

Emily made an ick face at the sound of Caroline's name and followed her into the bathroom. She sat on the toilet and watched Jaci finish getting ready.

"So, tell me," she whined.

Jaci followed Xander's directions and didn't mention the murderer who allegedly stalked her and boiled the situation down to the here and now. "I had to get away for a while. Clear my head." Jaci paused. "I think I'm in love with Xander."

"Oh I knew it. I knew it," Emily squealed. A smile exploded over her face.

Jaci interrupted Emily before she said anything more. "He's made it clear he's not interested in a romantic relationship. Said he'd rather be my friend and take care of me until I don't need him anymore."

"Jaci, he loves you, too" Emily responded with pure confidence.

Jaci turned to look at Emily and shook her head. "He didn't come right out and say it, but told me he didn't, in a nice way, but he let me know I'm firmly in friend status."

"He may say that he doesn't love you, but that's a load of crap. I saw him while you were gone. He was miserable, desperate almost." She paused, scrunched her forehead and bit her bottom lip. "I've known him a long time and have seen him around a lot of women. They seem to always float around the periphery of his awareness, like they are barely there for him. But with you, it's different. His gaze follows you. He's totally aware of you, every movement, every subtlety. He's never been like that with anybody else. And I've never seen him with a girlfriend. I haven't even seen him have a conversation with another woman, except for Diana. And, she was taken--unavailable.

"Oh, he's totally fallen for you. Trust me. The question is, why is he fighting it?"

Jaci would have taken this new insight to heart if she hadn't known that it was his job to watch her. As it was, nothing Emily said changed anything.

There was another knock at the door. "Will you get that while I finish in here?" Jaci asked, "It's probably Caroline." She wagged her finger at Emily. "Be nice."

"Sure," Emily said with her mischievous eyes twinkling as she left to get the door. "It's Caroline," she called a few moments later.

"Okay." Jaci heard the two women talking for a moment. Then, silence. She smiled at herself in the mirror. Those two had nothing to say to one another.

She stepped out of the bathroom and gasped when she found Emily lying on the floor with a syringe protruding from her neck. Caroline reentered the room from the kitchen with a knife in her hand.

"Oh my God! What are you doing?"

Caroline turned. "Have a seat, Jaci." She motioned toward the bed.

Stunned, Jaci didn't move. She stood looking back and forth between Emily's unconscious body and Caroline. Her wheels turned until everything clicked into place.

"Have a seat," she barked. Her eyes were wide and Jaci detected the adrenaline pumping through her.

Jaci sat on the edge of the bed. Her pulse throbbed at the base of her throat as she watched Caroline lean over Emily's body and retrieve the syringe. "This was meant for you," she said, holding it up before putting it in the front pocket of her jeans.

Then, without a moment's hesitation, Caroline plunged the knife she carried into Emily's chest.

Jaci screamed and jumped up from the bed to create some distance between her and Caroline. "It's you," she accused. "You're killing the fallows."

Caroline pulled a switchblade from the same pocket she'd put the syringe into and laughed. "No, Jaci. This is an obvious case of another fallow going crazy, but this time, killing someone else before killing herself. Now, come on. I've got a surprise for you." Caroline moved toward Jaci stepping over Emily's body and the broadening blood pool on the floor. "This is how it's going to work. We're going to leave the apartment and go for a ride."

Caroline's fingers gripped Jaci's wrist like the talons of a falcon sinking into its prey. She dragged Jaci out of the apartment into the hallway, turning the opposite direction from the elevator. They were going toward the stairs and there was nobody standing between them and that door. Jaci tried to wrench her wrist from the woman's crushing grip and yell for help toward the group of people standing at the other end of the hall. Caroline jerked Jaci, digging her fingers painfully into the flesh of her wrist and pulled her through the stairwell doorway.

There were so many doors open, so many people at the other end of the hall. Somebody must have heard her, noticed that she was being dragged away. But, there were no sounds of people following as they descended the cool, echoing stairwell.

They went through the emergency exit at the bottom of the stairs and Caroline pushed Jaci into the back of a waiting car. The door slammed shut behind her. Immediately, Jaci searched for a way out. There wasn't one. The car was a police car on the inside complete with metal screen dividing the front seat from the back.

Caroline got into the passenger seat in the front. "Drive," she said to the man behind the wheel.

"Caroline," Jaci said. "We have to go back. We have to help Emily. If we go back now, everything else can be worked out."

"I don't want to help Emily and everything is working out fine. Emily being in the way tonight was an added bonus for me. She was getting to be a problem. She had a vague sense about me that would have grown and become a pain in my ass. I'm glad you killed her." Caroline laughed.

Jaci was silent, thinking. How had she gotten a hold of this car? There were no privately owned cars in Amber. "Whose car is this?"

"You haven't figured it out yet, Jaci? Really? Your IQ scores were so high. It must be true what they say, book smarts don't mean anything if you don't have common sense. It's the Gov's car, sweetie," she said in a sickly sweet tone, obviously mocking the pet name that Xander used more and more often. "And so as not to hurt that pretty brain of yours, yes, it's the Gov that wants you dead. Not me."

"Why? I haven't said or done anything wrong."

"Don't take it personally. They're cleaning up future liability risks. You know, information leaks. That's my best guess, anyways. But I have to admit, when they recruited me for this job, I didn't ask why. I did what I was told so I wouldn't end up like you."

The car approached the Sapphire border crossing. But, instead of stopping for proper clearance to enter the Sapphire Zone, the car was waved through.

Jaci's jaw dropped.

"Where are you taking me?"

"To your parent's house. It's the perfect place to end this, no rush, no worries about Xander or anybody else showing up.

"Your parents are out for the evening. They won tickets to the Fourth of July concert and fireworks program in the Emerald Zone. How lucky are they?" Caroline said with an even mix of evil and sarcasm that told Jaci it wasn't luck at all that took her parents away from home that evening.

* * * *

Rock sat with Brady in the ninth floor apartment that was used as their task force base of operations. He and Brady relaxed while they listened in on Jaci and Emily. As far as Rock was concerned, it had already been interesting listening to Emily without her having the slightest clue that his ears were all over that place.

His amusement was precisely the reason that he didn't catch on immediately to what was happening after Caroline arrived. His stomach sank like a stone when he heard Jaci identify Caroline as the murderer. As soon as he realized what was going down, Rock flew out of the apartment, hoping he wasn't too late. He sprinted his way down to the fourth floor, directing Brady, who was right behind him, to com Xander and Jordan.

Rock's heart drummed furiously and his ears rang as he made the excruciatingly slow descent from the ninth to the fourth floor.

Shit. Shit!

He pushed through a small crowd after the elevator door opened and rushed to the apartment. The door was closed and locked, but Xander had the foresight to reprogram the palm scanner to allow all of the task force team to get in.

When the door crashed open, he saw Emily immediately. She lay face up with her wide eyes staring right at him as he came through the door. A dark red pool of blood surrounded her on the floor. The knife she'd been stabbed with still stuck out of her chest.

"Oh fuck, Emily!" he roared as he ran over to her. "No! No! No!"

He assessed her condition in a split second. She was still alive. Her gaze tracked him as he moved around her.

Frantically, he looked around for something to stop the blood flow and ran to the bathroom for a towel before returning to her.

He knelt in the sticky, red puddle surrounding Emily's body and pressed the towel around the knife wound, trying desperately to stall the flow of blood.

"Stay with me, Em." He looked into her eyes, and she looked right back at him, a glimmer of a smile on her face.

"S-sorry…" She took a labored breath and made the cute frown face he loved so much. "We're not married now."

"Are you finally saying yes to me? 'Cause if I'd known this was all it would take, I'd have stabbed you a long time ago."

Her eyes sparkled when she smiled at him. "Too late, I think."

"It's going to be okay, baby. It's going to be okay," he whispered as he stroked some curls away from her face. "I got you now." Her face was pale. Sleepy.

"Love you, Rock." Her words gurgled and then she coughed, spraying blood from her mouth.

Rock brushed his lips over hers. "You're going to be fine. Help is on the way." He pressed his cheek against hers. It was cool compared to the heated skin of his face.

He stayed there with her, cheek to cheek, eyes shut tight, whispering encouragements in her ear and stroking her curls with his free hand. The warm, wet stickiness of her blood seeped through the towel he held to her wound and through the denim of his jeans.

Blood was everywhere. He was drowning in it. Cupping the back of her head, he lifted it slightly off the ground as the thick, garnet puddle inched closer to her hair.

His lips stayed right next to her ear. "I'm so sorry, baby. I should have protected you better. Stay with me. Please, Em. Please." He kissed her temple. "Don't leave me. Do. Not. Leave. Me." He was desperate and tormented by the thought that tried to take root in his mind. She was dying. "God, I love you. Don't do this. Please," he roared. The guttural sound rose from the fresh place of pain that swelled inside of him. It bounced off the walls and the floor, echoing back at him, mocking him.

"Please."

There was a soft touch on his shoulder. "She's gone, Rock."

He felt wild inside and turned on the man standing behind him. "Get away from me, Brady. I mean it. Get the fuck away!"

Barely hearing the man retreating out the apartment door, Rock sat on the floor, pulled Emily into his lap and gingerly removed the knife protruding from her torso. He comforted her lifeless body, rocking her and whispering in her ear. "You're my beautiful girl, Em. You'll always be my beautiful girl." Tears rolled and sandwiched between his cheek and hers.

At that moment, he couldn't imagine ever being able to leave her. He couldn't bring himself to break the contact, because he knew once he did, he'd never touch her again. His heart told him letting go of her was not an option.

He stayed with her forever in the silent emptiness of that room. From the noise, he was vaguely aware of the activity on the other side of the apartment door. But nothing mattered except these last moments he spent with her alone. He was grateful for them.

When Rock finally pulled his cheek away from hers, she stared up at him with unseeing eyes. He closed them and kissed her lips. "Love you, Em."

* * * *

Xander placed his ear bud into his ear and turned on his com when he left his mother's house. He was met with a barrage of coms from Brady and Jordan and stopped listening to them after the first couple. He wanted to talk to a live person instead.

"Call Brady."

Brady answered immediately. "Dude, where have you been? Never mind. Meet us at headquarters. We're on our way there."

"Is Jaci okay?"

"I'll see you in a few." He disconnected.

Panic with a side of nausea ambushed him. Something had gone to shit and whatever happened was bad enough that Brady didn't want to talk about it over the com.

The transport seemed to take forever to get to headquarters, and he spent that time trying to prepare himself for the worst. Wasn't that how life worked? Just when it seemed as if everything he'd ever dreamed of was within reach, it was jerked violently out of reach. He closed his eyes. It was as if he'd sentenced Jaci to death as soon as he'd decided to love her forever. He shook his head, assuming the worst.

When he finally got to headquarters, he found the team in the briefing room.

Rock sat in the corner of the room, staring off into space and covered in blood. Xander couldn't hold back the explosion that had been growing inside of him.

"What the fuck! What happened? Where's Jaci?"

Brady stood, grabbed Xander by the arm, and pulled him into the corridor. "Emily's dead."

He stopped walking and looked at Brady. "How?"

"Caroline stabbed her in your apartment. It's Caroline, Xander. Caroline is the one killing the fallows."

"Jaci?"

"Caroline has her. Took her to Sapphire. We tracked her com there. Xander, they were moving so fast, they had to be in a car. It drove right through the border crossing. Never stopped."

Finally, the random pieces parts of information regarding the fallow cases mixed and solidified into a concrete fact. The Gov was behind the fallow murders. And the Gov was the only threat he could not protect Jaci from.

* * * *

Jaci was relieved to see her parents' house was dark when the car pulled up the driveway. She tried to escape the insane woman's grasp when the rear door opened, but she had no place to go. Caroline pulled

Jaci from the back seat by her hair and the driver gripped her arm to help drag her inside the house.

"Go park the car down the street and wait for me there. I'll be done here in a few minutes." The driver nodded and left without a word or glance at Jaci.

Caroline still gripped a huge tangle of Jaci's hair and easily controlled her with one hand. She pulled her knife from her pocket and brandished it in the other.

"Nice," Caroline said, looking around the kitchen when they walked in. She tugged on Jaci's hair. "Take me to your bedroom."

Slowly, Jaci led her down the hall and into her old room. Caroline laughed out loud when they turned and entered. "Looks like they couldn't wait to get rid of you," she said, when she saw the newly redecorated office.

The comment cut deep, but it also did something else. It pissed Jaci off, changed her frame of mind in a rudimentary way. With every passing second, her anger grew exponentially, until rage boiled under her skin.

She was done being a victim. She refused to cower in fear. If she was going to die, she was going to go down with a fight.

Without another thought, Jaci allowed her survival instincts to take over. She fisted her hand and landed a hard right hand punch to Caroline's eye. The bitch's grip on her hair loosened immediately. Jaci yanked her head free from Caroline's grasp with a rip of pain as her hair freed itself from her scalp.

She ran full speed back down the hall toward the kitchen and then yanked the knife drawer open, finding a wide assortment, from butcher to steak.

Caroline had been stunned, slowed down, but now as Jaci turned toward where she'd left the other woman, her figure stepped into the hallway.

"I'm going to kill you." Caroline snarled. She cupped a hand over her eye and continued down the hall toward the kitchen.

Jaci grabbed a knife from the drawer and whipped it end over end at Caroline. The knife sailed wide right and slapped against the wall next to the doorway that led down the hall. She'd missed completely. Jaci grabbed and whipped another one and this time it connected. It was still wide right, but it grazed Caroline in the shoulder before falling with a clank to the ground.

"Not good enough, bitch," Caroline jeered, as she sped up her gait, rushing forward toward Jaci as she made her third throw. This time, with Caroline merely feet away, Jaci's aim was true. The knife landed in Caroline's throat and stuck there.

The woman's surprised look was the last thing Jaci saw as she escaped the house through the back door at a dead run, doing her best to keep to the shadows of the dark backyard.

She ran and did not stop, didn't look back to see if anyone followed her and didn't have a clue as to what to do next. Changing direction, she headed toward the Amber Zone, staying off the streets and sidewalks. She wove her way through the shadows of the neighborhood she grew up in, hiding from the beams of occasional headlights and darting away from any people she saw.

After twenty minutes of running, Jaci wheezed with her lung's demand for more oxygen. Her legs trembled and grew more feeble with each step.

She needed to stop.

Jaci hid behind a strip mall dumpster and touched her com. "Call Xander."

"Where are you?" His voice was frantic.

"I got away from Caroline. I'm making my way back to Amber. I'm going to need help getting back through the border gate. I'm heading toward Gate One. Can you help me?" she asked, breathless and panting from her run.

"Jaci, listen closely, dump your com now and move as far away from it as possible. If you can, put it on something that's moving away from your location. Somebody will meet you at Gate One. Go along with what they're saying when you get there. You got it?"

"Yes."

"You're going to be okay," he said calmly and with authority. "Now, go get rid of it."

"Xander? I--" Jaci choked on a sob.

"I'll see you in a couple of hours." He disconnected.

Jaci looked around. The street was empty and dark.

She quirked her lips into a scheming smile. She knew exactly where to go to get rid of the com. She ran another block up and entered the only fast food restaurant around. Jaci entered through the side door, and the greasy aroma of tacos flooded her nose.

She slipped into the single person ladies room and locked the door behind her. She pulled the com from her ear, threw it into the toilet and flushed. She watched it to go down, and then flushed again to make sure it would stay down. When Jaci opened the door to leave, she turned the lock in the doorknob before pulling the door closed behind her. Just in case the com didn't go far, they would have to waste a few minutes getting the door open before they realized she wasn't there.

She snuck out of the restaurant, wondering if anyone was following her yet. She speculated as to how long that man would wait down the street for Caroline before he went looking for her. Caroline had to be dead. The knife blade sank deep into the base of her throat. She'd gone down fast. She wondered if he would leave her lying there dead in her parent's kitchen, or would he call the police or National Guard to cover their tracks?

Jaci walked at a good clip toward the border, sticking to the shadows. Her skin was cool and a sheen of perspiration from her full out running coated her skin.

The understanding that the Gov would never stop looking for her suddenly sunk in. She was a murderer. At best, she would be redesignated Onyx and be put outside of the city walls. At worst, she'd probably disappear into thin air, like the people Xander told her about.

She wanted to see Xander again before that happened.

That thought alone strengthened her tired body and ragged spirit. She kept going, finding points in the distance and making them goals. She promised herself she'd stop and rest once she made it to the goal. Then, she renegotiated with her tired legs and searing lungs, refocusing on another goal and telling herself she would stop and rest there.

Jaci didn't know how long it took her but she guessed it had been at least two hours since she commed Xander. Now, border crossing gate one was in sight. Jaci stopped and caught her breath. She wiped the perspiration from her face with her forearm and raked her fingers through her hair in a desperate attempt to not look like the way she felt.

As she approached, she saw Jordan standing at the small booth talking to a couple of soldiers. She was in uniform. Jaci never saw Jordan in uniform before. She was laughing and so were the two soldiers.

Jordan caught sight of Jaci's approach before the men did. She smiled wide at Jaci and raised her eyebrows. "Oh there she is," she said, pointing and laughing. "Could you be any more of a pain in my ass?"

Jaci's mouth was parched and her heart played the rhythm of her fear as she approached, pasting on her best smile. "I know, I know, guilty as charged."

"And, so you know, I'm not coming here to pick you up again," she said as she pulled Jaci through the narrow pedestrian gate.

"Go wait for me in the cruiser. I'll be there in a sec," Jordan said, winking at one of the men in uniform.

Jaci rolled her eyes and turned away from the soldiers. "That's what you said the last time, yet here you are," she called over her shoulder.

Now that her back was to them, she forced herself to squash the overwhelming urge to run to the waiting police car.

After a minute, Jordan walked back to the cruiser, drawing the appreciative looks of the two soldiers she'd been talking to.

"It took a considerable bit of flirting to get those guys to let down their guard enough to let me hang out and wait for you, but I think I made some new friends," she said as she slammed the car door closed.

"Emily?" Jaci croaked.

Jordan hesitated then took Jaci's hand. "Emily's dead, Jaci."

"Oh my God. No. I can't believe this." Jaci moaned, holding her hands over her face. Her head hung low as they rode together in silence for several minutes.

"I killed Caroline. I have to hide." Jaci was deadpan. "You can't be seen with me, Jordan. I'm going to be put out of the city when they catch me."

"Well, they'll have to find you first."

Chapter 16

Xander had been waiting for hours when the two women walked into the vacant apartment in building twenty-eight. Jaci rushed to him as soon as she saw him. He took her into his arms and held her tight.

"Thanks, Jordan," he said, his lips close to Jaci's ear.

"No prob."

"It's late. Jaci and I are staying here tonight. Captain Rush scheduled a meeting for all of us tomorrow at nine."

"See you guys tomorrow then." Her gaze flicked toward Jaci for a split second, silently checking whether it was okay to leave.

Jaci mustered a smile. "Night, Jordan," she murmured.

After Xander closed the door and turned the lock, he turned and held Jaci captive in a relentless embrace. Then her composure shattered. She withered in his arms. Each grieving sob filled his ears louder than the one before.

"Emily's dead, Xander." Jaci clawed at his shirt in an attempt to remain standing instead of curling into the ball her body seemed to demand.

He picked her up, laid her down on the bed and slid in next to her.

In the inky darkness of the room, Jaci's spastic sobs echoed off the walls and floor. He held her tight while she released her grief and fear, burrowing into his body, as if for shelter. Her despair mangled Xander's already wounded heart.

There were so many questions he wanted to ask her. So many things he wanted to say. But, now was not the time to do it. Not for either of them. Because as he lay there consoling her, he suffered his own feelings of loss.

He'd remained stoic at headquarters. Strong for his friend. Professional for the team. Now, in the sanctuary of their hiding place, under total cover of darkness, Xander took the time he needed to process the reality of Emily's murder. Thoughts of her tightened the muscles of his throat.

Emily was his friend. She genuinely cared for him and he felt the same. Whenever he was around her, she went out of her way to pull him into her orbit, giving him a prominent place in her panoramic world. She created a tornado of spontaneous fun, outrageous individuality and unbridled passion that swirled intensely around her. It was hard not to get caught up in it.

He never worried that he sent the wrong message when he was with her. She would never have mistaken his friendliness for anything more. She was Rock's, so he was always safe to be himself.

Xander snapped out of his own grief and noticed Jaci had stopped crying. He listened to the slow, rhythmic in and out of her breath. She was sleeping. Her warm exhalations of air played over his chest.

It seemed an eternity since the conversation with his mother. He thought of what he'd promised her, that he would grab onto his love of a lifetime and never let her go. He looked back down at Jaci.

He did love her.

He had been an idiot. He'd purposely tried to drive her away, and he'd knowingly hurt her in the process. Yet, she was still here in his arms. Safe. For now.

The Gov wanted her gone, her and the fallows before her. Those in power were so afraid that the extent of the oppression in the Amber Zone would become known, that Ambers would begin to gain sympathy through the close family ties the transferred fallows had with their families, that they killed to sever those ties. What they'd been doing was a violation of the Amber Accord. If this information got out, Ambers would be outraged. They would be within their right to organize and fight the Gov.

Xander considered what life would be like in Onyx. Maybe he should take Jaci and leave before she was targeted again. At the far end of the huge medicinal garden behind the wellness center stood a large section of the wall that encircled all of New Atlanta. They could scale it and make a go of it in the Onyx Zone. But the unknown of what was on the other side was as intimidating and dangerous as the Gov. Ideas floated and wove their way around his half-asleep brain. Plans developed and were foiled before ever being given the chance to be executed.

He woke from his ethereal half sleep with intangible plans for their escape, the solution to everything just beyond reach of his conscious memory. As the outside world came into focus, the brief respite gained from his hour or two of sleep dissipated and the stress and fear of remembering the events of the day before returned to their proper place, descending like heavy weights on his chest.

Throughout the night, Jaci positioned her body as close to him as possible. Now, her rear pressed firmly on his morning erection. This time, instead of moving away from her as he'd done every morning since their first night together, he stayed where he was and caressed the brown, wavy ribbons of hair away from her face. He would never force himself to distance his heart or body from her again. Of this, he was absolutely sure.

Xander leaned over and whispered in her ear, "It's time to get up."

Jaci released a soft, whispery sigh and was motionless again.

Then suddenly her eyes flew open. He watched her as she hastily took in her surroundings and then remembered the events of the night before. Her face fell. She turned her head to look at him.

"What time is it?"

"I'm not sure but I think we're probably already late for the meeting." Neither one of them moved. "Don't worry. We'll figure this out together. We have a lot of things to talk about too," he murmured as he wrapped his arm around her waist and pressed himself into her. He kissed her exposed neck.

Her gaze met his. He saw the confusion and pain in her face. She drew in an unsettled breath and closed her eyes on the exhale as if she were silently thanking God for the moment or maybe committing the moment to memory. He couldn't be sure. "But we'll have to save it for later. Come on." He rose from the bed and took Jaci's small hands in his, pulling her out from beneath the blanket until she sat on the edge of the mattress. He ambled to the bathroom while she started to comb her fingers through her hair.

Once in the bathroom, he looked around. No clean clothes, no toothbrushes, not even any soap. They both were going to look a bit rough. Well, he would anyway.

He commed headquarters, requesting a patrol car to meet them outside Circle City to give them a ride. The trip from the apartment to headquarters held an awkward silence, and Xander took a breath of relief when they walked into the briefing room. Everybody from the special task force was already there. They were crowded around the screen at one end of the room watching the morning news feed.

As Xander and Jaci joined them, they caught the remainder of the reporter's story.

"...hero Officer Rock Dunham killed suspected serial killer, Emily Taylor, in the Amber Zone last night while she was in the process of trying to murder her next victim. The intended victim, whose identity has not yet been released, is reported to be doing well this morning. This is the first identification of a known serial killer since the pandemic.

In related news, a Government spokesperson announced that Officer Dunham has been granted a special petition designation to Emerald due to his police work and heroism in this case. He is the second Amber Zone citizen to be granted Emerald status this year…"

The screen went mute and everybody in the room returned to their places around the table in stunned silence.

"Well, at least we know which way the Gov is playing it," Captain Rush said as he sat down. He looked at Jaci and stood back up. "I'm Captain Rush." He stuck out his hand and she shook it. "I think you know everybody else here." He motioned for her to have a seat. "Give us the run down from start to finish on what happened last night."

Jaci told everybody what happened while she was in the Sapphire Zone, while Xander sat, feeling like he was going to explode. He felt murderous. He couldn't believe that Caroline worked for the Gov. She'd been hiding in plain sight. The task force didn't think twice about her during their investigation. They'd screwed up on basic detective work, and Emily had paid the price for their mistake. He wanted to scream.

Xander looked over at Rock. He wore the same bloodstained clothes from the night before. His eyes were rimmed in red with dark circles hanging underneath. A day or two of beard growth darkened his face. He was there, but not really. His eyes were empty, his body language said, "I'm broken inside and out."

Xander knew Rock blamed himself. He hadn't put everything together in time to save Emily. Xander also knew there would be no consoling Rock's grief. There were no words he could utter that would ever change the depth of the agony Rock suffered. But Xander would still try.

The meeting ended with the consensus of all involved that they would release Jaci's name as the intended victim of the serial killer. They felt it would protect her from further targeting by the Gov, reasoning that having the Amber population know she was a target for murder once may prevent her from being a target again.

There didn't seem to be any more loose ends. Captain Rush officially called the case closed and silence descended on the room.

Nobody congratulated anyone else. There were no feelings of accomplishment or a job well done.

"Rock, come back to the apartment with us," Xander said.

He shook his head in response, still staring into space. Xander motioned for Jaci to wait for him in the hall and then knelt in front of his friend. He tried to tell Rock all the things he knew a good partner, a good friend should, but as predicted, he was inconsolable. At the moment, he possessed the presence of his namesake--a rock.

"Go away. Just go away," he finally said to Xander, not with anger, but with pleading expressed in his eyes.

Xander stood. "Okay." He sighed. "Com me tomorrow."

Rock didn't even acknowledge that he'd spoken.

Xander rejoined Jaci in the hall and caught a ride back to building seventeen. They waited until they got into their apartment and closed the door behind them to start talking.

"Somebody cleaned up," Jaci mumbled as she walked further into the room and looked at the spot where Emily had lay dying. She turned to look at him.

Xander couldn't hold back anymore. He advanced on Jaci with long strides, backing her up until she was sandwiched between him and the wall, his chest against her chest, her hair caressing his cheek. His cock pressed into her.

Jaci looked up at him wide eyed, surprised. She attempted to push him away. He grabbed her wrists and shackled them with his hands to the wall above her head.

"No, you're going to listen to every syllable of what I have to say before I let you go." Xander's voice started as a thick, throaty rasp. "There won't be any more mixed messages from me, Jaci. I was fighting it. I was fighting the concept of being a part of an us. I'm not fighting it anymore. I want you. In my mind and heart, you're mine already." Xander growled his words into her ear. His body still hard against her. "I'm sorry. I'm so, so sorry for betraying your trust, for hurting you. It won't ever happen again." He whispered the words over her lips. Their eyes met, and then Jaci turned her face away from him.

"Look at me," he ordered.

Hesitantly, she turned her head back to him. Pain and confusion swirled in her eyes. "I want to spend the rest of my life telling you how much I love you." He kissed the side of her neck. He sucked and roamed raising goose bumps on her arms. "Making you feel good, hearing you shout my name when I make you come." He practically breathed the words into her ear, and then he brushed his stubbled cheek against her temple. When he stopped speaking, he looked down at her. She was breathing heavily. The look on her face seemed like a mixture of agony and ecstasy. He gradually released his grip on her wrists and waited. Their bodies melded together. The sweet feeling of being next to her without guilt or hesitation empowered him. She was where she belonged, his to love and protect until…until he no longer could.

"Why, Xander? Why did this have to be such a painful process?" She paused and shook her head. "I'm raw. I am so raw from trying to form this bond with you and trying to form friendships with others. Nothing has been what it seems since I got here." She placed her hands, with her fingers spread wide, on his chest and pushed him away gently.

"I've been sliced open and had the hope for my future cut right out of me. I've been duped by you and Jordan, betrayed by Caroline, all people I cared for and trusted. The one and only honest friend I've had since I got here was murdered right in front of me." Jaci's tone was even, but her look accused him. "And you, you dismissed me. Shut me down hard before ever giving us a chance. I can't give in to you so easily anymore. At the very least I need to know why. I'll never be able to open myself up to you if I'm afraid you're going to wake up tomorrow and throw me away like a bad card drawn in a hand of poker." Jaci's innocent gaze searched his, groping for an explanation, and he knew she deserved one.

Xander exhaled a long breath and looked away from the regret plainly visible on her face. He had to have this conversation with her now, even though the only thing he wanted to do was feel her skin next to his.

She wasn't mad. She hadn't raised her voice. It was fair, he thought. A fair assessment and a reasonable demand. His stomach turned at the thought of revealing his secret to her. "Come on, sit down." He pulled a chair out for her at the small table and grabbed a couple of beers from the refrigerator before he sat down opposite her. She raised her eyebrows in surprise.

"It's not even eleven AM." Then she turned her concerned gaze toward him. "What is it, Xander?"

"I have an automatic disqualifier, too." Xander watched her eyes widen and jaw drop for a moment before she reined her reaction in. "It's the same as my dad's. Growing up, I watched my mom take care of him hour after hour, day after day. From my perspective, the perspective a little boy, it was overwhelmingly unbearable…his disease, and my mom's constant devotion to a man that wasted away right in front of her until she had nothing.

"After my testing--after I found out that I would develop the same disease that took my father after so many long and desperate years. I made a vow that I wasn't going to ruin the life of the woman I love, like he did," he mumbled and then sighed. "So I promised myself no serious relationships. I don't want to be taken care of like an infant. I wanted to protect you from it."

She looked at him, eyes wide, shaking her head. "I don't care about that," Jaci said softly.

"That's pretty much what my mom said last night. Jaci, I won't push you away anymore. I can't. I don't have it in me." He sat silently looking at her. She didn't meet his gaze.

Jaci was quiet for a long time, too long, in Xander's opinion.

He wanted her to rush into his arms, but he knew her silence was the consequence of his earlier stupidity. While he waited, he was overly aware of his breathing and was keenly conscious of his newfound vulnerability. It brought with it a deluge of growing anxiety, coiling around him and tightening its grip with every silent second that passed. Her next words could be either the best words he would ever hear, or the worst.

Chapter 17

When Jaci sat down at the small table in their apartment, she honestly thought there would be nothing Xander could say to erase the tightly guarded shield her tender feelings hid behind. But as the words tumbled out of his mouth, his personal burden and the choices he made, made sense. Things he had said to her that she previously thought were cruel, took on a different meaning. In his reality he tried to shelter her from his future.

"Don't you know me by now, Xander?" She looked up into his gorgeous brown eyes. "I would take care of you whether you were in love with me or not." Jaci reached across the table and took his hand. "But, you're going to have to show me more than a half hour of interest before I completely open myself up to you again. I know how I feel about you. From the very beginning, I knew. But I'm going to need more consistency from you. I don't want to get hurt again."

"So you want me to work for it?" Xander's tone hinted at more than a touch of irritation.

"If that's the way you want to look at it. But I think of it more like you actually acting like you care about me and my feelings before I give myself to you completely."

"Oh, you're mine completely," he said, and then fell silent. His expression was hard and the muscles of his jaw flexed and released like he was grinding his teeth. Jaci could tell he was rolling the situation over in his frontal lobe. Xander had never known any restrictions on his sex life. When he wanted it, he went out and found it. He was clueless about what it took to have a relationship.

"Fine," he said finally. "I deserve some skepticism. But I'm not going to accept it for long. His expression was stern. "There are also some things I want." A devious grin spread over his face and her stomach fluttered inside her, where the empty hole had been just yesterday.

"Like what?"

"You have to promise to be open to all the things I can teach you, all the variations of pleasure. You have a lot of catching up to do."

"Xander, I don't even know what that means," she said, rolling her eyes.

"I'll show you what it means. Are you open to it? All of it? Because if you want me, truly want me, you're going to have to get to know and accept my sexual preferences." His statement was followed by a return of the wicked smile it seemed he had a hard time containing.

"Xander...I don't know. I don't think I could stand another--"

He rose from his chair and knelt beside her. "Shh." He rubbed the pad of his thumb over her bottom lip and met her gaze. "I promise you have my heart, Jaci," he said in a baritone purr, rubbing her back. He unhooked her bra with an easy flick. "You always have." He pushed her shirt up, leaned in and captured a nipple in his mouth, sucking it in hard. It was a good thing she was sitting, because the circling motion of his tongue in combination with the pulls of suction weakened Jaci's knees.

She tried to push him away. "No, Xander. I'm not ready for this, this..." She searched for the right word. "Whatever this is," she yelled.

He cupped her face with his palm and gently kissed her. "I love you, Jaci." Their faces were mere inches from one another's. He caressed her cheek with the back of his hand. "Hold back if you have to. Say the word and I'll stop. But don't, if you're only doing it because you're scared. I will never push you away from me again."

Jaci was torn. She wanted to be with Xander so badly. Her heart ached with the need to love him and to be loved by him. She wanted to experience everything he wanted to give her, and to give back to him everything she was. But only a stupid woman made the same mistakes over and over again and expected a different outcome. Plus, being around her could be dangerous when the Gov decided to pursue Caroline's killer.

No. She couldn't be with him, at least not now.

With tears in her eyes and a broken heart, she shook her head. "I'm sorry." She leaped up and ran to the bathroom.

Jaci sat on the cold white tile of the bathroom floor.

The man of her dreams offered his love, the love she'd longed for, and now she couldn't do it anymore.

The bathroom door opened, and Xander stood over her, glaring. "Don't run from me," he warned. "Don't ever run from me again. Your allotted time for skepticism about my feelings is officially over. And don't think for one minute that the Gov will come after me. They won't. Captain Rush wouldn't let them get away with it and they know it."

He pulled her up from her spot on the floor, picked her up and threw her over his shoulder.

"What are you doing?" Jaci squealed.

"We have to start somewhere. You can wait to have sex with me until you're feeling less skittish. It's okay. It will give me some time to fill you in on some other talents I have and skills you're going to need as my girlfriend."

Jaci giggled. She couldn't help herself. Deep down inside, this was what she wanted. She wanted him to overrule her. To not take no for an answer. She wanted him to fight for her and she was unbelievably relieved that he was doing just that.

"Think it's funny?" Xander slapped Jaci's ass.

"Ow."

"No laughing."

"Is this going to be more sex that isn't sex?"

He growled and she giggled again.

"You said you're open to everything. Have you changed your mind?"

"No."

"Good." Xander threw Jaci on the bed and went straight for the button of her pants. He opened and unzipped them, then jerked the pants off with a savage yank that pulled her half off the bed. He followed it with an easy tug of her shirt over her head. "Lay in the middle," he ordered, as he undressed himself. Jaci reacted to his authority. Her nipples puckered, and goose bumps rose on her arms. She swallowed hard with a dry mouth. This was insane. She was nearly panting as she crawled on the bed, giving Xander a perfect glimpse of her from behind, before she lay in the center.

"Now you're teasing me?" he rumbled. "You're going to pay for that."

Jaci looked at him as he entered the bed beside her. His expression was dead serious. His gaze surveyed her like a king would survey his empire.

"Put your hands above your head."

Hesitantly, she did.

He leaned over her, placing his cock mere inches from her face. She lifted her head closer, wanting to swipe it with her tongue but she couldn't reach.

Jaci heard the clicks and felt the cold metal around her wrists simultaneously. She was cuffed.

"Now, you're mine," he said, backing away from her.

"What are you going to do?" she demanded.

"What do you want me to do?" he countered as he ran the pad of his index finger from between her breasts to her belly button.

"I--I don't know."

Xander leaned over and placed his lips right next to Jaci's ear. "Don't worry. I won't fuck you no matter how much you beg me. After all, it's going to take time for you to open up to me, to trust me again, right?" A slow, deep chuckle emanated from his chest and as the warm breath hit her ear, Jaci's body responded with a rush of liquid heat warming her sex.

He rose from the bed. His nude body was breathtaking. Perpetually tanned skin, a gift from his Greek ancestry, highlighted the architecture of his build. She followed his movements as he strode to his side of the room. His erection bobbed and her blood boiled.

He was absolute perfection. Her heart had known it from the start and through it all had refused to relent in that conviction, even when her mind wanted differently.

When he opened the top drawer of his dresser, her stomach twirled with nervousness and excitement. That drawer contained sweet torture and wild orgasms.

He chose a handful of items and threw them on the bed next to her. Jaci looked and drew a sharp intake of breath as she identified what was there. Maybe she was over her head. This was all so new to her. Yet, she felt it, the inescapable awareness that she would embrace all his needs and become everything he needed her to be. She loved him. God, she loved everything about him, including this.

She jerked her head back toward him to find him with a satisfied grin at her reaction to the toys and lube he'd thrown down.

"Any objections?"

Jaci didn't answer. She silently succumbed to him, knowing the pleasure he took from her apprehension. She was turned on. She wanted him to fuck her now. But he knew that didn't he? She was not going to give him the satisfaction of asking him for it. He knew that, too.

Smug fucker.

"I'll take your silence as a no." He took his time as he crawled into the bed beside her, stalking her like prey. He palmed the back of her neck, lifting her head, and kissed her savagely. His tongue invaded her mouth, explored it, and dueled with hers. He bit her lip.

She wanted to pull him closer to her, and put her arms around his neck. She wanted to pull him on top of her and swore when the metal of the cuffs stopped the movement short. She had already forgotten her hands were bound.

He stopped his dominance of her mouth, noting her attempt to move with a smirk. "Want out already?"

"No, I just forgot for a second." She was out of breath as she spoke.

He leaned his body against the length of hers. His erection pressed into her hip. He dipped his head and took a puckered nipple into his mouth and then flicked it with his moist, hot tongue. Jaci moaned. Her breath was ragged. She arched up toward him, her body wordlessly asking for more.

"Good girl," he encouraged her. "What are you going to say to me if you want me to stop? He waited, intent on her answer.

"Stop." She whimpered.

He nodded ever so slightly at her answer, a brief flicker of satisfaction played over his features. Then, he shifted himself to the area between her legs. "Look at me." The deep rumble of his voice was like rolling thunder.

Jaci opened her eyes and found Xander on his knees, erection in hand. "You see what you do to me? I haven't had sex with another woman for weeks. It's for you, Jaci. From now on, it's completely for you. Now's as good a time as ever for you to begin learning how I like to be touched." His hot gaze trailed up and down her body, devoured her. "But, I don't want you to lose your need. So, let's see." Xander looked over the toys lying next to her on the bed. "This should do."

Jaci had no idea what he'd chosen. Her eyes widened as he backed up and positioned the rounded oval end at the opening of her pussy. He inserted the item inside of her in a slow gentle glide.

Jaci gasped. "What…"

"Shh, sweetie." He held a small box in his hand, and with a slow smile and a flip of the switch, the thing vibrated inside of her.

She gasped.

"Good?"

"Oh, yes," she whispered.

"Good." He shot her a wicked smile. "I'm just going to leave it on low. I don't want you coming while I'm teaching you how to handle me."

Jaci closed her eyes and felt the exquisitely slow vibrations inside of her. He was right. It made her wet, made her want him, but it wasn't enough to make her come.

"Open your eyes." She watched him grab the bottle of lube, squirt some in the palm of his hand and stroke it onto his cock. It was ruddy and veined. Big, even in his large hand. She wanted the vibrating thing out of her and his cock in.

"Oh, fuck--Xander." She tried to move her hands again.

"What's wrong?" She met his sober gaze. He leaned over between her legs, his lubed erection laid on her stomach. "Are you okay?" His hot breath fanned her ear.

She was panting, trying to catch her breath. The slow vibration in her vagina made her crazy. His hot cock laying on her stomach made it worse. "Get on with it," she pleaded.

He returned back to vertical. "You'll probably have to use both hands to circle completely around it." He gave a demonstration of the technique. Long, firm strokes from base to tip. "But one hand is good too." He dropped one hand to cup his balls.

Jaci watched as he stroked himself more roughly than she would have done. He sped up his strokes little by little and never took his gaze off her face. He made sure she was looking, taking it in. Learning. And she was.

"I can't wait until it's your hands on my cock, sweet Jaci. Just thinking about it makes be want to come." Xander worked himself with his hand roughly, and then his body went rigid. "Oh fuck." She watched as his head rolled back and he came. The warm spurts arced into the air and landed on her breasts.

He slowly stopped his hand and returned his gaze to her. She was out of breath. Her air slipped past her parted lips in short, hot pants.

"Now, I can focus on you," he growled as he wiped her down with a towel. "How do you like the egg?"

Jaci couldn't talk. The vibration was torture. She was close. One touch could send her over the edge. "Please," she moaned as she arched her back.

Xander leaned over her body. "Please what?"

"Finish me."

"Oh, baby, we just got started." Xander rolled Jaci onto her stomach. He leaned over her, covering her body with his, supporting his weight on his forearms. He brushed her hair away and placed soft kisses on her neck and shoulders. He stopped for a moment, and then the vibration of the egg inside her increased.

He leaned back over her and covered the junction where her neck and shoulder met with his mouth. He sucked and tongued the same spot relentlessly. He was marking her. She felt the pull right down to her clit.

She tried to rub herself into the sheets underneath her, until she felt a slap on her ass.

"No, sweetie. Not until I say. Hold still."

Xander wrapped an arm under her hips and hiked her ass into the air. From his place between her legs, he grabbed the bottle of lube again, putting another thick quirt onto his hand and picked up another item she'd never seen before. "Okay, sweets, let's see what else gets you excited." He lubed the teardrop shaped toy and slowly slipped the blunt end into the tight opening of her rear.

"Holy fuck," she cried as the toy became larger the further he pushed it into her. "No. I can't do this."

He leaned over her. "Relax," he whispered. His physical closeness comforted her, melted her doubt and calmed her panic. He remained there, covering her until the tightness of her muscles loosened, until she released her angst and trusted him.

"This is a plug. It's made for this. I'm going to push slowly. I'll stop again if you tell me to."

Jaci nodded her assent, giving silent permission to continue.

The ever-widening diameter stretched her slowly. She focused on the low rumble of pleasure emanating from behind her. All she wanted to do was make this man happy.

Just as she was about to make him stop again, it popped into place. The vibrating egg created an entirely new sensation with the thing he'd put in her ass. Xander rolled Jaci back over to her back. He smiled at her. His eyes were hooded, seductive. He slid a finger into her pussy, and then two, skimming over the egg.

"You're so wet for me."

The walls of her cunt clamped onto his fingers as they plunged in and out of her. Xander lowered his head to her clit. It throbbed with want. She was almost coming at merely the thought of his lips sealing over the place she needed him most. He encircled the bud in his mouth and then lashed, pressed and swirled it with his tongue.

Her cries of pleasure were strangled as the shuddering waves of her climax overtook her. Everything, the vibration, the plug in her ass, his plunging fingers and his tongue working her, combined, made the orgasm bloom deeper inside of her. It was like nothing she'd ever felt before. He continued to work her and she continued to peak shuddering, quivering and wailing his name. She came and came. It was the longest, most mind-blowing orgasm in her life.

When the pleasure slowed, so did Xander. He withdrew his fingers. Then, she felt him pull the egg out. She lay there, a pile of loose gelatin with a frantic heartbeat. The cuffs clicked and her hands were free, but she didn't move. She attempted to calm herself as she felt the bed dip beside her. Xander's strong hands encircled her waist, pulling her to him He curled his hard body around her and draped an arm over her.

"That was the best not sex I've ever had," she declared drowsily. They dozed together.

Jaci woke to the smell of food. Xander was cooking in the kitchen. The afternoon sunlight streamed through the window giving the white of the apartment a cheerful atmosphere. It only took a split second for her to remember the second round of sex that was not sex she'd had with Xander prior to her snooze. She smiled. He didn't let her run from him and he'd withheld himself as punishment her for her insecurity and hesitation. It worked. She'd never wanted his cock inside her more.

Fucker. He knew more about the way women worked than she gave him credit for. And he used that knowledge to show her, to make it crystal clear, just how much she wanted him

She shifted to watch his movements in the kitchen.

He was naked, but she only glimpsed snippets of rear end and lower abdomen as he moved around behind the bar that separated the living area from the kitchen.

Oh God. Her stomach twirled and her pussy became wet for him all over again.

She admired the cuts and indents of his muscles as he moved. Her gaze then returned to study his face. He was brutally seductive. All man. Just looking at him changed who she was inside in a primitive way. She was still Jaci, but now she was his Jaci. She felt like she belonged to him. He'd marked her, claimed her, and somehow she knew neither one of them would change their mind about that.

She was so intent on the object of her affection that she didn't notice right away that the apartment door opened. Not until she heard the stern male voice.

"Jaci Harmon?" She startled and turned to look toward the direction of the voice. The soldier who spoke stood in front of a group of soldiers. They all entered deeper into the apartment and spread out, guns drawn, covering Xander and her.

Both Jaci and Xander were caught off guard. Jaci's stomach contents transformed from butterflies to stone. It hadn't taken the Gov long to catch up with her. They'd all been naïve to think this ordeal was over. "I'm Jaci Harmon," she said, sitting up and pulling the sheet up to cover her nudity.

Xander stood frozen separated from her by the bar. She saw the thoughts rolling around in his head. In his expression, she glimpsed the impulses he stuffed, not wanting to make it worse for her. The telltale sign of his anger, the muscle working in his cheek was present, but other than that he didn't betray his need to crush the piece of shit that leered at her into the clean white floor.

"Palm?" he said approaching her.

She held her hand up so that the soldier could scan her code. He checked to make sure he was detaining the right woman. "Get dressed. You're wanted for questioning."

"Could she get some privacy?" Xander asked through barely veiled rage.

The leader looked over his shoulder at Xander and smiled. "No. Animals don't have modesty."

Xander attempted to move, but a group of three advanced on him and pushed him back into the far end of the kitchen against the wall. He struggled violently against them, bringing more soldiers into the tiny space.

"Xander, don't! It's not worth it. Please!" The scuffling slowly stopped, but more likely because Xander was completely overpowered, not because he'd heeded her request.

With a sigh of resignation and as much grace and pride as she could muster, Jaci got up from the bed in front of the gathered soldiers, dressing in jeans and a t-shirt. She slid her feet into her flip-flops and glanced at Xander as she walked toward the group of soldiers. He was flat against the back wall of the kitchen. His gaze followed her despite the fact that a soldier's hand smashed his face, and a forearm pressed across Xander's neck. A different soldier held a gun to his head, touching his temple. Even from across the room she saw the vein in Xander's neck pulsing with the rapid beat of his heart.

"Let me go," he barked at the three men restraining him.

When she turned her back to a soldier so that he could cuff her, she lifted her gaze to meet Xander's. "Love you," she mouthed, as a loop was slipped over her head and tightened around her neck, before she was roughly turned and led into the corridor by the pole attached to it.

"Jaci!"

She heard Xander call her. Then, she heard the fading sounds of a scuffle. She looked at her feet as she walked down the hallway. She was a spectacle, an example for all those who cared to look.

Chapter 18

When the half dozen Guardsmen finally cleared out of the apartment, leaving Xander alone, he sprung into action. He tapped the com in his ear to contact Rock. Instead, he found a com waiting from Rock.

"Play."

"Xan, sorry I missed you. The Gov showed up to transfer me to Emerald. So, I guess this is it. Take care of Journey for me. She's going to be scared. Jaci will probably have to help you at first." He cleared his throat. "When she gets back. So, yeah…later, brother."

Xander tried to reply but got a message reporting that the com he was trying to reach was disconnected.

"Fuck!" Xander picked up the pan of fried potatoes he'd been making for their breakfast and threw it across the room, leaving a greasy mess over the wall and floor.

Then he commed his captain.

"Rush here."

"Cap, the National Guard took Jaci." There was silence on the other end. "Cap?"

"I'll get someone to get the team together and I'll send a cruiser to pick you up in…half hour?"

"Yeah, okay. Oh, Cap?"

"What?"

"Rock's gone to Emerald."

"Yeah, I know. Half hour. Be ready."

Xander sat on the edge of the bed. His mood was black. He felt desperate and lethal. The room was consumed by utter silence with only the sound of his own blood rushing through his veins, filling his ears. He'd never known of a person being returned to the Amber Zone after the National Guard picked them up. His blood boiled with the need to find and save her. Every second that passed was a second too long to be away from her.

He didn't know what a team meeting would do to help Jaci, but at least he would be able to find out where she was taken. He was going to get to her, and he was going to kill anyone that stood in his way.

The decision made, Xander stood focused and determined. He wiped up the mess on the floor and then slowly, deliberately dressed in uniform. He checked and holstered his gun.

He was calm. Like a man who'd decided to commit suicide and knew the pain would be over in a moment or two. He would save Jaci or die trying. Either way, his anguish would be over soon.

He sat stoic in the passenger seat of the cruiser that picked him up and did the same as he waited in the briefing room of Amber Police Headquarters. It had been less than twenty-four hours since the team met to wrap up the case. It hadn't occurred to him at the time that Rock would be transferred before they saw each other again. Already, it seemed like a lifetime ago.

When Captain Rush, Brady and two other Amber officers entered the room and headed straight for Xander, he had no idea what was going down until they were done. The two officers overpowered him and cuffed his right hand to the stainless steel cuff bar attached to the wall.

"What the fuck are you doing?" he shouted.

Captain Rush thanked the two officers and dismissed them. Then the cap and Brady sat at the table. Jordan entered a few seconds later.

"I'm saving your life." Captain Rush said as he sat back in his chair. "You are still under my command and you will follow my orders. I know you well enough by now to know you're planning on going rogue." The Captain leaned forward in his chair and leveled a glare at Xander. "You'd be dead before you even found her. We do this my way." He leaned back in his chair.

Xander seethed. "Let me the fuck go!"

Captain Rush ignored him. "Okay, I've made some calls and finally made contact with General Morgan the acting commander of the New Atlanta peacekeeping force. He was already aware of Jaci's detainment. She's currently being interrogated. He said that she may be charged with Caroline's murder, pending any disclosures she may make during the interrogation. I advised him that we were aware of the Gov's involvement in the termination of Amber fallows and the attempted murder of Jaci. I reminded him that the Gov's actions were a violation of the Amber

Accord and that he risked an Amber uprising if should this information to get out to the public.

"The general wanted to see what proof I had of their Accord violations. Brady is putting together audio and will e-mail it for the general's inspection. That's where we are now."

Xander took a deep breath and blew it out slowly, eyes closed. A slight wash of relief and gratitude flashed over him. They weren't going to lay down and pretend none of this happened. They were actually going to try to do something to help her, to get her back. "Do you know where they have her?"

"She's being held on the peacekeeper's compound in the Emerald Zone. I don't know exactly where."

Over the next few hours, they waited for Brady to gather all the evidence and then they waited to hear back from the general together. Eventually, after Xander surrendered his gun and promised not to do anything stupid, Jordan released him from the cuff bar.

A nagging impulse to go to Jaci, to save her, persisted, but he knew the captain was right. He'd never even make it to the Emerald Zone, let alone onto the peacekeeper's compound.

It was almost a complete day before they heard back from the general's office. He would discipline the people responsible for the Accord violations. Jaci would be released to Amber upon completion of her interrogation.

It was a long wait, and Xander had more than enough time for his mind to reason and rage. Finally he'd come to a surprisingly easy decision. Never again would he or someone he loved be a helpless victim to the Gov. He left police headquarters without a word to anybody.

An hour later, Xander walked toward the rear of the wellness center's garden, closing in on the wall that separated the Amber Zone from the ungoverned Onyx Zone. The pillowcase he carried was laden with canned food from the commissary.

A while back, he'd learned of the black market that enterprising Ambers developed between their Zone and people in Onyx. Reportedly, they threw bundles of goods, with notes included inside, back and forth over the walls, creating a cooperative food for goods that could only be found in Onyx trade.

When he arrived at the twelve-foot cement block wall topped with loops of razor wire, he called to anybody who may have been on the other side. He got no response. Turning to put about ten feet of distance between himself and the wall, he held the pillowcase with two hands and spun in circle after circle, giving the bag more and more momentum, before he released it. The bag skimmed the gnarl of wire at the top. He heard the *thunk* of the bundle hitting the ground on the other side. He waited for a minute, and then he heard a reply to his enclosed note.

"Tomorrow at sunset."

Xander smiled. He'd made a connection and if it turned out to be a reliable connection, life as he currently knew it would change drastically. Not only for Jaci and him, but maybe for all of Amber.

* * * *

Jaci had been in the dark, literally, for what seemed like days. Her stomach growled its displeasure at being empty for so long. It was a low, angry complaint. But being hungry was the least of her worries. She'd die of dehydration long before her hunger became unbearable. The inside of her throat was parched and had been void of any saliva for at least a day. When she opened her eyes, her lids felt like sandpaper scraping over her eyeballs.

The shade of the blackness she stared into changed only slightly with her eyes open. She had to be underground. It was the only way to achieve the dank air and complete darkness that surrounded her. She no longer knew if it was day or night as she lay on the cold, hard cement, shivering and wishing for more of the blissful escape sleep provided.

She thought about a lot of things in the complete absence of any sensory input. But, mostly it was Xander that lingered in her mind. She knew by now he would be out his mind with worry. She prayed he would realize quickly that she wasn't coming back so he could start the healing process and move on.

Jaci knew she was going to die, if not directly at the hands of the Gov, then from dehydration. She had another day, maybe two, and she would be dead. Thank God.

She was so happy to end it with the love that she and Xander shared. For a moment, she'd seen what it could have been like with him. She replayed their last day together in her head over and over. It was amazing. She smiled. It would have been so good with him. It would have been a new chapter in her life. It would have been her fairy tale.

That last night had been too good to be true. Some part of her knew it all along, because she'd easily accepted the fact that the life she wanted with him would never happen. It hadn't taken much to remove all expectations of happiness, and totally break her of her will to live. Jaci told herself she wasn't giving up, she was being realistic. If she expected to ever go back to Amber again, she was kidding herself. If the time since she'd been designated Amber taught her anything it was that she had no control over her life anymore, and her existence was meaningless to most everybody.

Her throat tightened as she tried to hold back an avalanche of grief. She prayed that Xander didn't feel as much pain and sorrow as she felt. She shouldn't have mouthed *I love you* to him before she was taken away. It was selfish, and if she were thinking at all, she would have realized it would be harder for him to get over her after that. She shook her head and berated herself for so many things she'd done and not done, said and left unsaid. In the end, though, she guessed it was better that they'd just started their relationship. They hadn't, technically, even made love yet. She didn't want to be a source of pain for him. This way, given time, she'd be easily forgotten.

Jaci jumped, startled by a light flicked on somewhere away from where she was being kept. The dim illumination carried to her, faintly cutting through the thick blackness. Footsteps approached. Her heart sped up. She'd waited to be questioned when she first got there, but nobody ever came. So, she assumed that they were going to leave her down there until she died. She was almost there.

"Get up." A soldier ordered as he came up to her cell.

Jaci staggered to her feet, using her hands to walk up the cement block wall for support.

"Put your wrists together through the bars."

She was cuffed and then walked down a long corridor toward the light source. The soldier shoved her into the center of a room. He grabbed the few links of chain between her handcuffs and dropped them onto a metal hook dangling over her head. Jaci was strung up on a hook like an animal carcass. She was forced to stand on wobbly legs or bear the entire weight of her body dangling from her wrists. The soldier stood back and leered at her, raking his gaze over her body. His terrible smile flooded her with feelings of dread. She looked down at the floor to escape it.

The light switched off again and the soldier's footsteps faded away. With a snicker, Jaci recognized the irony of wishing for the cold, dark place she'd been kept in before.

She stood for as long as she could before her legs gave out. The excruciating pain of being hung by her wrists made her cry out. The air seemed dead around her. The air--or the room--she wasn't sure, seemed to gobble up every sound she made. Somewhere in the far reaches of her mind, it occurred to her that she may be hallucinating. Before long, she gave up her screaming, and eventually, she passed out.

Jaci woke to the sound of the door opening. She found her feet again and supported her own weight. It was a lame show of strength, but it was the best she could do.

The uniformed man who entered pinned her down with a piercing, blue-eyed, savage glare. She would have considered him handsome if it weren't for the air of evil that followed him in.

"Good morning, Jaci. I'm General Morgan."

She didn't reply. She only followed his movements with her gaze.

"You've caused me a fuckload of trouble over the last two days."

"By not dying when you wanted me to?" she rasped through her arid throat.

Out of nowhere, he slapped her face with a powerful swing. She hadn't seen it coming and the impact swiveled her head around.

"Shut your nasty, stinking mouth, Amber bitch." He slapped her again. "Don't mistake my manners for weakness." His tone was lethal.

"You're lucky that I let a piece of shit like you in the same room as me, let alone spend two days of my life on this stupid bullshit." He paced the inside the room for a minute, before he continued in a calmer tone. "I have a few questions." He sounded more dangerous now than when he'd slapped her. She held her breath.

He took her chin and lifted it, trying to meet her eyes. "Who else knows about Caroline?"

Jaci refused to look at him while twisting her head away from his grip. She kept her gaze focused on the open door behind him. She pressed her lips together, remaining silent.

"You don't want to talk to me?"

"No," she croaked.

"Your choice," he said as he turned the light off and left her dangling in the dark.

She smiled. That was the most fun she'd had in days. The thrill of the defiance wore off about ten seconds later.

She had been there so long. The days without food or water began to have its desired effect. Jaci's weakness grew. The muscles in her legs trembled under the weight of her body. Even though the air was damp and cool, a fine film of perspiration coated her skin. It cooled her to the point she was shivering. After several hours, her teeth chattered and the cold was bone-deep. She wouldn't be able to stand for much longer before she would have to dangle again.

When her legs finally failed, she hung from her wrists with the cold metal digging into her so deeply it felt as if it was slicing her hands off.

She knew she was dead already. She tried to mentally prepare herself for what was coming because she sure as hell wasn't going to say anything that would hurt anybody she knew in Amber, no matter what they did to her.

It seemed like days before the general returned. His vicious blue gaze took her in. A finger of dread aroused her to full consciousness. He walked up to her and grabbed a fistful of her hair.

"You are going to talk to me, or I will go back to your apartment and take your roommate into custody. I heard that neither one of you were clothed when you were picked up." He chuckled as he crowded Jaci's face with his own. "Is he your special friend?" Jaci noticed the Emerald band around the man's wrist as he released the grip on her hair.

"No," she croaked.

"Good." He indicated to another soldier standing outside the cell. "Take her down."

She was unhooked and shoved into a chair. The relief of pressure on her wrists didn't feel as good as she thought it would. In fact, the renewed blood flow to that area seemed to increase the amount of pain she felt. A few seconds later, she was in agony. "Aaah," she cried, rocking back and forth, cradling her wrists in her lap.

General Morgan pulled out the chair on the other side of the table and sat, crossing his legs and staring at her, apparently waiting for her to stop crying out. It took several minutes before she quieted herself.

"Who knows what Caroline was doing?"

"Nobody." Her voice was nearly gone. Her throat was on fire.

He rose from his chair, stepped forward and slapped Jaci's face with so much force that she fell out of the chair. He picked her up by her cuffs and sat her back in it.

"Who else knows?"

Jaci shook her head. "Nobody."

The man slapped her again. "Who else knows?"

"Nobody, dammit! I didn't tell anyone." Jaci tried to yell, but the words sounded more like pathetic squawking than defiant refusal.

"Who else knows?"

Jaci didn't answer the question. She closed her eyes and braced herself for the next strike. It didn't come.

"How did you get back through to the Amber Zone?"

"I walked."

"Did you go back through a gate?"

"Yes."

"Which one?"

"Gate One."

"Did one of the border guards let you go through without scanning you?"

"No, I snuck through."

"I doubt that," he said, scrutinizing her face closely. Then he rose, stepped out of the cell for a moment, and exchanged words with the soldier stationed there.

"I had my sergeant go get you some water. It looks like you're thirsty." He leaned against the wall with his arms crossed over his chest. He stared at her. Silent.

Jaci knew this wasn't over by a long shot. He was planning his next move. The soldier returned with a paper cup of water and a syringe. He handed both to the general.

"Here, my dear, have some water." He placed the paper cup on the table in front of her and tipped it over, spilling it. His lips twisted into a smirk when she looked up at him. He was fucking with her, and she wasn't going to give him the satisfaction of watching her lap up water off the table. Then, after a long stare down, his eyes narrowed.

"We can do this easy, or hard." He looked at her as he removed the plastic cover over the needle of the syringe he held. Jaci didn't fight. It was futile. She knew he would be successful one way or the other. He injected the liquid directly into the vein of her arm. It burned for a moment, and then Jaci melted. She was an instant marshmallow. Every part of her drooped. She was in a state of almost sleep.

She closed her eyes and only seconds later she was knocked out of her chair again with another strike to her face. She wasn't alert enough to soften the fall with her hands, and her head cracked on the hard cement. She was yanked up and back into the chair almost immediately.

Jaci slumped. The trickle of blood from the fresh gash on her head dripped into her lap. A thread of drool hung from her mouth.

He slapped her face again. "The police were watching you?"

"Yes."

"And you knew it?"

"Yes, after a while."

"What happened in your apartment that day?"

"Hmmm?"

He grabbed Jaci's hair and brought her face close to his. "What happened in the apartment?"

"Caroline stabbed Emily." Jaci's words slurred, but she couldn't seem to correct the problem.

"Why?"

"'Cause Caroline was a bitch." Jaci sneered.

"And you killed Caroline?"

She didn't answer him.

Jaci was yanked up from the chair and her back slammed up against the wall. General Morgan clutched her face in his hand and squeezed. His fingers clenched, gouging the yielding flesh of her cheeks. "I'm getting tired of the fucking games, Miss Harmon." His body was pressed up against hers. "Tell me."

His cock was hard between them. He was getting off on this. Jaci's expression must have reflected that revelation.

He chuckled. "That's right, you know what's next." He grabbed the front of Jaci's shirt and with a savage heave, ripped it, partially exposing her breasts. Then, he threw her to the floor.

She landed hard, her forearms and elbows taking the brunt of the fall. He stood over her. "You killed Caroline?"

"She was trying to kill me," Jaci croaked.

"I know that, you stupid bitch. It's unbelievable. You Ambers get more simpleminded every time I have the displeasure of having to speak to you." He squatted down next to her and ran his hand inside her shirt to cup her breast. "As far as I'm concerned, you're only good for one thing."

Jaci sucked in a breath, and attempted to back away from him. But he grabbed her with his other hand, holding her in place. He released a deep, frightening chuckle.

"How did you get through the border back to Amber?" he growled, as he ran a thumb over her nipple.

"I snuck through."

He wasn't appeased by her answer because he pinched and twisted her nipple brutally hard. Jaci screamed from the pain. He didn't let up. He kept pinching and twisting until Jaci wailed and sobbed for him to stop. "I snuck through. I snuck through," she yelled over and over.

Finally, he eased the viselike grip.

The general stood. "I think we're through for now. But this isn't over, not by a long shot."

Jaci curled into herself, tucking her legs up to her chest as he turned to leave.

"Oh, and Miss Harmon," he turned back to look down at her. "Don't flatter yourself. You stink like an animal. I would never stick my dick into a filthy, diseased Amber like you." He spat on her, the warm wet fluid landing on her cheek and then he walked out.

The soldier stationed outside the room extinguished the light and closed the door before leaving her alone and in the dark again.

Chapter 19

Xander was practically out of his mind. It had been over three days since the message from the general. He started to wonder if they were going to give her back. Then, he finally got the news that Jaci had been released to Amber Border Gate Two.

She was a heap on the dirty floor of the border guard station when Xander walked through the door.

He immediately spoke into his com. "We need a VN at the apartment when we get there."

"Visiting Nurse. Roger that," was his response from Jordan.

Xander rolled Jaci onto her back. Her face was bruised and swollen. She was unconscious. He checked her pulse.

Her hair was bloody and matted against a gash on her scalp. Her t-shirt was ripped, her breasts exposed.

"Motherfuckers," he roared. His anger was uncontainable. He looked up and eyed the two Border Guardsmen that watched. They were smug and didn't bother to hide the amusement that washed over their faces.

"Looks like they used interesting interrogation techniques," one of them said, laughing.

The only thing that kept Xander from snapping the asshole's neck was Jaci's need for medical attention. But he still looked at the Guardsman good and hard, memorizing the man's face. Xander would see him again.

He picked Jaci up from the floor and carried her outside to the cruiser where Brady waited. He laid her gently on the back seat and quickly got into the passenger side of the car before it sped off toward building seventeen. He peered over the seat and looked at her. Bruises mottled the dirty, blood covered skin on her face. The skin that wasn't bruised was ashen. He wasn't sure which bothered him more.

Jordan and the visiting nurse were waiting at the apartment when Xander carried Jaci in. After a cursory examination, the VN inserted an

IV to hydrate her and then closed the gash on her head. She left saying there was nothing else she could do, and gave directions to call when Jaci regained consciousness.

It was a waiting game. Again.

Somebody commed his mother and Gwen. They arrived while the VN examined Jaci. He didn't talk to them. He couldn't, not without losing it, but they stuck close to him and did what they do best, love and support him.

Not long after, Xander kicked everybody out of the apartment with quiet thank-yous and promises to call. As he closed the door behind the last of them, he turned toward the bed. He was near a total loss of control. He took the minutes he needed to clamp down on his emotions and focus on his responsibility.

He walked around the bed and surveyed the battered form of the woman he loved. She still looked near death, despite the assurances from the VN that she would be okay.

She was a mess. After filling a bowl with warm water and grabbing a washrag, he began cleaning her. With a tentative hand, he tenderly wiped her face with the warm water, washing away the blood under her nose and the grime from her cheeks. His hands trembled with unreleased rage that he forced himself to push away as he continued his task. But that emotion was quickly replaced by another. His throat tightened, the muscles squeezed away his ability to swallow. He cut her shirt off so as not to disturb the IV in her arm. Earlier, he saw the ripped shirt, but his mind, at the time, rejected the direction of that train of thought. But now, he let himself go there. If they'd raped her…

Tears rolled silently down his face while he methodically cleaned her arms and torso. Her wrists were marred by deep bruises and worn away skin from being cuffed too tightly and for too long. When he cleaned the dried blood on the inside of her arm and found the needle mark underneath, the sudden surge of rage that he felt made him want to kill. They drugged her.

This had not been 'questioning', this had been plain, old school torture. His hands were shaking as he finished her arms and upper body. He dumped the dirty water in the kitchen sink and refilled the bowl before returning to her.

He braced himself for what he might find when he took off her pants, but he found that the bottom half of her body was in much better condition than the top. As he cleaned her, relief dulled his anger. They'd not let her go to the bathroom. Her pants were stiff with dried urine. But otherwise, she seemed untouched everywhere below the waist.

He dumped the dirty water and pulled off his own clothes. Gingerly, he lay down next to her and pulled her to him. He curled the full length of his body around her to give her the comfort and healing of his touch. He covered as much of her skin as possible with his and held her without moving underneath the soft blanket of their bed.

For hours, he relished the feeling of his skin on hers as well the even in-and-out of her breaths. What a dumbass he'd been trying to keep her at arms length. It took almost losing her to truly understand the huge part of his heart she owned, and to realize how much of his life was her now.

She was his. He would not leave her vulnerable again.

It was then, in those quiet hours of holding her in his arms, that Xander was finally able to think past getting Jaci back and start considering the larger implications of the events that had taken place. The Gov would expect that Amber authorities had been mollified by Jaci's return.

He wasn't. This time was different from every other injustice the Gov had done to Amber. This time they had concrete proof of the Gov's outright murder of Ambers.

They were growing dangerously brazen after more than two decades of the population's utter submission to their authority.

The Gov's absolute authority needed to happen during the dire circumstances immediately following the pandemic. They needed control and cooperation to do the things necessary to create order, provide for basic needs, and protect the survivors flocking to the city.

But their society wasn't struggling like it had been twenty-five years ago. The genetic qualities that were near extinction back then, were thriving now.

Many of these restrictions, these measures to safeguard humanity, were no longer necessary. If the Gov went unchecked by its citizens much longer, the United States would no longer be a democracy. The country wouldn't grow as it did the first time when settlers in covered wagons set out to populate the land beyond the borders of their cities. It would be a military dictatorship that never loosened its control over the population.

The more he thought about it, the more he was willing to bet that the Gov controlled the lives of all its citizens, from Ambers to Diamonds, in more ways than anybody realized. The fury faded and determination gathered within him. Changes needed to be made. Now was the time to start.

He looked down at his woman, caressed the hair away from her cheek. Xander was overcome by the intense love he felt for her. He understood why Amber women gave up control, gave up authority to the men around them. Without that small submission, every man in Amber would be impudent with no control on any aspect of their lives. It was a true gift and it was time that the men took that gift and did something with it, did something to truly protect their females, themselves, and their country.

* * * *

Disorientation crowded Jaci's brain as she came awake. Her last memory was being left on the cement floor in the opaque blackness of her cell. But now, there was no pain from the cuffs, no cold seeping into her bones from the floor. She was still drugged or her body was shutting down. It would be over soon.

She knew she was still in the dark because there was no suggestion of light on the other side of her eyelids. She tried to open her eyes. They wouldn't cooperate. Her lids were heavy and felt suctioned to her eyeballs.

A flood of memories surrounding the interrogation rushed to her mind. She had been as strong as she could, never giving up Jordan's actions at the border gate. She was proud of herself.

She smiled. "Ow." She lifted an arm to her face. Smiling was out.

She felt the slightest of touches on the skin of her arm. "Jaci?" A whisper.

Her doped brain heard Xander's voice. She was hallucinating. And then a rushed thought pushed its way forward in her brain.

"Oh God!"

He knew. General Morgan knew about the relationship between Xander and her. Jaci began to panic. He wasn't safe. A spontaneous, keening sob escaped from her soul. It filled her ears. She'd put him in danger. She'd accepted her own death, but only as long as he was going to be okay.

"Jaci," she heard again.

Anguish careened through her, culminating in a crescendo of uncontrolled sobs. She covered her ears with her hands and tried to drown out his voice with her wails. It hurt too much to hear him.

A hand grabbed her arm. She screamed, panic stricken. There was someone in there with her. She scrambled away and then screamed again at the sharp pain in the crook of her arm and enormous crash behind her.

"Jaci!"

A light flicked on. She saw it behind her eyelids. She tried again to drag her lids up. Her right lid complied.

Xander's face filled her field of vision. "What…" She whipped her head from side to side taking in a quick glance of her surroundings.

She was confused.

Xander pulled her to his lap and cradled her against his chest, rocking her like a mother rocks her newborn baby. "You're home, Jaci. You're home. You're home," he whispered into her hair over and over again. The warm drifts of air from his words raised goose bumps on her arms. The safety of his embrace anchored her body as her brain labored to make sense of what was happening.

It took an eternity for her mind to take in and process where she was and what had happened. Eventually her sobs quieted and the steady sound of Xander's beating heart under her ear calmed her thoughts but she still shook uncontrollably. She took a deep breath and tried to relax her rigid, shuddering muscles but it was no use. She had no control of them.

Xander flicked off the bedside light. "Come on, let's lay back down." He scooted her off his lap and laid her down next to him. He enveloped them both with the blanket and as the warmth and safety of being next to him surrounded her, she slowly settled. They faced each other with their heads on the pillows and their legs entangled. Xander's hand rested in the dip of her waist.

"What happened?" she finally asked.

"Captain Rush negotiated your release."

She was silent while she rolled the information over in her mind. "They didn't want the information to get out about their involvement in what Caroline was doing."

"Exactly."

"They're not going to put me out of the city?"

"No."

"Captain Rush agreed to drop the matter if they gave me back?"

"Essentially."

"But that's not right. People should know what they're doing."

"I agree."

They lay in silence then, looking at each other in the barely there light of the room. His eyes roamed her face. "My face, is it bad?"

He lifted a hand to her cheek and caressed it softly. "You're beautiful."

"I think that's because we're in the dark."

He smiled at her attempt at a joke and then his expression turned as hard as stone. "Tell me what they did to you," he said in a strangled voice.

Jaci shook her head. "No." She loved him too much to give him a blow by blow. She couldn't do that to him. "I don't want to talk about it." She knew he'd respect that answer and not press her for details. At least, not now.

He pulled her into him, and she curled into his chest. "Make love to me Xander."

He chuckled. The sound under her ear comforted her. "I don't want our first time together to be like this, sweetie. We'll have our whole lives to make love to each other."

"Please," she whispered.

"You're hurt, Jaci," he said in a deep rasp.

"I need your touch to heal me. Please, Xander."

He released a long shuddering breath. "I don't want to hurt you."

"As long as you love me, there's nothing you could do that would hurt me." She turned her head to look up at him and placed her hand behind his neck pulling him toward her for a kiss.

He stopped the forward motion of his head before their lips met. He looked into her eyes. "I do love you, Jaci."

Not waiting for a reply, he leaned in for a firm, full kiss. The contact of his lips made Jaci's stomach twirl. Joy lightened her heart. She wanted to do everything with him. Be everything for him.

His tongue possessed her mouth while he rolled her over onto her back.

His hand cupped her breast and the thrill and triumph she'd been experiencing faltered, and then stalled. His hand on her breast momentarily called to mind the general's hand on that same breast. She knew a pained expression crossed her face with the memory. Whether Xander saw it or sensed it, she didn't know, but he stopped short. He closed his eyes as if to compose himself. When he opened them, safety and love shone in them. He leaned his head in and rubbed his cheek lightly the sore breast. "It's me now," he said in a soothing voice. "Just me."

He turned his head and brushed butterfly kisses all over it. Then, he trailed his hot tongue over the peak. He cupped the breast gently before he lifted his head to meet her gaze. He branded her with his intense gaze. "You're mine and this is mine." He took the tightly beaded nipple and bit down. Jaci was about to cry out from the pain when he released it and rolled his tongue over the throbbing peak.

"Anywhere else?"

She looked at him for a moment, trying to process what he was asking her? Oh…had she been violated anywhere else? "No."

Syvia Ryan

He moved over her and nudged her knees apart to a wide stance so he could fit in between. He rubbed his thumb over her clit and lowered his hand. He slid a finger inside of her. She was slippery and ready for him.

They both moaned at the same time. The blunt end of his cock lingered at her opening for only a second before he slid inside of her. He knelt between her legs, inside her to the hilt, then he slowly wrapped her legs around him. He filled her completely and as he began to move, her pussy clamped around him tightly. He hissed and stilled himself while he slid his finger over the swollen bud of nerves that laid open to him.

She looked up toward the beautiful man who began his slow, gentle thrusts again. She wanted this, had wanted it for so long. His touch was sparks on her flesh. She stiffened, tightening her legs to pull him even further inside of her.

Their eyes locked. "Stop. I'm going to come."

"That's the idea," he rumbled, as another swipe of his fingers played over her clit, strumming the slow rhythm of a perfect love song. He brought her to the top of the peak.

"Oh, fuck!" She bucked as the overwhelming rush of her orgasm tore through her violently. She gripped the sheets of the bed as if trying to brace herself from the relentless ecstasy crashing into her.

As the shudders and writhing receded and the world came back to her, she opened her eyes and looked into Xander's loving face. He had been watching her while she climaxed. She felt her face redden. "I don't think I've ever come with a man watching me before." she said, closing her eyes, embarrassed.

"You're beautiful when you come," he said as he moved over her. He supported his weight on a forearm as his other hand slid between her ass and the bed. He kneaded the flesh there, guiding her ass up to meet him in time with the slow advance and withdraw of his cock. His breathing was ragged and his voice barely audible. "You feel perfect, so tight around my cock." The base of his cock rubbed against her clit as he ground her into him. His strokes were slow and even.

"You're testing my restraint, Jaci."

"Don't hold back. I need more of you." She dug her nails into his back.

His stroke quickened and became more demanding while the hand underneath her ass easily lifted her to him, ground her into him, to the rhythm of his penetration. Her muscles gripped his cock harder as she neared another orgasm.

"Come with me, Jaci. Come on." He pumped her hard. With one final collision of their bodies, Jaci froze. She spasmed, grabbed at Xander's cock with tenacity and then the pleasure of his body inside hers was all there was. She called out his name when she felt the hot spurts of his cum and heard the bass rumble of his satisfaction. Felt it vibrate from his chest as she clung to him. In that magnificent moment, while they were locked together experiencing the ultimate pleasure for the first time with each other, it felt like her world would never be the same and she silently thanked God.

When their bodies stilled, he stayed inside of her. She felt the mad thumping of his heart against hers. Their ragged breathing was in unison. He kissed her neck and shoulders lovingly.

"I don't want you to leave my body. I feel whole connected to you like this," she whispered into his ear.

"I'm not going anywhere." They lay joined until Xander finally retreated from her. She was half asleep when he rolled to his side and pulled her into him, surrounding her with warmth and safety.

Chapter 20

A sharp knock at the door startled Jaci awake. Brilliant sunlight glared through the window. During her confinement underground, her eyes had become unaccustomed to bright light. She threw the sheet over her head to dull the brilliance of it. Xander moved beside her. She peeked at him as he lifted himself out of bed. His nude form was broad and muscular. She admired the muscled round of his ass as his legs propelled him toward the pair of jeans folded over a chair. As he stepped into the legs, her glimpse of his hard-on made her thrilled with anticipation.

"Get rid of them," she whispered.

He looked up from zipping his fly and flashed a hot, magnetic look at her until his concern overtook his passion and cloaked his face. He stepped toward the overturned IV pole and righted it before he walked to the door.

"Captain Rush sent me to get a statement," Jordan said as she held up a camera, "and document." Without a word, Xander swung the door wide for Jordan to enter and she followed him into the room.

"How you doing?" she asked, when she saw that Jaci was awake and sitting up.

"Okay. A little worn out and sore."

"You look like shit," Jordan said with her usual matter of fact tone. "I have to take your statement and document your injuries. Which do you want to do first?"

"Neither." Jaci glanced over at Xander and held out a hand. "Help me up. I want to go to the bathroom."

Xander walked over and assisted Jaci as she gingerly slipped off the bed and assessed whether her legs would bear her full weight. They did. "See, I'm fine," she said back over her shoulder to Jordan.

Jaci walked naked to the bathroom and locked the door behind her. She examined the marble of black, blue and red spread over her face and tested her ability to open her swollen left eye. It looked worse than it felt. It was sore, but only hurt when she prodded the tender flesh with her finger. As she did that, she caught sight of her gruesome wrists and the dark bruise in the crook of her arm.

"Xander could you get me some clean clothes?" she called through the bathroom door. She started the shower and waited for the water to warm. Xander's soft knock prompted her to steel herself before she opened the door.

"Thanks," she said as he handed the clothes in to her.

"Let me in," he demanded, almost growling.

"Why?"

"I want to talk to you while you're in the shower."

Jaci appraised his face. "It's over, Xander. I don't want to talk about it."

"Open the damn door!"

Jaci sighed, stepped back and let the door swing open.

She didn't look at him as she stepped over the edge of the tub into the swirling steam of the shower. She didn't want to see the look on his face as he appraised her body in the light of day.

A moment later, he stepped in behind her.

"What's going on?" She could tell he was deliberately trying to use a patient tone. She smiled. He wasn't very good at it.

"Nothing. I just don't feel like reliving the last…however many days of my life. Especially when it's for no real purpose."

"It is for a purpose."

Jaci picked up the bar of soap and started rolling it in her hands. "What purpose? There's nothing anybody can do. It's the Gov. They do what they want to do. Nobody holds them accountable."

She handed Xander the bar of soap and rubbed her bubbled hands over her arms. Xander turned her away from him and then washed her back.

"One day, Jaci, when people grow tired of the Gov's absolute power, and the corruption and abuses that go along with it, we may have enough documented proof of their ruthlessness that people would be compelled to act, to change Amber's subjugation and prevent our extermination."

Jaci tried to turn back to face him. He stopped her. "Let me wash your hair. Look up toward the ceiling a little bit."

She followed his directions while his hands, slippery with shampoo, moved over her head, working her hair into a mass of bubbles. He stayed well away from the gash as he scrubbed her scalp with the pads of his fingers. It felt amazing. She lost track of what she was going to say.

"Rinse," he directed softly as he soaped up his own body.

"Do you think it's over? With me, I mean. Do you think they'll leave me alone?" Jaci's eyes were shut while foamy streams slid down her face. She was disappointed she missed his expression, because he didn't answer her right away.

"I would kill to prevent them from taking you from me again."

"No," Jaci snapped. "No. I could never live with myself if you put your life in jeopardy because of me."

He stepped in closer to her so the shower spray hit both of them and pulled her into his arms. "And I could never live with myself if I didn't." He dipped his head and kissed her. "Do this and it will be over. Then we'll only have to look forward after that," he said tenderly.

Jaci nodded her head in wordless acquiescence.

"Thank you, sweetie."

After urning off the spray, Xander grabbed towels for both of them. "Put your pants on, I'll send Jordan in to take pictures of your injuries before you put on anything else." Jaci grabbed for her clothes while he finished dressing and left the bathroom.

The pictures and statement took about two hours. Jaci was not traumatized by the blow by blow of what happened, but Xander was. His fury simmered under the surface barely contained. It was thick in the air by the time the interview was over.

Jaci closed the door behind Jordan when she left and turned to look at Xander. "You okay?" she asked. She wasn't sure what she was going to do with the infuriated man standing in front of her.

"Other than feeling like grinding something or someone to a pulp? Yeah."

She grabbed him by the front of his shirt, fisting it in both hands. "Let's make use of that slow boil." She jerked him down toward her and kissed him, then shoved him away.

He looked stunned for a split second before he advanced on her. He burned her with his gaze, but that look was quickly replaced by an unmistakable expression of sadness and…fear?

"After what you've been through, Jaci, I'm not sure that you would find some of the things that turn me on as pleasurable for you anymore."

"Xander, it's behind us. You promised me we only look forward, remember? I don't want you to treat me differently, to settle for lesser satisfaction because you're afraid to do what you really want to do. It will kill me if you treated me differently because of this."

"But Jaci," he whispered, cupping her bruised face lightly "I like to be rough, to be in control. I'm not sure--"

"Stop! If you can't put it behind you, I don't want to be with you." She looked at him defiantly. "I am not less of a woman, less of a lover because I got knocked around. If I let that happen, I've given them the power to destroy my life, to taint our love." Her voice escalated to the point that she was yelling at him. She was determined. "I can't let that happen, Xander."

Xander paused looking at her. Seconds passed as he processed what she'd said to him. "Take your clothes off." His deep voice was need that sizzled the air between them.

Her gaze met his. He was himself again. His look scorched her. His breathing quickened. Her nipples hardened just thinking about the new sexual adventure she was about to embark on with this hulking, smoldering man. She pulled her shirt over her head and to his credit, the only emotion she saw flash across his face was desire. If it had been anything else, she wouldn't have been able to go on.

He started to unbutton his jeans and then looked at hers. "Take them off," he ordered.

Jaci complied. As she stripped, so did he. Then, he walked over to his side of the room and opened the drawer in the nightstand next to the bed.

He looked to her and seeing that she was fully naked, he crooked his finger at her. "Come here."

Instead of walking around to his side, she crawled toward him on the bed. He groaned.

When she reached him, he palmed his erection for a moment, thinking, studying her. "Hmm, suck me while I decide what's right for you today." He put the crest of his cock near the opening of her mouth.

He rattled around in his drawer while she covered the head of his cock with her mouth and sucked with enthusiasm. Only a slight pause betrayed the sensation he felt. He appeared absorbed in his decision making about what to choose in the drawer. She sucked him hard, down to the back of her throat, trying to get some response. He gave none except for throwing some lube and another contraption that she'd never seen before on the bed next to her.

"Oh fuck, Jaci." He slapped her ass. "You like my cock in your mouth, don't you?"

Her moan was a long, drawn-out vibration on his cock.

He withdrew from her mouth with a pop, because she didn't want to let it go. He wrapped his arm around her waist and lifted her off the bed, moving her more toward the middle. Jaci's lust surged at his easy show of strength and mastery over her. He lay on his back and turned her around over him so that her knees were on either side of his head, and her mouth was mere inches away from his cock. He wrapped his arms around her thighs and pulled them further apart so her pussy lowered to his face. Jaci sucked in his cock like a long strand of spaghetti and cupped his balls with one hand.

It was hard to concentrate on giving him pleasure. Her mind jumbled as she scoured his cock with her tongue, scrubbing and polishing with the most savage lashes of pleasure she could deliver. He was doing the same, matching her strike for strike, sucking on her clit as hard as she suctioned him. With his arms wrapped around her thighs, his fingertips ended right at the crack of her ass. His hands worked her. He swiped his finger down the valley created by her cheeks. She jumped at the touch and tried to move, but his arms kept her in place. She tensed. She lost track of what she was doing. Her moans against the cock deep in her mouth resonated through the room and filled her ears.

"Xander, I need your cock inside me." He ignored her at first, but then her hushed plea had him rolling her off him.

"You'll have it soon enough." His low, guttural tone twirled and flipped her insides in excitement. She felt danger and anticipation, possessed and cherished. He placed her on her stomach and jerked her hips up into the air. She felt the cold squirt of lube and the gentle rub of fingers down the crack of her ass. Jaci squirmed into his touch as he penetrated her rear with his finger.

She sucked in a gulp of breath.

"I'm going to slide my cock in there." His voice was throaty. Slightly panicked she looked over her shoulder at him.

"Xander--"

"Relax, sweets. Just relax. You took the plug. You'll be able to take me. I'll go slow."

Jaci turned her head back to a comfortable position and closed her eyes. When his fingers finally stopped, she felt the head of his cock at her opening. He slid it in slowly. The sexual turn on from this was new to her. It seemed like it was more for him than for herself. But she would do anything, give him everything he wanted from her as his sexual partner.

When he was all the way in, his big hands gripped her hips, holding her still. She looked over her shoulder again. The gleam in his eye as he looked down at her quickened her heart. He placed a pillow under her and then spread her legs wide. His cock was thick, stretching her to the brink of her tolerance.

"So tight, so incredibly tight," he rumbled. He took large, ragged heaves of air into his lungs.

Reaching around her, he massaged her clit. The tiny nub of nerves was throbbing, screaming for his attention. Her hips moved into and away from the rhythmic petting of the pad of his thumb, and then the rest of him joined the choreography with the tight slide of his cock.

"Oh God," Jaci wailed. She was stretched tight around his dick, feeling every fine movement, every infinitesimal ridge and curve.

His rhythm sped and the pressure of his fingers increased as he rolled over her clit. The sound of their bodies slapping against each other filled the room.

Jaci stiffened and floated for several seconds before she erupted. She fell apart with quaking swells of pleasure completely drowning her. The world receded. There was only her and him. His curses filled her ears as he shot hot jets of cum into her.

* * * *

Xander stood solemn and stiff in his uniform as he scanned the room. The gathering was large as people filed in and paid their respects to Emily's parents. The entire Circle City police department made an appearance. Those officers who had been friends with Rock and Emily still remained. Xander stayed as proxy for Rock.

Rock would receive no comfort or closure from this memorial. He would have to suffer his loss alone. Xander missed his partner already.

He glanced toward the door where his mother and Jaci were leaving together. Jaci's body and spirit were healing, but she still didn't want to wallow in the grief she felt for Emily, fearing regression to where she'd been emotionally a couple of days ago. It made Xander's heart sing as he watched them walk through the exit, holding hands. He liked that they were spending time together and getting to know each other.

He was glad they'd left. He needed some time alone to grieve privately and find his own closure. He never told Jaci of his sexual encounters with Emily and he never would. Not that he wanted to start their life together with secrets between them. He didn't. But, the past was past and nothing good could come of revealing that information. They needed a fresh start with each other.

He stood motionless, lost in his own head for another hour before he decided to leave. He had a bundle to pick up before he joined the large group gathering in the common room of building twenty-eight. Most of the police force had spent their morning silently searching for and cleaning the room of bugs. They'd found three. Now they were confident that the meeting would take place under the Gov's radar.

This would be the first meeting of the New Resistance. The only people in attendance would be cops and the people that those cops trusted one hundred percent.

Xander didn't know, exactly, how they were going to go about taking back their civil liberties. But the country was no longer in a state of emergency, and it was their responsibility to all the men and women throughout history who'd fought for the freedom of the US as well as to the generations ahead of them, to force the Gov to return to the Constitution and make sure the US remained a free country.

He'd contacted several men who'd been in the original resistance movement right after the pandemic. Knowing the details of the past would give them a good idea of where to start. Obviously, what they'd been doing back then had been effective because it led to the Accord.

When he arrived, his arms strained under the weight of the large bundle he carried. He stopped and took in the room. It buzzed with the low level conversations of at least a hundred men. He was amazed at the turnout. They were men of courage who would take up the challenge that was going to be put on the table for them today.

For years, Xander, like many men, preferred to lurk around unnoticed, under the Gov's radar, reasoning that if the Gov never noticed him, it couldn't victimize him. They used fear to keep the Ambers in line. Every man in the room today would have to choose to throw off that fear of being noticed, of being targeted by the Gov, and not blindly accept what's been crammed down their throats their whole lives.

The room became increasingly quiet as he made his way deep into the gathering. He waited expectantly for everybody's attention. When he'd got it, he opened the bundle and spread its contents on the table. The array of guns he'd acquired from his contact in the Onyx Zone caused a hush to fall over the room as the men saw the contents.

Xander spent the next hour detailing the crimes against Amber citizens the Gov had gotten away with. Then, the original resistance members detailed their covert methods of waging war against the Gov prior to the Accord. The acts of rebellion were small, but once compounded with growing Amber participation, it worked, making the Gov fear losing its control.

Leaders were voted in and teams were formed. Captain Rush was elected the leader of the movement, and Xander was second in command. His primary duty would be coordination between all the committee heads, identifying needs and assigning new Resistance members to their teams. They were, in essence, forming their own army with goals that ranged from recruitment, to developing safe houses that would provide protection to any Ambers that were labeled as subversive by the Gov.

The group's first identified goal was to begin finding and destroying all intelligence gathering technology the Gov used to monitor them. The longer this New Resistance kept their own secrets, the easier it would be to catch the Gov off guard.

It was a good start. When the meeting was over, Xander's mind was heavy with ideas and hope as he walked back to building seventeen.

Upon entering his apartment, he found his mother teaching Jaci a family recipe in the kitchen. Gwen and Journey chatted with them from the other side of the counter. He couldn't help the huge grin that plastered itself on his face when he saw his three women together.

Jaci beamed back at him when their eyes met. She was gorgeous, even with the purple and green remains of bruises on her face.

"Right in time for dinner," she said as she stood on her tiptoes to kiss him on the cheek. She examined his face. "Are you okay?" Only Jaci could be concerned about someone else while her body was full of bruises.

"I'm good," he said, kissing her back. He walked over to his mom and kissed her, too.

"Well," Jaci said. "I have some interesting news."

"And what's that?" Xander brushed Jaci's arm on his way over to Gwen.

"I just received a new job assignment."

"Yeah? What is it?"

"I am officially the new Sit-In Team Leader for Circle City."

He smiled at her. "They couldn't have made a better choice, but I predict you won't be working much. Soon, fallows will be a thing of the past."

* * * *

Jaci took a moment and looked around the room. They all had closed ranks around her after she was dumped back into the Amber Zone.

She'd been working hard to put the past behind her and it was easier with Allie doting on her and welcoming her into the family, literally with open arms.

Allie acted as though it was a given that Jaci and Xander were going to get married. After Jaci corrected her several times saying that Xander hadn't asked her, and having Allie wave the statement away as if it were a technicality, Jaci stopped correcting and went with it.

Later, Gwen explained that Xander had never even talked to Allie about a woman he was involved with, let alone introduced one to her before. It helped her to understand and make allowances for Allie's excitement. Truth be told, she hoped Allie was right.

Jaci always felt Xander's eyes on her. She glanced in his direction and his possessive gaze met hers. Lately she found herself wishing the rest of the world would go away so they could connect. She wanted him all to herself.

He flashed her a look that tickled her insides and warmed her core. She liked the person she was when she was with him.

Jaci's mind wandered back to the day she walked into their empty apartment, distraught and wanting to die. It was a million years ago. Back then, she could have never imagined how happy she would be being

Meet the Author

As an avid reader, I'm always on the hunt for that next amazing story. Those unforgettable books with the perfect balance of action and passion are hard to find and even harder to write. My hope is that *Being Amber* has given readers a few hours of happiness while they savor the gradual discovery of each character and how their story unfolds. I usually fall in love with the hero and heroine in the books I write by the time I've written the last page. If I've done my job well, you've fallen in love, too. So many times I find myself not wanting a book to end. I crave more of the story, wanting to know what happens after the happily ever after. If you're like me and want to read more about Xander and Jaci, the epilogue to *Being Amber* is posted on my website at www.RyanBooks.net. Stop in and find out how their story ultimately ends before moving on to Jordan's story in *Being Sapphire*.

And from the bottom of my heart, thank you for reading.

www.ingramcontent.com/pod-product-compliance
Lightning Source LLC
Chambersburg PA
CBHW022152260626
47155CB00017B/1843